a cut so deep

thornes & roses

DANI RENÉ

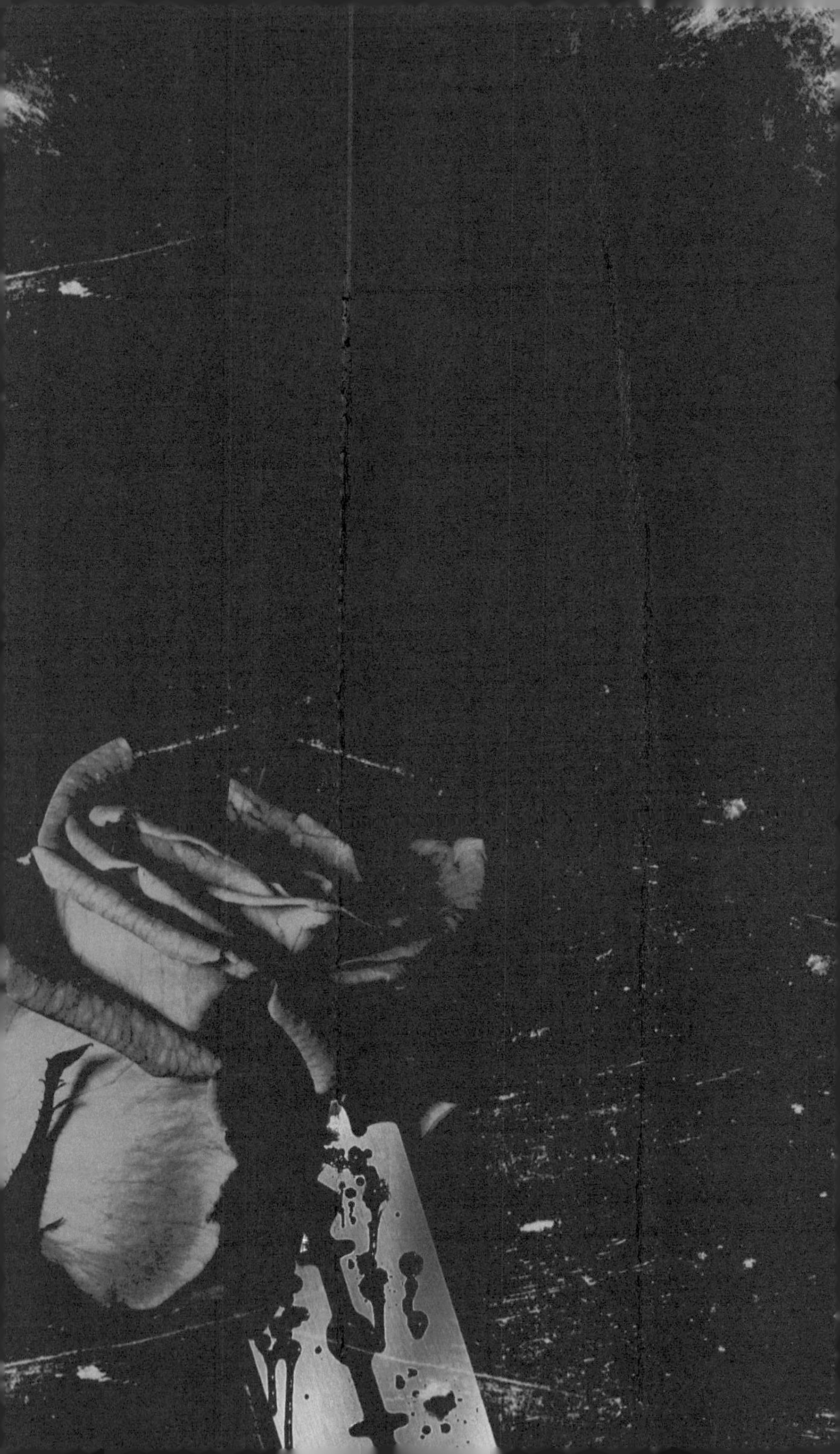

She was chaos and beauty intertwined.
A tornado of roses from divine.

- Shakieb Orgunwall | Quotes 'nd Notes

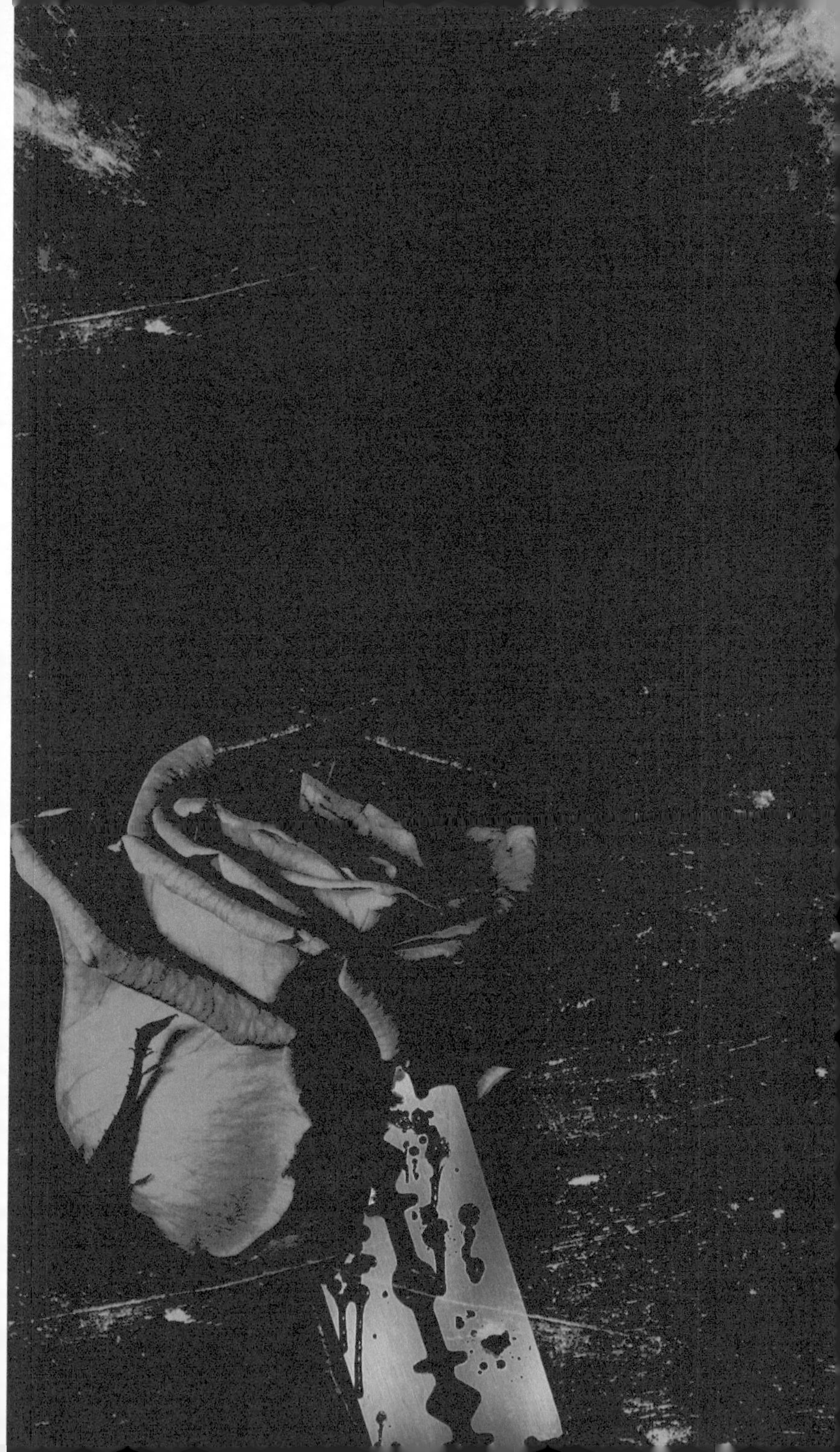

playlist

Cut - Plumb
If These Scars Could Speak - Citizen Soldier
The Devil Within – Digital Daggers
What I've Done – Linkin Park
Irresistible – Fall Out Boy, Demi Lovato
Heaven Help Me – RAIGN
Saints - Echos
My Demons - STARSET
I Miss the Misery - Halestorm
Bring Me to Life - Evanescence
Monster - Skillet
Numb - Linkin Park
Right Here - Chase Atlantic
If That's Love - Shawn James
I Got You - Corvyx
Mansion - NF, Fleurie

Find the full playlist on Spotify

THORNE

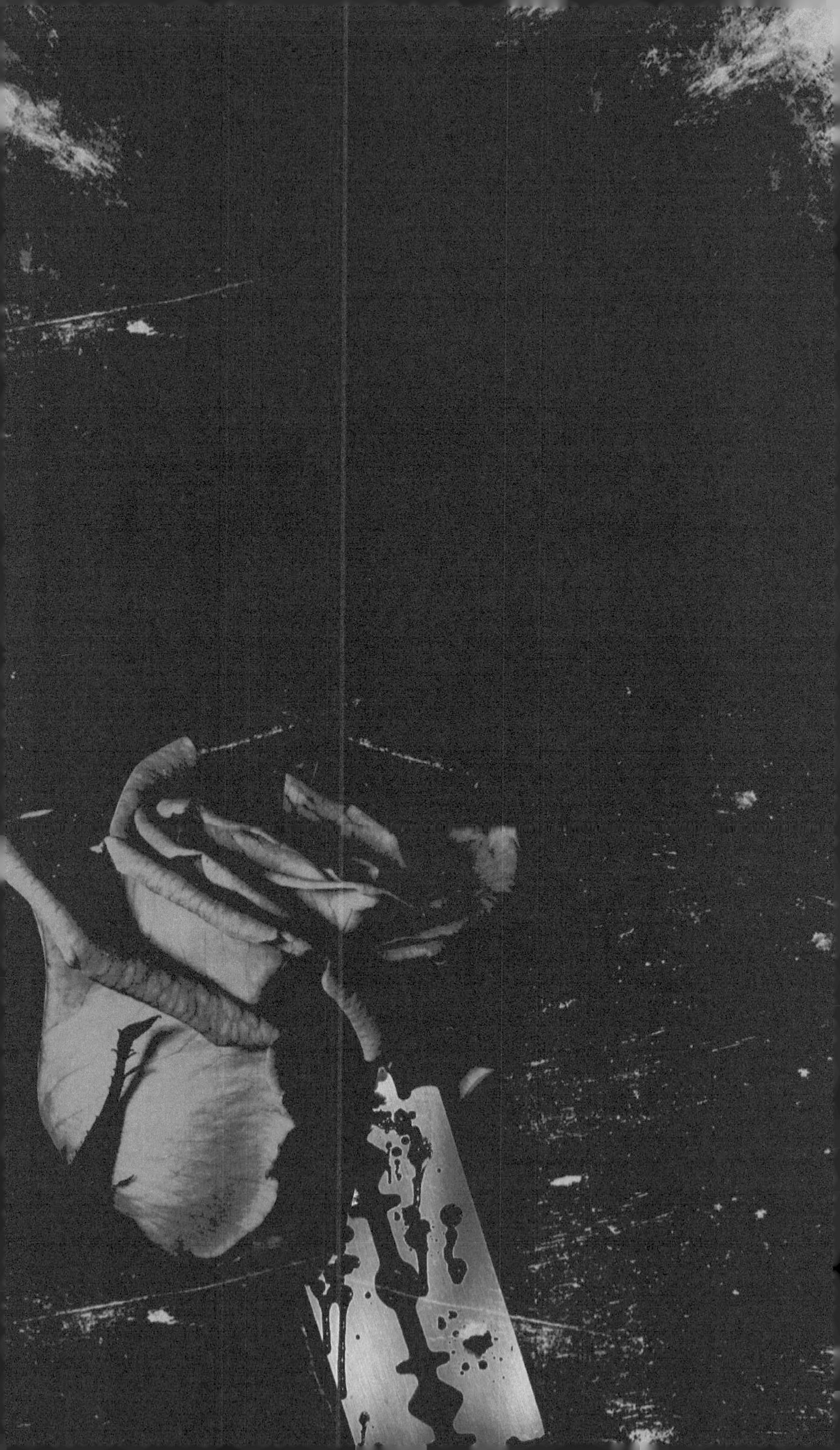

dedication

To the girls who were broken long before their hearts knew
about love. And to those same girls who crave the bad boy
who will find them in the darkness and not save them
but swim in the murky waters with them.

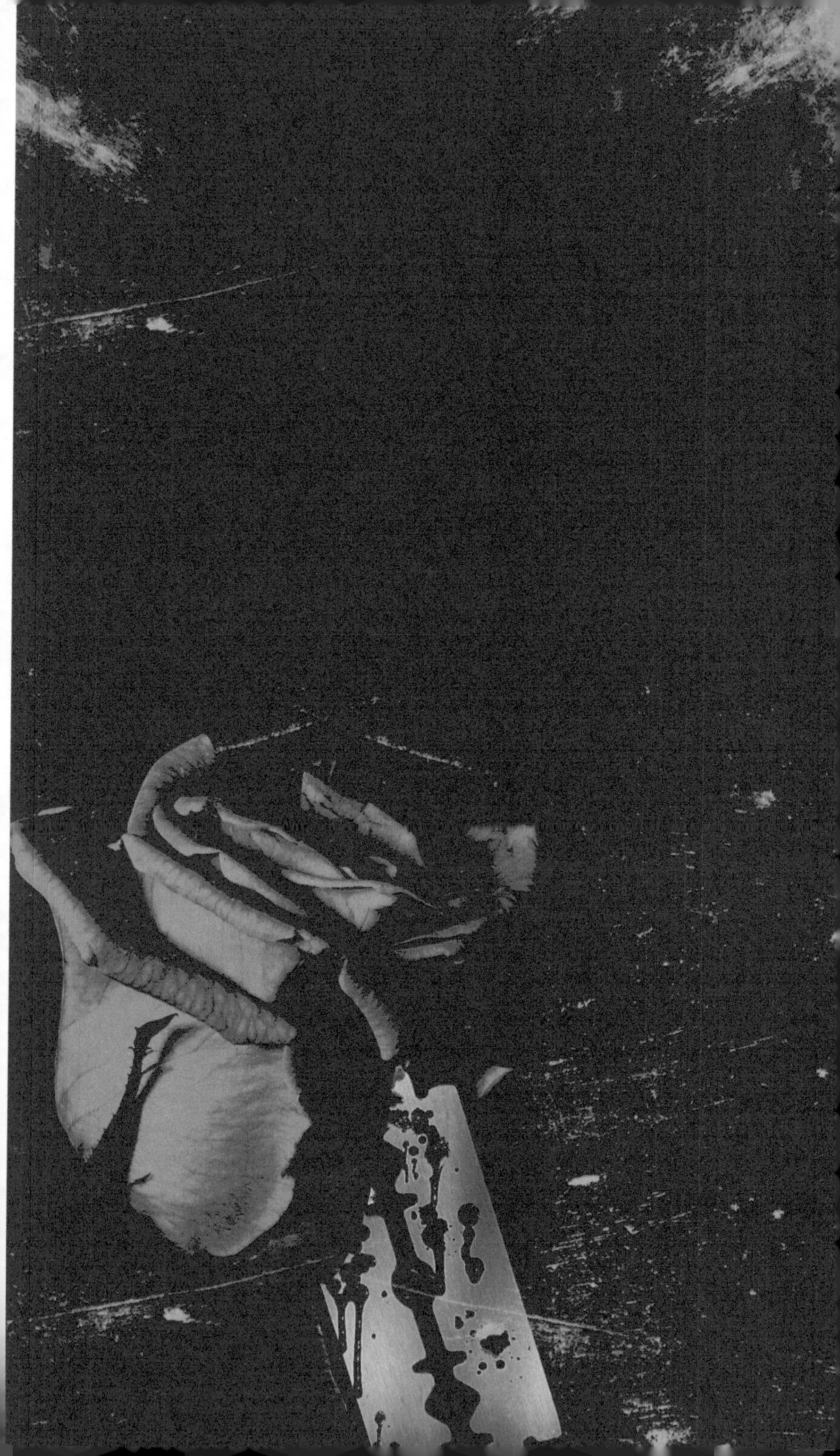

prologue
Nesrin

Sixteen years old

ONE THIN SLICE.

Just one touch of metal to flesh.

Inhale.

Exhale.

Pain. A pinch.

And then, freedom.

It's only the second time I've done it, but I already know that it's going to be so much better than talking to some rich bitch who makes notes on her iPad about my well-being. Not physically, no, she's testing my mind to see if I'm 'normal.'

I laugh.

It's low. Nothing more than a giggle.

Everything around me comes alive as I feel the warmth coat my skin. My hand is shaking, the blade drops from between my fingers, as pure relief shoots through my veins.

I've heard all about how it works. The internet is an amazing thing. Anything I need or I crave, I can find it there. I'm no longer shaking. I feel at ease with the world. Like everything is going to be okay.

Opening my eyes, I glance down at the incision I made, and a tear drops into the dark liquid. The deep crimson dribbles slowly. Languid in its path down my leg. As it escapes the thin slit, it takes my anxiety with it.

The trickle slows, creating pretty patterns over the tanned flesh of my inner thigh.

The euphoria is inexplicable.

My body is so free. Relaxed. I've only ever felt like this when I accidentally cut my hand on a broken glass.

It happened so suddenly.

But the moment the sting caused me to whimper, it forced out the worries, which plagued me for months, years even. I'd been so numb, so empty, the cut forced breath back into my lungs. The anxious knot that constantly twisted in my gut eased, and it was a release of all the stress and fear that held me hostage.

I was made to feel. Not expected to.

Every day, I have to be polished, poised, and beautiful—the perfect daughter of the perfect couple, who lives in the most perfect house. Everything the media sees; all the photos are made to look like we're happy.

But we're not.

My father fucks half his company—all the women, obviously.

My mother spends her days at the country club, where her pool boy tends to her needs that my dad no longer does.

When they come home, they smile and play happy family, loving parents, and honest people. I've numbed myself to it all, I've emptied my soul and shoved it into a box that I'll never open again.

I have one year left before I can leave. Twelve months before I walk out of this place and never come back. The fancy rooms, the hefty bank account, the exquisite gifts, everything about it is fake; nothing more than a shiny surface for a filthy underbelly.

The need to be away, far from my life, from the normal that I've become accustomed to burns through my veins, reminding me that I can never be loved in the way I need to. Not from my parents, and not from the boys at school.

I've made my choice.

It won't take much for me to walk away because I want

to leave this place and never come back. I want to find my own way, without the rules and regulations that my parents have imposed on me, where I have to be perfect all the time.

Perfection is not real. It's a myriad of broken pieces fit together just to shimmer when the light hits it. But, in reality, it's broken, it's shattered. Nothing more than an illusion to show off a poised, polished person that you can never be. Under scrutiny though, the fissures show up, and each time you fear someone might notice them, you add more jewels, add more makeup, more expensive clothes, hiding the ugly truth underneath.

I look at the cut on my inner thigh, it's not deep, but it's enough to release the pent-up frustration that's taken hold of me. Enough to make me feel alive, real. I push off the floor and wince when the skin tingles and stings.

It's high enough to be hidden from view. Only I know it's there. Only I can see the truth of what I've done, and that's how I know it needs to stay. I apply the plaster gently over the wound and pull the leg of my shorts down.

Time to be the happy child they created. Time to be the perfect doll my parents have portrayed me as since I was born.

And that all starts right now.

Happy birthday to me.

Nesrin

Two years later

THERE'S NOTHING MORE DANGEROUS THAN TIME. People come and go and, sometimes, they go before you're ready to let them. When you have no choice but to say goodbye. It's been a year since my father died, twelve months since I first found solace in the actions that I've become addicted to.

I can't explain why, but I need it. Anxiety tightens my stomach when my mother knocks on my bedroom door. It's my eighteenth birthday, and even though I can legally move out of the house and get an apartment, she hasn't yet allowed me that freedom. Her argument is that I'm safer in the home I grew up in. For now, I'll indulge her.

That might sound strange to someone else, but my mother isn't a normal mom. She's one of the most famous faces in America. And now that she's getting remarried, she's become a household name. People follow her around daily; the paparazzi never leave her alone. There are times I'm fearful of her life being endangered, but she loves it. Every moment is like a godsend for her, even when she receives stalker mail. I've seen some sordid messages from people who call themselves fans, but they're more deranged from what they've said.

Each time she opens one of those envelopes, a cold shiver takes hold of me because I half expect them to walk in any second and I'll be an orphan. Without a dad, losing my mother would more than likely hurt like hell. Not that we've ever been close. We've always had a volatile relationship.

But I've learned that behind the Botox and pearly white smile lies the depression she struggles with behind closed doors. That's how I've grown up, knowing that when you're in public, you fake a smile, giggle when you're asked personal questions, and air-kiss people you don't know but act as if you love them dearly.

"Nesrin Anne Ellington," my mother's voice calls to me from the other side of the door. Whenever she uses my full name, I know shit's about to go down. Groaning, I push my blankets off and swing my legs over the edge of the bed. It's not even sunrise yet, but I know summer will be here soon, and we'll be drenched in the sticky heat.

I wanted to move to Washington State, or farther north, maybe Canada, where it's cooler, but Mommy Dearest loves to be baked under the hot California sun.

"If you don't—"

I swing my door open, interrupting the angry tirade I know she was about to spew at me. Arching a dark eyebrow, I meet her steely gaze. I look nothing like her, taking after my father—olive skin, pitch-black hair, and gentle hazel eyes.

"I'm awake," I tell her nonchalantly because I enjoy fucking with her pristine, polished appearance. Nobody knows what she's really like. Only I've seen the ugly bits, the parts she doesn't show to anyone else.

"We'll be leaving for the church in an hour," she huffs. "I've had the biggest fight with your father," she sighs.

"He is not my father," I bite out, anger raging through me at her inconsiderate words. She's convinced I'll accept Bradford Thorne as my father, but what she doesn't know is that nothing she can do will ever make me want to call him Dad. And that's what she can't understand. I mean— he's wealthy, influential, and he has connections—her words not mine. I've heard rumors of Bradford, the man who owns the world.

Okay, maybe not the world, but he does own half of America, and from what I've garnered, he also has Europe, Britain, and most of Southern America in his pocket. A man who knows that money can buy anything, and the next item on his list is my mother.

"You need to learn about respect," Mother bites out, and I know she's talking about me actually accepting some asshole as my new father. She didn't even wait for Dad's corpse to go cold before she was diving onto Bradford's dick. I shudder at the thought. At least I know for sure I won't have any surprise siblings because my mother had her tubes tied after she had me. And I only know this because I overheard a fight between my mom and Dad when I was younger; she was adamant one child was enough; whereas, he wanted another.

"I'll respect the man, but I will not call him Dad. He is *not* my father," I retort. Anger sizzles through my veins, and I'm ready for another one of our infamous arguments when Jeannine, our maid, nears us.

"Ms Ellington, the car is on its way." Her voice is low, and I know she's scared of my mother. Everyone in this house is afraid of the wrath that Marcia Ellington spews.

"Thank you, Jeannine." Mom doesn't look at her. Those luminous green eyes are still pinned on me. "Get ready." She spins on her heel and leaves me glaring daggers at her back. If only one would pierce her, just to show her how much it hurts.

"Are you alright?" Jeannine asks, regarding me with her gentle smile. I wish so much she was my mother. If only.

"I am." I nod. "I have to get ready, you heard the queen," I bite out, causing Jeannine to grin. More like an evil queen.

"Take care of yourself today, don't let her upset you."

The warning in her voice sends a cold shiver down my spine. She's seen me broken by my mother's cold words, by her constant berating comments. Her time spent in this house has led her to learn just how my mother *loves* me.

I nod, stepping back and closing the door, as Jeannine makes her way down the hall toward the staircase.

Sighing, I head into the bathroom with my mind on the upcoming nuptials. I don't want to go, but when your mother gets married, your attendance is expected. Frustration blooms in my chest. I wish I could go live with my aunt. She's, at least, someone who I can get along with. Someone who I can talk to; whereas, my mother is more focused on her career and making headlines.

Marcia and Mallory are sisters, but they couldn't be more different. Even though they came from the same womb, three years apart; Mallory, my aunt, is a gentle, affectionate woman. My mother, on the other hand, is cold, aloof, and hates being a *mom*.

Time to get ready. Time to see just what this new man I've never met has in store for us because my mother agreed to marry him before I even had the chance to come face to face with Bradford Thorne.

The church is massive, filled with guests, people I've never met. My nerves are shot. I hate being in the public eye, and I honestly wish my mother had chosen a more intimate event. All my life, I've struggled with anxiety, especially in crowds like this, but Marcia always enjoyed pushing me outside my comfort zone; hence the scars I bear that nobody will ever see.

The man sitting at the large organ starts playing a song I don't recognize, and the doors slide open. I'm standing at the altar beside the priest. Opposite me are two boys; well, men actually, but they can't be older than twenty-five. They're gorgeous, and I can't stop myself from sneaking peeks at them. My new stepbrothers.

We haven't officially met but I know, soon enough, I'll be thrust into a family where I will have three older brothers. Which has my mind wandering to where the third son of my mother's new husband could be. Perhaps he's as against this wedding as I am, and he won't show up.

My mother slowly moves down the aisle, gliding as if she were floating on air. Her smile is pristine and perfect, and I wonder how real it is. Bradford looks absolutely smitten with her, as he watches her walk toward him, and when she finally reaches us, he leans down to kiss her cheek. A chaste kiss.

Mother hands me her bouquet, and I'm thankful to have something else to focus on, other than the eyes that are now on us at the front of the church.

"Welcome guests; today, we celebrate the union of Bradford Jeremiah Thorne and Marcia Anne Ellington." The priest's voice filters into the background as I glance up, and in the darkness of the church, right at the back, behind all the people, I see a dark figure. I can't make out his face, and I certainly can't see if he's in a suit or not, but my gut tells me that I'm looking at the eldest son of Bradford Thorne.

Deep down, I wonder why he's hiding, why he'd come to the ceremony, only to watch from the back. I blink, and when I open my eyes once more, he's gone.

Damien

The shitty LA air is stifling. I want to go back home to Thorne Haven. It's the only place I feel myself. Where I can allow myself to indulge in the silence that the city doesn't offer. Even though I know he's happy, something doesn't sit right with me. The woman he's vowing his life to is a fucking gold digger, and no matter how much I try to tell him the truth, he doesn't want to listen.

When he first told me he was getting married, I admit, I threw a shitfit. The rage I felt was nothing compared to that of my mother's, when she walked out on us, leaving her husband and sons behind.

I watched her breakdown.

The volatile relationship they had was nothing short of a hurricane tearing through the house, leaving only destruction in its wake. At twenty-seven, I shouldn't even be bothered with what my father is doing, but what he doesn't know is I've looked into this new wife of his.

She's nothing more than a Botox filled plastic doll that he's marrying to make himself look good. She's in the public eye twenty-four-seven, and I know she loves it. I've seen the photos online. What I don't understand, though, is what her daughter does. Granted, she only just turned eighteen, but I've not seen her in the photos I found of her mother.

And that is why my gut is churning with anxiety, and my mind whirling with questions.

When I pull into the parking lot of the hotel, I kill the engine of my raven-black Camaro and slide out of the driver's seat. My phone is already buzzing, and I know it's one of my brothers. They were both standing at the fucking altar, smiling at Dad, as he kissed his bride, but they didn't know I was there. I didn't want anyone to know, and then the girl looked at me.

Her daughter.

My new stepsister.

Pulling the cell phone from my pocket, I flick the green button and press the device to my ear. "What?"

"Dad would've liked that you were here." Cassian. Even

though I'm older, you'd think he's the eldest because he's more levelheaded than I am. He thinks things through before acting on impulse, whereas I like to jump in headfirst. Not thinking about the consequences has always been my mistake, and you'd think I would've learned by now, but no. I'm still like that, even at twenty-fucking-seven.

"I don't think Dad even noticed I wasn't there." My tone is cold and biting, but I know my brother won't notice it. And if he did, it wouldn't matter because he'd still give me shit for not being there.

"Finn and I think you should come back, spend the reception with us." I know he's trying to keep the peace. That's what Cassian is like, always making sure everyone is happy, but this time, he can't fix it.

"Cass, I know what you're trying to do, but I can't deal with this bullshit. Even though our mother walked out on him, I've watched him latch onto every woman who's offered him a smile since I was fourteen. He claims to be in love, but that's pure lust. Love doesn't exist." Even as I voice the words, I can see Cassian's expression, he's probably wincing at my biting tone. Cassian is the only one of us, besides our father, who believes in love. Even though he's single, my brother is a serial lover. He falls for girls all the time, and yet, he has never kept one around for longer than a month.

"I know you're angry—"

"I'm not angry, I'm actually quite happy, Brother," I tell him with a smile. "I've booked the plane; I'm heading to London to see what Thorne Industries is doing over there."

"How long will you be gone for?"

"I don't know. Why don't you take care of our little sister while I'm away?"

Cassian sighs. "Fine. But don't stay away too long. She seems like a nice girl. Perhaps we can find peace in this madness." And there he is, the peacekeeper.

"Tell Finn not to fuck her," I bite out, as I recall the girl standing at the altar with the bouquet. She looked so out of place, not because she wasn't beautiful, but the expression of worry that painted her features was enough to tell me she didn't want to be there.

"She's our stepsister, Damien," Cass reminds me, with an exasperated tone that has me chuckling. "Sometimes I worry about your sanity."

"It's not mine you have to concern yourself with, you know what Finn is like." The corner of my mouth quirks when I think of our youngest brother. He would fuck anything with a pair of tits. Not only that, I know for a fact that Finn has experimented sexually with guys.

Another sigh from Cassian. "I hate being stuck between you two dickheads," he tells me, but I can hear the smile on his face.

"Sure, you do, some girls say the same thing." This time, I hear him laugh out loud. It's true, though, Finn and I have had the same girls in our beds, but none of them were ever around long enough to learn more about us. It was one night of fun, and before the sun rose on the next day, they had to leave.

Finn is a lot more like me than Cassian would like, but you can't stop someone from acting like their hero.

"You're such an asshole," Cass tells me then adds, "Okay, I have to go. Have a good flight."

"Always, Brother." I grin, knowing I've only just annoyed my brother. But I end the call before he can warn me from breaking hearts while I'm over the pond. I head into the hotel, making my way up to the room to pack. Having a private jet at our disposal comes in handy for trips like these. But even if we didn't, I wouldn't stick around to see my father fawn over some woman who is only with him because he's got more money than god, and knows how to spend it.

I'm about to walk out of the hotel room when my phone buzzes once more. Cursing, I pull it from my pocket and see my father's name glaring brightly at me. *Jesus,* I can't catch a break today. Cass usually will allow me my freedoms, keeping my plans quiet from our father, so there must be a reason he's gone to the old man to get him to call me. And I know he did because Bradford wouldn't spend a moment of his wedding day on the phone with me.

"Dad," I answer, keeping my voice cool and calm, already knowing what my father is going to say.

"I hear you're flying to London," he sneers. The darkness in his tone tells me that something else is about to happen, and me flying across the ocean isn't one of those things.

"Maybe."

"I want you at Thorne Haven," he tells me. "My honeymoon is coming up, and I will be away." There's no debating with him. If he's made his mind up about something, then that's what's going to happen. I learned a long time ago, after my mother walked out, that Bradford Thorne is a man who's no longer soft and caring: he's cold, calculating. He's nothing more than a grown-up bully with narcissistic tendencies.

"I wanted to check in on the offices," I tell him.

"That can wait. Listen to me, Damien, you're the eldest. Your brothers need you, and your new sister is going to need help finding her way. You should be there to get to know her." There's a warning in his tone that tells me he doesn't trust me around her; which begs the question, why is he forcing me to stay at the house *with* her?

"Fine," I sigh in resignation. To be fair, I can leave her

in Cassian's hands since he's the least likely to want to get into her panties. "I'll be home when they arrive." I think about the drive home, and I look forward to it. Thorne Haven is nestled in the middle of nowhere. Which is exactly what I like about it. Forests, mountains, and not much else. Our home is one of the oldest properties in the Pacific Northwest.

Seventeen fucking hours.

"Thank you, Damien. You know, if you can do this for me, I'll ease up on the restrictions in place for you taking over Thorne Industries." He's taunting me with promises I know he won't deliver on. I don't understand why he can't be honest and tell me he doesn't want to let go of the company.

"Don't put yourself out. I'm not doing this for you. I know you may not realize this, but I do love my brothers, and leaving them with some new girl who doesn't know shit about our family isn't something I'll do."

"I would like you at the reception tonight, don't be late. I don't want to have to call you again," he tells me, then hangs up immediately, ignoring the rest of my tirade. I'm left with a command I can't ignore and anger racing through my veins.

Thorne Industries was started by my grandfather. A company built with old money, with the blood, sweat, and tears of those who came before us, and Bradford believes he can just walk in, rule the roost, and not do shit in the office. When I turned eighteen, I begged him to allow me to work for him, interning while I was studying, but my father has always hated me. I know he sees my mother when he looks at me.

Black hair, blue eyes, I'm the spitting image of Mommy Dearest, and that's why my father hates me. The day I turned twenty-one, he gave me my inheritance and told me to do what I wanted with it. So, I did; I invested it, and I live off the profits. He thinks I'm young and stupid, and I'll blow it all, but what he doesn't realize is that I learned how to do business from him.

Be shrewd.

Be calculating.

And, be an asshole.

After sliding my phone into my pocket, I grab my keys, wallet, and suitcase, and head for the door. Time to grab something to wear tonight since it looks like I'll be in attendance to celebrate the happy couple, even when I don't want to be. Also, I'll have some time to think about just how much hell I can give this new girl when I meet her.

I'm coming, little sister.

I hope you're afraid of the big bad wolf.

Nesrin

Present Day

The lavish party plays on as I make my way down the stairs and into the main dining hall of our beautifully stylish home. The room has been changed, making it look more like a party venue than a space where the family would sit down to eat. This house, the same place that I grew up in, and the only place I've ever called home, feels vastly different.

Three floors of Italian marble, infamous original artworks hanging against the walls, and carpets handwoven by the most prolific weavers around the world. Crystal clinks as the guests cheer and smile at each other. Each one as fake as the last. My mother has changed into a sleek silver dress that hangs to the floor.

Her wedding reception is in full swing with the guests mingling, most of them circling my mother and Bradford as if they're the newest celebrity couple. People hang onto every word from my mother's new husband.

The gold-rimmed railing of the staircase is confirmation enough of how wealthy my mother is in her own right. And it's also a stark reminder of how drastically life can change. I can't find it in myself to smile, but I know if I don't, she'll be on my case.

I really should be happy for her, and I am, to a certain extent. If I believed she truly loved him, I would smile and play the dutiful daughter, but I don't.

As I was changing, I once again google searched the man. It seems like he's more powerful than god, which makes me think that throwing money at anyone and everything is what he enjoys doing, because the lavish party is drenched in gold and crystal, diamonds and silver. Perhaps he believes his wealth can right the world of all its wrongs.

How I wish it were so.

It's not.

I move toward the crowd. People smile at me, tilting their flutes as I pass by, and I paste on the happy expression that's expected of me. I'm not averse to parties, but I prefer being on my own. Tonight, especially, I feel out of my depth. Perhaps it's because I'm nervous about meeting my new *family*, as my mother put it earlier.

I find my mother in the living room that's been decorated—luxuriously and lavishly—filled with sparkling banners that wish the couple a Happy Marriage. Gold shimmers from every corner, balloons that are color-coordinated to my mother's specifications float above everyone's heads. Knowing my mother, she probably drove everyone crazy, making sure it was all set up perfectly. Even the hors d'oeuvres that are being served have a mini edible candle-shaped breadstick coated in gold glitter, as per my mother's instructions.

"Nesrin." My new stepfather smiles at me happily, and I have to grant him his dues. He's vowed to love my mother for the rest of his life, that's commitment with eyes closed because he's not seen her at her worst yet. The coldness she exudes when she doesn't get her way, the biting words that attack like knives. "I hope that we're able to get to know each other when your mother and I get back."

"Thank you." I smile at him, but I don't feel the assurance that I should.

"I've spoken to my sons, they'll be with you at Thorne Haven, while we're away. Just so you don't have to stay here alone. I wouldn't want you to feel as if you've been abandoned."

I don't know what to say. I never thought my mother would agree to me leaving this house. But when she moves up behind Bradford, there's a grin on her face that makes me feel as if this was planned long before tonight.

"I think you'll like it up there, Nesrin," Mother says. "Bradford told me it's one of the oldest houses in the area. You've wanted to move up to the Pacific Northwest."

My heart stutters in my chest. *What?* "We're moving?" I croak.

My mother is about to respond when two Thorne sons, the two best men who stood witness to the marriage stroll up to us. "Hey, Dad." One with a buzz cut of dark brown hair grins. His eyes are a soft blue, with a twinge of green. A sharp jaw with a light dusting of stubble. His full lips capture my attention for a split second, and I notice the lower one more so than the top.

"Here they are." Bradford smiles happily. "This is Cassian." He points to the boy with the teal-colored eyes. "And that is Finn." I notice the boy farther back who has a mischievous grin on his face. His hair is longer on top and buzzed short at the sides. His eyes, however, are dark brown, like hot chocolate on a cold winter's night.

"Hello." I smile at them, but I can't stop my stomach flipping, as they stare me down, as if I were something beautiful to look at. I've grown accustomed to people staring at me, but never men who looked like *them*.

"Nice to officially meet you, little sister," the one called Cassian says with the corner of his mouth tipped into a smirk. He holds out his hand, which I accept.

"It's good to meet you, too," I respond, feeling nervous at everyone looking at me. I want to hide, to not have their focus solely on me, but I can't with so many people around me, and I feel my stomach twisting with anxiety.

"I'm the handsome brother," the other boy says suddenly. Although, I can't call either of them boys because they're men. He offers me a wink, and I laugh, it's a real honest to goodness chuckle, and I'm shocked that he's brought it out of me.

"She's our sister, for fuck sake," Cassian bites out through clenched teeth, before rolling his eyes at his brother. I don't know who's younger, but from their banter, I guess it's Finn.

"Language," Bradford admonishes his son.

"Sorry, Dad," Cassian says. "You can call me Cass," he informs me, then tips me a salute before making his way to a pretty blonde that I now realize is waiting for him.

"Sorry about that," Finn says, as he steps forward, "Welcome to the family." I'm expecting him to shake my hand, but instead, he pulls me in and wraps his arms around me. I can't see his body, but I can feel every ridge and dip of his muscles.

Finn has his hair falling over one eye, making him look even younger than I would guess he is. His smooth jawbone is angular, with a sharp nose and full lips. Where Cassian is stoic in his expression, Finn smirks like a bad boy personified. And I have a feeling he lives up to that title.

Finn steps back as he pins his focus on me. His chocolate brown eyes dance with mischief. Their father has salt and pepper hair, with piercing blue eyes, and I wonder if their mother had dark brown eyes which would match Finn's perfectly. It's intriguing.

"It's good to meet you," I say, looking up at Finn.

"I think it's time for a drink." The young man winks then heads off to grab some bubbly from a passing waiter. My gaze follows him, taking in his broad shoulders in a crisp white shirt.

"Why don't you grab a glass of champagne? Only one," Bradford warns, playfully, as he taps me on the nose, and I fight not to cringe away from him. It's far too personal for someone I've only met once.

"I'm going to get some fresh air before everyone starts with the speeches," I tell him with a smile, ignoring my mother's heated glare burning into me because I'm not doing as I was asked.

I move through the throng of people, stifled by the amount of perfume that's invading my nostrils. I push through to the patio doors and step out into the rather warm night. I've always hated this weather where you can shower one minute, then sweat the moment you step outside.

Soon enough, I'll be in the Pacific Northwest. I should've asked about where they live. All I gathered was that it was in the middle of nowhere, and my mind runs riot with images of a large mansion sitting on a hill, overlooking a beautiful forest.

My heart thumps at the thought, and I smile as I make it onto the porch, without more awkward hugs and fake smiles. Closing my eyes, I lean against the pillar that holds up the balcony on the second floor and rest my head against the concrete.

I hear a giggle from somewhere in the garden, my gaze snapping open, as I try to make out where it came from. Our grounds aren't filled with too many trees, so it would be easy to spot someone from here. Another laugh dances across the warm breeze toward me, and I take a step off the patio and onto the mushy grass.

Following the sounds, I find myself at the greenhouse that my father had built for my mother. She hasn't used it at all since he died. I suppose the heartbreak was too much for her to bear. And perhaps that's why she's always been so cold and heartless. But she never allowed me in to learn about her, to get to really know her.

I always wondered why she never had it destroyed. Taken away. Deep down, I wonder if she's holding onto hope that it will rekindle a flame that's long since been put out. I step quietly into the glass structure, and that's when I see it.

Even in the dim light, I can see a guy leaning against one of the shelves of potted plants. His hair is as black as night; I notice from the illumination of the garden lights that circle the perimeter of the glass housing. He's dressed in a dark suit, what looks like a crisp white shirt, and a black tie.

His head is tipped back as pleasure clearly paints his face. I watch with rapt attention as the head at his crotch thrusts back and forth. His one hand tangled in the red curls that spill down her back and his mouth parts as a groan escapes his perfect lips.

There are choking sounds coming from the girl, and he lifts his head right at that moment, his heated gaze landing on mine. He doesn't make a move to let her know they're being watched. And he doesn't stop her either. Instead, he watches me. His stare bores into me, burrowing itself into the depths of my soul, as the corner of his mouth tilts upward, and deep dimples appear. A smile, dark and devious, turns my body molten, and I can't stop the tremble that shoots through me.

Stupidly, I don't run. I don't move. I'm not even sure

I'm breathing at this point. But the stranger's face is filled with pure ecstasy, as he holds the girl steady and moves his hips.

The filthy, sexual sounds bounce off the glass walls. My breathing hitches in my throat, and my heart is drumming wildly in my chest. The ache that starts low in my stomach twists tighter with every second that passes. The pulse between my legs is erratic, and I want nothing more than to touch myself.

"That's good," he growls, keeping his eyes on me, and it's almost as if he's talking to me, but I know he's not. "Keep going," he tells her but doesn't stray his gaze from mine. "I'm going to fill your pretty mouth with cum." His voice is low, gravelly, dripping with lust and desire.

My nerves are shot; they spark with electric energy that has my feet slowly moving backward, but I never leave. I don't look away from his beautiful, luminous eyes. I can't tell what color they are from here, but all I know is they're fucking flawless.

He grunts, his head tipping to the side, as he regards me now. His hand is still in her hair, but his eyes are burning me from the inside out.

"That's what you like. Isn't it?" he says, but this time, I'm not sure which of us he's speaking to. Another grin from his mouth and she's standing up, which sets me in motion, as I run back to the house. By the time I'm indoors, with a glass of champagne in my hand, I'm still shaking. I'm not sure who that was, or why they were using my mother's greenhouse for something like that, but I know I never want to see that man again.

"Here you are," my mother snips when she finds me standing close to the corner of the room, where I can't see the patio doors. The thought of laying eyes on *him* again has my body both shaking and thrumming.

"I told you and Bradford I needed some fresh air," I tell her.

"Your aunt is here," Mom whispers, leaning in closer to me. "She wants to see you." Mallory is a godsend, and I can't help but smile when I think about her. The younger sister, the *harlot*. That's what Mom used to call her. They never got along, and I know it's because something happened between them after my mother got married. I never learned what, but one day, I know I'll find out.

"I didn't think she was invited."

"Well, you know your aunt." Mother shakes her head, as if her sister is a disappointment, just like me. It's almost as if I'm not allowed to have other family besides my mother and the people she approves. But I know it's more than that. "Come, say hello to her."

I follow my mother through the crowd, but my gaze continually flits over to the doors that lead out to the garden. I realize I'm waiting for *him* to come inside.

I want to see what he looks like in the light, without pleasure written all over his face. But, of course, he'd now have satisfaction all over his expression instead.

My cheeks burn, and I almost stumble into my mother's petite frame, when I don't realize she's stopped.

"There she is." My aunt, Mallory, grins playfully as she pulls me into a hug. Her body is warm, calming, not like my mother's who is cold and unaffectionate. I've gotten so used to it, that when Mallory holds me, I actually hug her back.

"I've missed you," I tell her with a genuine smile, knowing she'll understand the underlying pain in my words. Mallory is younger than mom by a few years and, at times, I wonder if that's why I get along with her better than my own mother. My mother trying to be the older, more grown-up levelheaded of the two, whereas my aunt is more frivolous, younger in personality and immature in her choices in life.

"I just heard you're moving up north to the cold and rain." She glances at her sister, and I can tell there's animosity because the tension between us is so thick, so heavy, it feels as if a fight is about to break out.

"I am, for a month, until mom gets back from her honeymoon, and then we'll see what happens," I tell her.

"Well, if you need to ever get away, you're always welcome at my house," she offers, but my mother's hand lands heavily on my shoulder in warning. She doesn't like the idea.

"Or she could focus on choosing her major and making sure she's chosen the college she wants to attend. Bradford is generously offering to pay for her studies. I think it's nice of him." My mother's tone is filled with fury, as she hisses the words.

My aunt's gaze sizzles as she regards her sister.

If I didn't feel halfway comfortable spending time with Finn and Cassian, I would've asked my mother if I could stay with Mallory; but with tensions running high, I think I'll just let it go for now.

"I'm actually looking forward to spending time at the Thorne house. Apparently, it's rich with history, and I'm dying to have some cooler weather." I turn to my mother who's watching our interaction, hoping she'll lay off. She sips her drink as I stare at her, and she offers me a smile of victory.

I'm the pawn in the middle of a game between the siblings, which annoys me, but I allow it to filter into nothing. If I did put up a fight and argue the fact, I know my mother would only force me to go to Thorne Haven.

The need to be anywhere but in LA is burning in my veins. I can be someone else, no longer the daughter of the infamous beauty that my mother is. When she realized I would never be like her, she gave up on me, allowing me to focus on my schoolwork.

"I'm glad you're taking this so well and not throwing a hissy fit in the middle of the reception," she finally responds in a slightly hushed whisper, and my lungs expel the breath I'd been holding. "But," she says a bit louder for everyone to hear, her voice stern, more serious than I've ever heard her, "If you don't go to college or choose your major while we're away, when I get back, you're coming into the studio with me. My agent has roles that would be perfect for you."

"I'm sure she'll figure out what she wants to do with her future, Marcia," my aunt tells her sister, her voice drenched in frustration. This is what it's like with them all the time.

"Seems I haven't met the beautiful ladies of the Ellington family yet." A deep and raspy tone comes from behind me, sending goosebumps skittering across my bare skin.

I know who it is before I turn around. There's no doubt that it's *him*. No man in this room sounds like *that*. A voice dripping seduction, and a tone that's laced with sin.

"You're far too kind," my mother gushes, her gaze locked on the man behind me. I can feel his warmth, smell the intoxicating spice of his cologne, and the hint of smoke that tells me he's had a cigarette outside.

I guess it's true what they say: after good sex, you need a smoke.

"This is Damien." My mother grins happily, causing my body to go into a flat-out panic.

"It's a pleasure to meet you." My aunt shakes his hand, and then I finally take a chance and glance over my shoulder. The moment I do, my breath is knocked from my lungs. Ice blue pools of glass are looking directly at me.

Where Cassian's gaze is a soft teal shade and less intimidating than Damien's icy blue one, I can't stop trembling at having his cold focus on me. Each brother unique in the features, and I'm sure in personalities too.

"And you are?" He quirks his thick black brow at me. It's now that I can see his hair is jet black, like a raven's feathers. His mouth is pursed, lips full and pink. His angular jawbone is smooth, temptingly beautiful. I want to touch it to see if he's really human. But I don't move. His sharp nose looks like it's been chiseled by an infamous artist.

"This is your stepsister, Nesrin," my mother answers for me, when I can't find my words. Frustration burns my cheeks because I'd never been so caught unaware by a boy before. Not a boy, really. This is a man. He is the eldest of the three, which would make him mid to late twenties.

"Damien Thorne," he says, reaching for my hand. I offer it only because I don't want to be rude, but the moment he brings my hand up to his mouth, heat coils in my stomach. His lips touch my knuckles, and sparks shoot through every inch of my body, from the top of my head to the tips of my toes. The pulse that was so boldly thrumming between my legs earlier is set alight by his touch. "It's a pleasure."

"It is."

Really?

That's all I can manage!

Damien

I MAKE HER NERVOUS. IT'S ALLURING. SHE PULLS HER hand away as if my touch burned her, and I wonder if she's thinking about what happened in the greenhouse. One thing I know for sure is that she won't be telling anyone what happened in there because she's feeling embarrassed for watching, but most of all, she's feeling guilty for enjoying it.

"It's good to finally meet you, Nesrin," I tell her, which only makes her cheeks darken, as she watches me. I've been around plenty of women and girls who fall to their knees for me or would like to, but nobody has ever captured my attention like this.

"Yeah, same," she responds, once more, and I realize

that my father has just ensured a month of fun and games for me. Granted, she is my stepsister now, and I know I can't do much about it or he'll probably cut my dick off, but I can certainly toy with her to my heart's content.

"I trust you'll look after my little girl while me and your father are gone," Marcia Ellington says, but I don't answer her. She's one of those fake beauties. Everything about her is plastic, even her heart. And I know I'll make my father see the truth, one way or another. Perhaps I can use the little rose in front of me to do it.

I'm going to kick Cassian's ass if he allows Finn to go anywhere near her because my youngest brother is a loose cannon when it comes to pretty girls. But I can see why he would go there. She's sweet and innocent, but far too young for me, even though I'd have her on her back in a few hours, if I really wanted to.

Even in her sweet innocence, there's more to her, I can tell just from her reaction to my touch. Beautiful, appealing, but even with all that shiny veneer, there's something *broken* about her. As if her petals could easily tumble to the ground, one by one. Wilting under the bright spotlights of fame that come with her mother's career.

She pins me with her hazel eyes, and I can't help but read through the glare to find something far darker than

I anticipated hiding there. Something I would certainly love to uncover.

"Well, then it seems I'll have a full car on the way back," I tell Marcia with a sincere smile. I can't wait to see what she makes of life in Thorne Haven.

"You will." Marcia grins happily, swaying on her five-inch heels. I'm sure she's had far too much of the sparkling gold bubbly already. My father should cut her off, but knowing him, he probably prefers her like this.

I don't know her well enough yet, but I have a feeling once she's living in Thorne Manor, I'll be moving out. I doubt Dad will mind; he seems happy enough with his new bride.

"Can I talk to you?" Marcia whispers to her sister, but we all hear it. I can read the animosity between them as if it were a page in a well-known book. I've lived around bullshit like that for so long it's become second nature to pick up on it the moment I walk into a room.

Soon enough, the sisters are gone, and I'm left with Nesrin. She looks like a deer caught in headlights when she looks up at me.

"Did you enjoy the show?" I ask, arching a brow at her.

The apples of her cheeks turn dark pink, and I can almost feel the heat coming off her. Her gaze dances along the crowd, not meeting mine. She's shy, but still, I can see the fire burning in her gaze when it sweeps over me.

"You know, I enjoy people watching. I would love to have watched you touch that pussy that I'm sure is still tight and pure." Another statement that has the same hue flourishing on her chest, and I'm tempted to lean in and get a taste of her flesh.

"You're disgusting," she finally hisses, but her voice is merely a whisper. "You do realize that I'm practically family now."

I tilt my mouth into a smirk. "*Practically* and *actually* aren't the same thing, Darling," I tell her. For a moment, it looks like she forgot about our new living arrangement.

"Are you really living at Thorne Haven? Aren't you a little *old* to be living at home with your father?" Her biting tone makes me hard. I can't help it. I love a woman with spirit. Makes it so much more worthwhile when I break them.

"I don't know about old, little sis." I shrug as if she hasn't struck a nerve. "You'll soon see just why we haven't left Thorne Manor, and when you walk through those doors, you will never want to leave."

"Is that a threat?" she gasps in shock, her mouth falling open and her pouty lips spread into a perfect O. My mind has taken on a whole new scenario of the pretty girl who's standing in front of me. I shouldn't be thinking about the filthy things I'd love to do to her mouth, but my mind is on a pathway straight to hell.

"Not at all, but remember one thing, we're all extremely close."

"Well, I'm not living with you. I'll be in my own bedroom or something." She folds her arms across her chest, which only serves to make her cleavage all the more prominent. She's slightly curvy, and the tips of my fingers tingle to touch her, to grip her hips and hold her steady, as I lean in closer to inhale her feminine scented perfume.

"Damien." My name drips with need and want from the woman who just swallowed my load. I used her for my pleasure. That's what I do. There aren't any second chances, not in my world. "You disappeared on me."

"I'm busy," I bite out, not turning my attention away from Nesrin, who's now pinning the redhead with a glare that would certainly kill if she had the powers to do so.

Jealous? I ponder silently.

"But I—"

"I. Said. I'm. Fucking. Busy." My words are low, but they're like silver bullets hitting her right in the chest. To the very heart of where she thought I was going to take her out for dinner and then fuck her into oblivion. I don't do dates, and I certainly am not boyfriend material.

"You're an asshole," the redhead spits. I chuckle, it's something I've known my whole life. I'm just like my father. I may look like my mother, but my charming and oftentimes misunderstood personality comes from Daddy Dearest. Cold, heartless, and narcissistic.

"Did you have to be so rude to her?" Nesrin's voice is a whispered gasp. Shock is painted on her pretty face, and I can't help but be intrigued by her. Even though I've never met her before, this is the first time I've come face to face with a woman who wasn't fawning over themselves for me.

"Yes," I answer simply. She doesn't need any more information than that. I glance up, noticing the crowd moving around, watching who's talking to whom. I notice Finn and Cassian, both have a woman on their arms, one more languid than the other, and I can't help but roll my eyes.

And, as the eldest brother, I take my responsibility seriously. But, sometimes, I let them do what they like. Even though they haven't spotted me yet, I know Cassian's going to give me grief for taunting our little sister.

"You're so confident that every woman in this room would drop to their knees and suck your dick. Aren't you?" Nesrin hisses under her breath, as she leans into me, and I bask in her scent.

"Yes, I am, because they will. When they learn my name, they'll even fall on their back and spread their thighs for me to fuck them into oblivion, just to say they've been with a Thorne."

Nesrin stumbles backward, into someone, before she spins on her heel, but she doesn't make it out of the room before she slams into my father's chest. I can't hear what they're saying, but it's clear he doesn't want her leaving.

I'm not sure why she's so shocked by my words. She's clearly not the innocent rose I thought she was. And her fragile exterior is nothing on the strength that shimmers in her eyes and has her squaring her shoulders.

Dad offers her a pat on the arm before he steps onto the small platform that serves as a stage. He grabs the microphone and holds up his glass of champagne. He takes in the crowd before smiling down at his new pride and joy—Marcia.

Nesrin

The Past

MY MOTHER'S ANGRY. I WATCH HER PACE BACK AND forth, her body rigid at my outburst. I hate being here, I never wanted to go to the stupid casting, but she insisted. I tried, I really did, but I just couldn't face those people prodding and poking at me.

Four faces, four sets of eyes were on me, watching me intently. They wanted me to perform like a dancing monkey, and I hated every moment. My anxiety curled slowly in my gut, twisting it painfully. My stomach tightened into a knot, it stole my breath, and that's when I started hyperventilating.

Nobody understands.

They all thought I was some crazy daughter of a well-loved actress, throwing a hissy fit. But I'm not. I'm old enough to know when I'm uncomfortable. So, instead of opening my mouth and telling them, choking out the words, I couldn't form any, so I ran. Right out of the room.

Why can't my mother understand?

"This is going to make me look like an idiot to the people I have to work with," she finally speaks. "Do you know how much you've embarrassed me?" Finally, she stops pacing, her glower on me makes me shrink back. "Sixteen! You're a fucking teenager, and you can't even open your goddamned mouth!" Her voice bounces off the walls of my bedroom, the sound burying itself in my mind; the words, filled with poison, slowly burrowing under my skin.

Every time she's ever insulted me, shouted at me and been angry at me feels like it's coming to the forefront and slowly rising up to the surface of my skin.

Sweat dots my arms, the nape of my neck. My stomach is aching, but I know if I move now, she'll only laugh at me, tell me I'm overreacting.

"I don't know how I got lumped with you as a daughter." Ice fills my veins, and I want to respond and tell her I don't know either. But I don't because it will only make her angrier.

She turns around, looking at my bedroom. My haven. I'm almost sure she wants to smash everything within reach, but she doesn't.

"You'll stay in here for the next two days to think about what you've done. I'll have your food brought to you." She spins on her designer four-inch heel and leaves the room.

I'm getting so used to people leaving me, that watching someone's retreating form is no longer scary, it's welcomed.

Pushing to my feet, I race into my bathroom and shut the door, locking it behind me. Leaning against the cool wooden surface, I close my eyes as the tears slowly trickle down my cheeks.

My hands shake as I try to calm down, but I know I won't be able to until I've opened the box. My feet carry me to the cupboard where I know I'll find what I need. My stomach coils with the promise of a panic attack. My breathing comes in short spurts of rushed expelled air.

With trembling fingers, I pull open the cabinet door and find the small box that's been my salvation, and I can almost breathe again. Flicking the lid, I pull out what I need and slide to the floor. My head falls back against the cupboard as I hold onto the box. Inside, I find what I need. Pulling my shorts up to the crease of my leg, where my panty line is visible at my hip, I sit crossed-legged and find a spot on my inner thigh.

I blink back the tears that fall. My body is shaking, but I know the moment I cut into my porcelain flesh, it will all be okay. My fingers shake as I hold onto the metal object. Gently, I press the silver blade to my skin and push harder, until I feel the release shooting through me.

The tightness in my muscles ease. Coiled anxiety which was a heavy looming figure racing behind me, ready to snatch me in its claws, dissipates. The dark cloud that felt like a storm hanging over me disappears as the sting skitters through me. The sky is no longer dark, the soft blue appears, and my lungs don't feel like I've run a marathon, they easily pull in air.

I watch my blood trickle from the cut, the small wound opening, and the pain and heartache from today spills along with the crimson to the floor. It's only a small cut, one that will heal quickly. I've never made bigger incisions because I was afraid I'd be really hurt.

When I read horror stories of girls who took it too far, who craved it so much they would cut longer, deeper, I focused myself on never going down that road. As much as it helps me clear my mind of worry and fear, I've scared myself into the realization that this could be fatal. And that has ensured I'm always careful.

Blood coats my fingers, but the freedom feels like

flying. It's what I imagined an orgasm to feel like. Like tipping over the edge and wings emerging behind you, keeping you up in the air while you soar.

It's the only way I can describe it.

Leaning my head back on the cabinet doors, I smile up at the ceiling, as I lift my fingers to my lips and taste the metallic flavor. I'm so broken, so fucked up from the way my body craves this, I doubt I'll ever have a normal life.

I can finally breathe.

The knot in my stomach is gone.

And I can happily stay in my bedroom without the anxiety hitting me again. My mother will never have to know what I've just done. Not that she'd care.

I know she flies out of the country in a day or two, so I'll be alone with my thoughts. I smile as I lean back against the wooden surface and close my eyes. I'm no longer twisted up inside. When I first started doing this, *cutting*, I went online, read about others who've done it. They explained how it felt to them, the suffocation of anxiety lifting the moment they made the incision. Some even mentioned it felt good, as if they were drunk. I don't know what that's like, but the relief is real, it's a force that holds me close like a warm blanket on a cold night.

I push up, standing at the sink and rinsing my leg. I tidy up the mess I made and go into my bedroom. On the nightstand, I find my cell phone and tap out a message to Isaac. He's been my tutor for three months, and even though we haven't done anything, his messages, along with the stinging on my inner thigh, have offered me a calm in the storm.

I smile when his response comes back—a photo of him in his boxer briefs, and a message, *thinking about those pretty eyes.*

I breathe deeply, sliding under the covers and snaking my hands between my thighs. Time to find another release.

Damien

Present Day

L AST NIGHT WAS LIKE A SCENE OUT OF A FAMILY SITCOM. Actually, more like a comedy of horrors. I wanted to disappear so many times. But I couldn't. When I finally slid under the covers last night, I was too tired to think about anything other than dreaming. And then, even in my sleep, blue eyes stared back at me. It was as if Damien was haunting me.

Sliding out of bed, I pad into the bathroom. The sun is just rising, bathing the room in a soft pinkish glow. I pull open the cabinet and find what I'm looking for. My muscles are stiff when I settle on the lid of the toilet.

I haven't turned to this for two long weeks, but after yesterday's fiasco, I need it.

My heart thuds against my chest at the reminder of what happened. The images of seeing Damien getting a blow job from some random redhead. The thoughts of sitting with him in the car today have my nerves shot to hell.

The first time I did this, I was young. I recall the release so clearly. It was as if it was yesterday. I had accidentally cut myself on a broken glass after hearing my father screaming at my mother, and mom, in turn, decided to smash his whiskey decanter all over his office floor.

My anxiety spiked. At the time, I didn't know what the feeling was, all I knew was that I needed to scream, but if I did, I'd only draw attention to myself, so instead, I crushed the fragile glass I'd been holding. My fingers had squeezed so hard that it shattered, slicing my hand open. The moment I saw the blood, I felt like I could breathe again. It was as if the world was no longer blurry, it was peaceful. When I was younger, I just knew it eased the ache in my body, it lifted the tension and pain, but now, it's different.

I pick up the sleek, silver blade. It's small, thin, and inconspicuous. Once, my mother found my box, she rummaged through the bandages and the Band-Aids, and she found the blades. At first, she went on a rampage, screaming at me, and then she broke down. I had never seen my mother cry, but that day, she did. I promised her that I'd be okay. It was the first and last time she acknowledged what she found. The days after, she ignored me, as if she never knew what I did.

After a couple of weeks, she sent me to therapy, not wanting to deal with it herself. I spoke to a stranger about my feelings, but nothing worked. The only thing that helped was the metal biting into the smooth, tanned flesh of my inner thighs.

I hate this.

But I don't.

It's a release that I never thought I could ever feel because nothing that was *normal* worked. Therapy. Medication. Even just focusing on hobbies didn't help me.

A cut was the only solace I found.

A harsh knock on the door sounds like a warning alarm in my bedroom. I go to it, opening it up, to find my mother smiling at me like the world is perfect. Her happiness makes her glow, and I wish that she was like this all the time. But I know it's a fleeting moment in time.

"We're getting ready to leave," she tells me, before pulling me into her arms as if we were always close and loving. Her affection is so foreign, it takes me a moment to hug her back.

"I hope you have fun," I whisper, still confused at her sudden *love* for me. She doesn't say anything; she just holds me.

When we finally break apart, she smiles at me, before telling me, "I hope you enjoy Thorne Haven. I hear it's beautiful. And the manor is just stunning."

"Yeah, I'm sure I will like it."

"And behave for the boys, they'll be looking after you." Her voice is stern, annoying, because I'm no longer a child. I'm eighteen, all grown up and ready to take on the world.

"Mom, just go," I tell her, hoping she'll stop this strange behavior. It's been so long since she's paid me any attention without insults, it's disconcerting.

"I just want you to show them that you were brought up with class." Her voice lowers to a whisper. "And no boys, school should be your focus. Make sure you're ready to choose your major by the time we're back. If you want to move to England and go to Oxford, like your dad did, then you can do that as well. I just don't want my daughter falling pregnant with some misfit's child." She doesn't say it, but I know she wanted to say, *like I did.* All my life I've heard about her finding out she was pregnant with me, which set her career back by a couple of years. And, all the while, I knew I was a mistake she didn't want.

"Hey, little sis," Finn saunters by, his gaze raking over my silky sleep shorts and tank top before he arches a dark brow. "We're leaving in an hour, best be ready, Damien hates waiting."

"I'll be there," I respond, with a smile. The thought of sitting in a car with the three guys for so long has me on edge.

"Have fun," Mother tells me, before planting a kiss on my forehead. Once I'm alone, I'm able to breathe. It's apparently going to be a long drive to Thorne Haven. We can't fly because they don't have an airstrip in the town. And Damien doesn't want to leave his precious car here, so it looks like a road trip is in the cards.

I guess it's time to face my three stepbrothers.

Damien

THE MOMENT THE ENGINE ROARS TO LIFE, I PUT MY foot on the gas, and we head down the driveway and out onto the road. I'm hyperaware that she's in my car, right behind the passenger seat. It's almost as if I can feel her looking at me, watching me. I don't turn; I focus on the road, but it's difficult.

Cass reaches for the radio, flicking it on to find something to listen to. I know he's going to end up linking his iPhone to the stereo, but I leave him to it. At least his taste in music isn't bad.

If it was Finn, I'd lose my shit. Sometimes, our youngest brother can drive us crazy with the tunes he has blaring from his bedroom. Flicking my gaze in the rearview mirror, I find golden eyes staring back at me. She doesn't act shy; instead, she holds my gaze.

I can't help but smile. I don't mind her shyness, but it's her feisty nature that seems to appear every now and then, which intrigues me.

"Are you looking forward to your stay in Thorne Haven?" Finn questions her, and I can't help but keep my ears pricked for her response.

"Yes, I've lived in LA my whole life, even though I hated it. So, I'm excited to see someplace new."

"Why would you hate LA? It's a fucking amazing city," Finn tells her.

I don't hear her respond yet, but I have a feeling she's just shrugged him off. "I don't know, I just don't like crowds."

Finn chuckles. "Then you'll love Thorne Haven, there's fuck all going on there."

"Except for the parties," Cass reminds him, in a sober tone.

Yes, the parties in our hometown are infamous around the area, bringing university students from all over the place. Even though we're secluded within a large forest, we're well-known around the schools from neighboring towns.

"I don't really do parties," Nesrin tells us. "I mean, I just don't like crowds in general, and, normally, parties give me anxiety."

"Don't worry, little sis," Finn tells her. "We'll keep you safe. Damien is definitely bodyguard material." He slaps his hand on the back of my seat, and I want to pull over and punch him the fuck out. Sometimes, my brother can be an asshole. More so than I am.

"I think you'll like it there," Cassian says once his phone is connected, and a playlist comes through the speakers. The somber melodies seem to lull everyone into silence, but I don't complain. It's easier than having everyone talking all at once. Even though I want to learn more about Nesrin, I allow it to slide for now. Being the eldest, I've always taken the lead when Bradford isn't home, and this time isn't any different; our little sister will learn that soon enough.

Five hours in, and I'm in the passenger seat with Cassian driving. Leaning back in the chair, I close my eyes and try to get some shut-eye. But my ears are attentive when Cass starts questioning our stepsister.

"So, tell us more about you? Did you ever want to get into acting like your mother?"

A sigh comes from right behind me. "No. Even though she insisted I go to castings, I never found a love for it like she had." There's an inflection in her voice, which has me glancing at Cass. His gaze quickly locks on mine, before turning back to the road, and I know he heard it as well.

"What about your dad?"

"He… He left when I was young. My mom and dad fought a lot. Things that didn't make sense to me seemed to be a daily argument. There were small things, at first, like who did the washing up, or why weren't my dad's shirts ironed." There's a waterfall of pain dripping from her words. "Then, one night, they had a huge falling out. I never found out what it was about; she never wanted to tell me."

"And you haven't seen your dad since?" Finn asks, shock clear in his voice.

"No." One word filled with so much pain, I feel it right down to my gut. I know how she feels. The heartbreak of a parent walking out sticks with you. My mind goes back to that night when my mother did the same thing.

Even though the sun's shining through the windows, our folks are screaming at each other. Thankfully, Finn's still asleep, and Cassian's in his bedroom. I don't want them to see this. I don't want them to witness the fight. Glass crashes from the living room, but I can't see what's happening.

"I'm done with this, Bradford," my mother's voice filters up to me, "I can't love you anymore. It hurts far too much."

"If you can't love me, then love the boys."

"I've met someone," she says suddenly, and another crash sounds up toward me, causing me to jump. My stomach is in knots. "I love him."

"You are not capable of love if you can leave your sons like this. You're nothing but a fucking whore running around and opening your legs for every man you see." My father's words are vile, filled with anger, and I realize he's trying to hurt her. I've never heard him speak to my mother like this.

"If that's what you believe, so be it."

"If you walk out of this house, you're not coming back. You will never have contact with the boys. They won't know you."

"They already know me. They also know what an evil bastard you are." More venom is spat between them. "They will always be my boys."

"Like fuck they will. Don't you ever try to return. Our love is broken, there's nothing that can bring it back. You've annihilated the trust between us. If you try to contact them at any point, I'll end you."

My mother laughs, shock lacing the sound. "You don't have it in you to kill me, Bradford, you love me too much."

"The love I had for you is gone. I always knew that it was a wasted emotion, even when you begged and pleaded for me to say it to you."

My lungs struggle to pull in air. They always seemed so happy. They played the part well because I would never have believed they never loved each other.

"Love is nothing more than a fool's errand. Get out of my house if you want to leave, but remember, they're my sons, not yours."

My mother walked out that night. She didn't return, and she never once tried to contact us. Not even when I hit eighteen and became an adult. I never tried to find her either. She was the reason our father turned into a tyrant, and I didn't want to allow her the decency of knowing me.

Cassian and Finn broke down the next morning, finding our mother gone, but I didn't. I knew what she did to our dad, and as much as I can't stand the asshole, I know his heart broke when she left.

Hence the fact that love is off the cards for me. It's a stupid fucking emotion that only gets you broken.

"I need to take a piss," Finn says from the back.

"Be careful what you say, we have a lady in the car," Cass admonishes him, but Finn's chuckle tells me that he doesn't give a shit if the Queen of England was sitting beside him, our youngest brother will say anything he likes.

"She'll need to get used to it," Finn responds. "Right, little sis?"

"Don't mind me." Nesrin's tone seems amused, but I

can't see her face, and deep down, I realize I'm dying to look at her. To study her features and take in those golden eyes.

"See," Finn says full of confidence. "Three guys and one girl. I like the odds." Something in his tone sets my body tight with tension. The games we've played with girls in the past spark in my mind, and I can't stop the images that play on a loop.

Perhaps we can introduce our sister to the game we like to play. And she'll become the rose amongst the Thornes.

Now that will be something to see in the dark.

Nesrin

IT'S BEEN A LONG, PAINFUL DRIVE.
Too many people in my fucking car.

By the time we pull up to the house, I'm out of the vehicle and sauntering toward it. Leaving Finn and Cass to deal with our new stepsister is my plan, but even as I push open the front door, I know I'm already hooked. Like a fucking teenager, wanting to know more about the girl he's intrigued by.

But that's not me, so I ignore Cass calling to me to help with her suitcases. Even though the rest of her belongings are arriving on the truck in a couple of days, I don't feel the need to be a bag boy for her.

I'm angry.

I'm frustrated.

And I'm hungry.

Heading straight for the kitchen, I find Joy at the stove. The older woman who's worked for my father, far longer than I can remember, smiles at me when I saunter in.

"There's my boy," she says, turning to me with a wooden spoon held up. "Taste this." The scent of tomatoes, spices, and something else fill the air. It's been a long nineteen hours on the road. Thankfully, with three of us driving, we didn't have to stay over anywhere. That wouldn't have gone down well.

I lean in and take the tip of the spoon in my mouth, and my taste buds burst with flavors. "That's good, Mama Joy," I tell her with a wink. Moments later, three bodies enter the kitchen, catching Joy's attention, and I glance over my shoulder to meet her gaze. The golden-brown shimmering eyes that draw me in hold me hostage for a moment, not too long, but long enough.

"And who is this young beauty?" Joy coos, as she races toward Nesrin. "I'm Joy, you can call me Mama, just like the boys do," she informs our new stepsister, which only irritates me more. She has no right to call her anything because she shouldn't be here.

I move through the space, pushing open the door and making my way out into the garden. I can't be in the same space as her. Even though I'm dying to inhale her scent, to delve into her mind and see what secrets she has hidden there, I can't. I know I can't because my father will kill me.

"Is there something you'd like to tell me?" Cass's voice comes from behind me, but I don't turn to regard my brother. I can't because, if I do, he'll notice that I'm affected by the new girl.

"What would there be to tell you?" Even as I ask it, I hear the inflection of frustration in my voice. Normally, I can play it cool, but the irritation that's got a hold of me has latched its claws in, and I don't see how I'll be free of it.

"I don't know, D," he says, stepping up beside me. Staring out at the garden, I realize now why my father had that atrocity installed. The greenhouse sits far behind our house, filled with plants and flowers of every color. But most of all, the roses that seem to blossom in their pots.

He chose to get it set up a month ago and had a variety of specialists in to set up the greenery. But it was only when he had those roses brought in that I was fascinated. Now I know why.

Our stepmother has a love of the flower. Naming her daughter Nesrin, which means Wild Rose in Persian, has to be a sign that he was trying to impress her.

"There's nothing to say," I tell him, finally facing my

brother. "I'm just making sure that I keep my distance like father wanted." I make a move to go inside, but Cassian is hot on my heels. In the kitchen, we find it empty, but I can hear Joy gushing over Nesrin.

I'm not sure where Finn has disappeared to, but I would hazard a guess that he's gone into town to meet up with one of his fuck buddies. Even though Thorne Haven is small, my youngest brother has found a way around it by fucking every girl within a ten-mile radius of Thorne Manor.

"You don't have to lie to me," Cassian says, causing me to stop dead in my tracks. He's trying to goad me, taunting me, so I will admit I find Nesrin attractive.

"And what lie would that be?"

"You know you can't go for her," he tells me, something that's glaringly clear to me. Even good old Bradford made sure that I was well aware the girl was off-limits.

"If you haven't noticed, I'm not averse to fucking beautiful women, but she's nothing more than a girl. That's all. And also, I didn't realize that keeping it in the family meant that she was even on the table." Tipping my head to the side, I narrow my eyes on Cass, whose mouth has quirked playfully. The fucker always gets to me, no matter how I try to ignore him.

"Just saying, big brother," he says. "Just saying." I watch him retreat toward the gym, and I'm tempted to join him, not because I want to work out, but just to focus on something other than the fact that her bedroom is opposite mine.

I head up the stairs, taking them two at a time. When I reach my bedroom door and shove it open, I'm tempted to turn to glance at hers. I wonder if she's inside, or if she's decided to shower before dinner.

Shaking my head to clear the images that the thought conjures, I shut my door with a kick so harsh, the wood reverberates sending vibrations through the walls. The first thing I do is flick on the music and strip off my clothes. In my attached bathroom, I turn on the shower and step under the spray, before it has time to heat.

The cold bristles against my skin. My lungs pull in a quick breath before I close my eyes and focus on everything other than the girl who's merely a few meters away from me.

Back in my bedroom, I pull on a pair of black jeans, my boots, and a navy-blue shirt that I button up, leaving the top four buttons undone. I roll up my cuffs to my elbows and stare at my reflection.

"I can do this," I shrug easily, but even as I say it, I'm not convinced. The drive here was difficult. Being so close to her and not reaching for her was one of the hardest things I've ever had to go through. But I did it. Now, all I have to do is ignore her, and I'll be fine.

I can't describe the need to be near her. Perhaps it's because I know I can't have her. Besides the fact that she's far too young for me, she's also my stepsister. She's too innocent for me to corrupt because if I were to partake of the forbidden fruit that's only a few meters away, I can't guarantee that I won't end up breaking her heart.

But that doesn't mean I don't notice her beauty. With her long dark hair, those luminous gold eyes, and her pouty lips, I was intrigued from the moment I first saw her. Counting in those incredible curves and her fiery personality, she's everything wet dreams are made of and more.

And I am a man. Certainly not a blind one.

When I pull open my bedroom door, I'm met with the golden eyes of Nesrin, as she steps out into the hallway. It's big enough to offer space between us, but it still feels too close for comfort.

"I… I don't know if it's time to go down for dinner," she tells me. I should appease her, tell her I'll show her down, but I don't. Being an asshole has always come naturally to me. This time, it's no different.

I offer a nod and turn to walk away. I'm halfway down the hall when Nesrin speaks to my back.

"You know, hating me because of our parents getting married doesn't change the fact that we're family." Her voice carries all the way to me. I turn my head, glancing at her from over my shoulder. I take her in from where I'm standing.

She's dressed in a pair of tight yoga pants, the color of soft gray clouds. Her top is tight, long-sleeved, thank god, but it accentuates her slight curves. She's nothing like the girls I normally go for, so it makes no fucking sense as to why I'm so intrigued by her.

"Hate is a wasted emotion, Nesrin. It only makes us weak."

"And what does love do?" she challenges. No woman, no girl, has ever challenged me. I can't help but smile at her when she steps closer. The soft, gentle scent of her perfume assaults me, and my body shudders with the need to pin her against the wall. My need to touch her is visceral. I can't explain it. I don't like it. I never want to be weakened by emotions.

I shake my head and chuckle. "Love is an excuse for people to get addicted, obsessed, and for them to change who they are."

"What if it doesn't change who you are? What if it only makes you a better person, bringing out the best in who you are?" she continues, her voice coming out strained.

"Does your mother love my father?"

"My mother isn't capable of love, never in my life have I seen her truly happy. When my father was alive, she didn't care if he came home or not. My father, on the other hand, he loved her, he would do anything for her—"

"Then, your father was a stupid man. He did everything for her, but she never wanted it. Did she?"

"I..."

"I know this farce of a wedding is nothing more than a leg up to gain exposure. If you ask me, I think they deserve each other. Both fake. Both cold and barren. And both only in it for the money and fame."

Nesrin's expression changes quickly, as if I'd just slapped her. I expect her to lash out at me, but she shocks me when she nods. "I know. And that's why I don't want to fight with you, or Cass and Finn. I don't have anyone in my life besides my aunt. My mother doesn't love me. She never has. I grew up knowing that I was never going to have a normal family."

"Well," I say, turning to regard her fully, "if you think moving in here will bring you a normal family, you're sorely mistaken." I spin on my heel and head down the hall, leaving her in the darkened space.

Damien

FRUSTRATION TRICKLES THROUGH ME AS I MAKE MY way to the greenhouse I spotted when we arrived. A memory assaults me with a vengeance the moment I step foot over the threshold. The last time I walked into my mother's greenhouse, I saw *him*. The way he was enjoying his pleasure had heat trickling through me, reminding me of just how inexperienced I am.

I watched a scene that hasn't left my mind since. The moment I think back on that night, jealousy burns through me, and even though I try to convince myself I was more angry than envious, I know it's a lie.

I can't deny I wanted to be the girl who offered him pleasure. To watch from my knees, as he took my mouth and used it for his pleasure. To have that power over him would be surreal. Every fantasy I've had since has confirmed to me that I wanted to be the girl who made him grunt and growl like a feral animal.

But I can't show him. I can't admit it because, if I do, I know he'll break me. He's not the type of guy you introduce to your folks. Not the type of man that my mother wants me to be married to. So, instead of admitting it out loud, that I crave his touch, I've only ever allowed myself to think it in the darkness of my bedroom.

Shaking my head, I focus on the task at hand. I tentatively run my fingers along the petals and smile. A beautiful, soft pink that looks too fragile to touch. I smile when I inhale the sweet fragrance, my eyes closing in enjoyment.

The sweet, lingering scent reminds me of my mother's garden before she became far too important to bother with it. I smile when I recall the past when I remember just how happy we were.

But then a more recent memory takes hold of me. One of which is the cause of my twisted need and darkest fantasies. The night of the reception. When I first laid eyes on Damien Thorne.

Even the gentle perfume of the flower doesn't change the feeling that's gnawing in my gut, reminding me that, even though I'm living in this impressive house, *he* will also always be around.

And for some reason, Damien Thorne has made it his mission to taunt me at every turn. As handsome, charming, and intelligent as he is, I need to stay away from him. But even though I chastise myself for thinking about him, I still find myself caught in his web.

Lured in by the sparkling blue eyes and charismatic smirk.

"You look good bent over like that." His deep, seductive voice comes from behind me. Spinning on my heel, I meet his cerulean gaze, and it burns right through me. The memory that scampered in earlier, now returning, as I look at the wolfish smirk that tilts his lips.

Dressed in a pair of black jeans, a crisp light blue shirt—which is teasingly unbuttoned, offering just enough smooth, tanned skin to taunt me—and heavy black boots, I wonder briefly where he's headed.

"What are you doing in here?" It's stupid to ask him that since it's his home. I'm the newcomer. He doesn't respond. Instead, he takes a few steps toward the opposite corner from where I'm standing and picks up a pot that holds a dark red rose. This one is alone in the soil, with thorns threatening anyone who dares come near it.

"Your mother enjoys looking at pretty things," he muses, as he twists the flower this way and that. His focus is on the plant, but still, my heart feels like it's about to break free from my rib cage.

"You didn't answer me." My voice comes out softer than I intend, but it causes him to turn around. When those deep blue eyes are on me, I feel like I'm being scrutinized. Perhaps I am. One thing's for sure, Damien Thorne doesn't play around when it comes to any actions he makes. I know this because his eyes narrow, assessing me before he sets down the rose and turns fully toward me.

He takes three long strides before he's inches from me. The scent of his cologne reminds me of rain and freshly cut grass. It's a refreshing scent that's mingled with citrus.

"I like pretty things, too," he murmurs, as he reaches for a loose curl that's escaped my messy bun. He twines it around his finger, until there's no more give, and then tugs hard until tears sting my eyes.

But I don't allow myself to make a sound. He likes toying with girls, I'm sure of it, just like he's doing to me. I'm convinced he can hear my thoughts because he twists his hand even harder, forcing wetness to form on my lashes from the sting. A sly smirk graces his classically handsome face, joy in my agony.

Perhaps he wants me to cry, to beg him to stop, but I won't give him the satisfaction of seeing me shed a tear or hearing me plead for mercy.

If only he knew why I can't cry. Pain prickles my scalp, for a moment, before Damien releases me as if I've burned him.

His eyes spark with a flame so destructive, it threatens to engulf me in its inferno. The way his mouth tilts, his full lips curling into a sinister smirk, makes every nerve in my body come alive.

"Are you going to be my pretty thing, Nesrin?" he asks, as he tips his head to the side. "Will you let me have you, enjoy you, until I've had my fill, even though I really shouldn't?" He regards me through a shrewd gaze. His question diminishes any need that burned through me seconds ago.

"You may be used to girls throwing themselves at you, but I'm not them, and I never will be." My words are filled with venom, but he doesn't seem perturbed at my retort. The smile that curls his lips only seems to brighten and the dimples that deepen in either cheek do nothing to stop the flurry of hummingbirds in my stomach.

It's stupid, really. I shouldn't be looking at him like this. And I certainly shouldn't be feeling like a teenage girl with a crush, but Damien Thorne is just that—something my young heart would love to learn more about. He's handsome, sexy, and he has a voice that could melt ice cream. Even though he's aloof most times, there's a seductiveness to him that I'm drawn to.

"Is that a hint of jealousy I hear in your voice, Nesrin?" he asks, as he tugs my lock of hair once more. The darkness of the impending storm gathering outside seems to encroach on us, filling the bright and sunny greenhouse with shadows.

I meet those ice-blue eyes in an attempt to seem unperturbed by his nearness. "Why would I be jealous?"

"Let me make this clear, I'm not going to lie to you to protect those delicate emotions of yours, Nesrin." His words still me. *What could he throw at me verbally to hurt me?*

"You don't need to protect me from anything, Damien." I push by him, wanting to put some distance between us, but he's fast. His hand shoots out to grab my wrist, spinning me around, until I'm flush with him, and his other arm wraps around my waist.

"Even from myself?" he challenges, with a glint of mischief that shines in his eyes. His dark brow raised, as those dimples threaten to have me falling deeper under his spell. "Because I'm the most dangerous one there is, Nesrin. And you have no way of fighting me off."

My mouth falls open, but no words come out. I want to tell him I hate him, to push him away, maybe even to knee him in the groin, but my body is rigid with shock and need swirling together.

He leans in closer, so close, in fact, I can feel the heat of his breath feathering over my cheek. My heart skids to a halt, then beats wildly against my ribs, when I feel the softness of his lips on the heated skin of my jaw.

His mouth brushes along my ear, leaving white-hot electric sparks in its wake. Then he whispers, "But something tells me you like that. You like the danger, the passion, the mystery. Which means, if I slipped my hand between those pristine, caramel thighs of yours, I'd find your panties soaked. Just for me."

Anger and humiliation rage inside me. A battle of hate and lust rages within, just like the strike of lightning that shutters outside—sparking the darkened sky with a streak of warning—and the silence is shattered, causing me to yelp in shock.

My heart is now in my throat, thick and ominous. I attempt to swallow, trying to force myself to shove Damien away, but I don't have to because, just as the white spark outside disappears within seconds, he moves away from me.

We stand in silence, our gazes locked, and I have nothing to say to him. My body is trembling from our interaction, and I know he can see it. Damien knows he has an effect on me, and he uses it to his advantage.

With a nod, he turns to leave. I watch his form retreating toward the door, but before he steps out, he twists his head, offering me only his profile to admire. His eyes burn with blue flames that dance with intent.

"I wanted to see you."

My brows furrow in confusion. "What?" I croak.

"You asked me what I was doing here," he tells me. "It was because I wanted to see you." His admission hangs between us, for a second, before he spins on his shiny heel and leaves me in the greenhouse, still trembling.

When I sit down at the table beside Cassian, he leans over and whispers, "Don't let Damien get to you. He's an asshole, most times, even to us, but he cares."

I don't know why my heart flip flops at his words. It's wrong to think about Damien in *that* way, but when he settles in at the head of the table, and my eyes find his, I know I'll never see him in a familial way.

"So, tell us more about you," Finn says, when he seats himself opposite me. "Any hobbies? Or favorite things to do?"

"I'm pretty much a homebody," I shrug. "I love being on my own, spending time with my books. Not really a party animal."

"That's unfortunate because we're having a party this weekend to welcome our new little sister to the family and the town." Finn grins at me, while he spears a piece of meat and shoves it into his mouth. "She's our guest of honor."

"I didn't know about this," Damien speaks up, looking at Finn with a glare, his blue eyes sparking to life, and I can't help but be pulled into that hard stare.

"I spoke to Holly and Mali," Finn says with a playful grin. "They're bringing the rest of the team, and The Black Knights want to head up here as well."

"Fuck that, I'm not having those assholes in this house again." Damien's voice lowers into a growl, and I can't stop the shiver that races down my spine as the warning drenches his words.

"Come on, D," Cassian says. "It's harmless fun. We'll keep them down here, we can lock the door from the kitchen leading to the rest of the house and just have them in the garden. The kitchen will still be accessible, we can keep the living room patio doors locked as well." He seems to have thought this through. "The pool house has a bathroom if they need it. I mean, think about it, we can keep them contained."

I don't know who The Black Knights are, but from the name alone, I can't help but want to agree with Damien. I'm not a fan of crowds, and this sounds like it's going to be big.

Blue eyes flash, flitting between the two younger

brothers, and I silently pray that he says no but, after some consideration, Damien finally nods and says, "Fine. Outside."

My heart leaps into my throat, as Finn whoops at the thought of having a bash in his father's house. I doubt their dad would be impressed if he knew about this, but I have no say. It's not my house.

"Looks like we're having a party, little sister," Finn tells me, with a satisfied grin on his face, and I don't know why my eyes sweep to Damien. He's watching me intently, and I wonder if he can see the trepidation I'm feeling.

I fake a smile, just like I've been taught to do all my life, and try to finish my dinner. Even though it's delicious, the anxiety churning in my stomach makes it difficult to eat.

"Have you decided on a major?" Cassian asks from beside me.

Shaking my head, I tell him, "Not yet. I'm thinking of perhaps doing a History major. Something different to anything my mother wants me to do," I tack on with a small smile. I can feel cerulean eyes piercing me, but I don't look at *him*.

"History. If you like that kinda stuff, Damien can show you around the manor." Finn grins as if there's an inside joke that only he can hear. "This place is fucking old, I'm sure it's haunted too." With a chuckle, he shakes his head, and I try not to look at Damien, who I know is watching me.

"I'd love to learn more about Thorne Haven and the manor. I've always been interested in learning about how towns came about."

"Are you musical at all?" Cassian poses, before taking a bite of his meal.

"Not really. More like tone-deaf." I smile at him. "My mother wasn't impressed that I didn't want to get into show business as well. All my life, she begged and pleaded for me to go to castings. Even though I've been to a few, I never got the part. I guess acting isn't my forte."

"Being fake, not your kind of thing?" This comes from Damien, drawing my attention to him. The corner of his mouth quirks and I see the dimple forming in his cheek. His dark brow lifts into a perfect arch, and those baby blues flash with a challenge.

"No, it's not. I guess being an asshole is your kind of thing?" At my challenge, both Finn and Cassian gasp, then laugh out loud, as they slap their hands in a high five across the table. But all the commotion doesn't break the eye contact between Damien and me.

There's a glint of surprise in his eyes. The shimmer of mischief, and then he smiles, and I'm not ready for it. Not my heart, not my body and, certainly, not my mind.

"Being an asshole takes a special kind of talent," he

says, leaning back against his chair. It's almost as if he takes great satisfaction in being such a dick. He slides his chair back, rises to full height, and I can't help my hungry eyes from drinking in every inch of him. He slowly rounds the table, making his way toward me.

When he reaches my chair, Damien leans in and presses his lips to my ear, which has heat shooting through every nerve in my body. My skin tingles with awareness of his proximity, and I bite back the whimper that threatens to escape.

"Don't ever underestimate me, wild rose," he murmurs in my ear. "I may be proud of it, but only those close to me are ever allowed to call me an asshole to my face."

My mouth goes dry, my throat struggles to work, but I find my words, even though they come out in a croak. "And what happens to those who aren't close to you?"

"They pay dearly," he mumbles, the tone of his voice dropping so low, it's almost as if his words vibrate through me.

He pushes up and leaves us in the dining room. I watch him for a long moment before I look back and find both brothers staring at me.

"I have to say, little sister," Finn starts, "you have some big lady balls." With a chuckle, he finishes his meal, offering us a quick salute, before he leaves the table. Cassian is smiling as he pushes his plate away.

"What?" I ask, turning to face the middle brother. He looks just like Damien, only his hair isn't as dark, it's more of a chocolate brown. He doesn't look like an asshole, whereas Damien has that aloof coldness to his demeanor.

"Oh, I've just never seen anyone challenge my brother like that." He sounds like he's impressed when he says this. I can feel him regarding me closely, and I'm sure he's trying to figure me out. It's the first time I've been scrutinized so wholly by someone. Even with my mother's job, I've steered clear of the public eye, for the very reason that people try to *figure you out* while they come up with their own conclusions on who you are.

"I think he should be called out more often," I say, but my hands tremble when I think about how close his mouth was to mine. If I had turned my head, I would've practically kissed him.

Cassian grins, as something flashes in his eyes. His smirk matching his brother's and I wonder, briefly, just how they can look so alike, yet act so different. At least, from what I've seen in the short time I've spent with all three of them.

"I like you, Nesrin," Cassian tells me. "I think you'll be a breath of fresh air in this family." He tips his head to the side before he nods and turns to leave. I watch him for a long moment before I take a deep breath, then let it out slowly. My feisty nature hasn't come to light in such a long time, that even I was shocked at my outburst with Damien. A small smile curls my lips when I think about how his eyes flashed with indignation at my challenge.

"How was dinner?" Joy asks as she enters the room.

"It was lovely, thank you," I tell her. "I was about to clear the table, the boys just left."

"Oh, don't you worry about it." She shoos me with a wave of her hands. "I'm here to do this, so please, why don't you go ahead and walk around, familiarize yourself with the house. It's big enough to get lost in."

"It looks like it," I tell her, with a smile.

For a moment, she looks at me as if she's about to say something important; her expression turns serious, but when her gaze flicks over my shoulder, it changes. "You'll like it here," Joy tells me before she grabs the stack of plates and scurries into the kitchen.

That was strange.

When I turn to leave, I find Damien leaning against the doorjamb, looking at me. He doesn't look at all perturbed, his arms folded across his chest. I notice he's now wearing a black leather jacket over the shirt he wore to dinner.

"I suggest you don't go out into the garden at night," he tells me, but there's a warning bite to his tone. "It's not safe out there."

"Why? Will wild animals eat me?" I retort playfully, causing his smirk to appear. His lips tilt into a seductive grin, and his eyes seem to light up at my words.

"Not animals, no." He leaves without another word, and his response slowly sinks in, making every inch of my body burn with the promise of what he actually meant.

Nesrin

THE WOODS ARE DENSE AND DARK, AND I KNOW they're dangerous, but it's not me I'm worried about, it's her. It's only been a short while that I've been around her, but the need to keep her safe seems to override the want to send her packing.

Being in the house with her only seems to make me *want* to be near her. The banter between us has become twisted, more than I expected it to. Her fire is nothing like any girl I've come across, which only seems to turn me on more.

And that's not a good thing.

She's eighteen, I tell myself.

She's an adult, I remind myself.

But each time, there's a heavy foreboding that our age gap is far too big.

I twist open the bourbon and swig back a mouthful. The burning liquid trickles down my throat, reminding me that I'm alive, that I'm not lost in the darkness of this fucking town.

"I didn't think I'd see you here tonight," the sultry voice says from the shadows. *Neither did I.*

"Yeah, the house is a shitshow," I tell her. But I don't look at her because I don't need to meet her hungry gaze. Genevieve has been one of my fuck buddies for years, and even when I left for college, she still waited for me. Love was never in the cards for us, and she knew that, but she never cared. I broke her heart more times than I can count. And even in those times, she would return, just to dance on my dick.

"Anything I can do to help?" she questions, in the tone that used to get me hard as fuck. Now, all I want is to go home, to taunt the little sister my father dumped us with.

"No." Another swig of alcohol, reveling in the burn, I focus my attention on the dark water that sits before us. The stillness of the stream offers solace. Genevieve doesn't take a hint; instead, she leans against the car beside me. She reaches for the bottle, and I allow her to grab it.

I finally turn to look at her. She takes a small mouthful, swirling the amber liquid, before swallowing it slowly.

"Is it another girl?" she asks, without looking at me. But I don't know how to answer her. Yes, it is; no, it's not. It's a girl I can't have because my father decided to stick his dick in her mother.

"Perhaps." It's the only thing I can offer in response. Genevieve hands me back the bottle and pulls out a packet of smokes. Even though I'm tempted, I don't ask her for one. It's one of the things that's never truly fazed me. Finn smokes on the odd occasion, especially when he's had a few drinks. But Cass and I have steered clear of it in recent years.

"I hope she's worth it," Gen tells me. "I mean, you could have so many beautiful women lining up for you."

"Are you one of them? Is that why you're here?" I'm challenging her, and I know it. There is no doubt in my mind that if I asked her to, she'd drop to her knees in front of me. But it doesn't offer the allure that it used to, so I take a long gulp of bourbon instead.

"I just don't like seeing you like this."

"Like what?"

"Broken."

I consider her words. I don't feel broken at all, perhaps more frustrated. And not only sexually, deep down, I know that being around Nesrin does something to me.

Something I never thought I would feel—at ease with myself.

"You're torn," Gen muses, before pulling in a lungful of smoke and keeping it there for a while until she blows rings into the dark night.

"I am." My admission should be a shock to me, but it's not. I knew it the moment I sat in the car with Nesrin. I was rocked by the intrigue she presented, and each time Finn or Cass asked her something, and she offered an answer, I found myself wanting to know as well.

"Perhaps you should ask her on a date," Gen teases, then giggles beside me, because everyone knows I'm definitely not the dating kind. I don't even spend the night if I'm with a woman. Being so close to someone will only hurt you in the end. It happened to my father, and it will happen again. I've seen lives torn apart, worlds shattered, just because people fell in love. They opened themselves up to it and then got smashed in the process.

"Why are you here, anyway?" I ask into the night. Even though this is my hiding spot, Gen is one of the only women I've ever been with who knows about it. Cass and Finn found me here once, so drunk, I had passed out. My father was looking for me all night, well into the day, and when my brothers found me, they thought it was funny. Finn's too young to remember the fights that ensued in the manor; Cass probably remembers the night our mother left, but I doubt he can recall the times I would sit up on the landing and listen to their screams.

"Wanted to see you. I heard you're back."

"Finn's an asshole."

"He didn't tell me. I overheard the girls talking," Gen says. I know there are a few girls who my brothers know well and keep around when they need to let off some steam. "The Black Knights were talking about you as well."

"Fuck them," I bite out, clenching my jaw so tight, I feel the ache in my cheeks. I gulp down another mouthful of alcohol before I hand the bottle to Gen.

"They want you back," she tells me. I know they do. They've been pandering around like lost sheep since I walked, but I'm not going back to that life. It's nothing I need. Especially now that I have a sister who's fucking with my head.

"I'm not walking backward in my life. Not anymore," I tell her, hoping she'll take the news to them. I know they'll be at the party we're having, and I don't doubt they'll force the issue of me joining back up, but it's not happening.

Kids in this town have always tried to find new ways to keep themselves entertained, and the Havens were well-known for the dangerous games. But I'm done playing them. I am all grown up and no longer want to get into the shit they do.

"Does this have anything to do with the girl?" Gen asks, the challenge in her tone mingled with curiosity is clear. I know she'll go back to them and give them all the information she's gleaned from me. I shouldn't have spoken about Nesrin, but I can't help it. I have nobody in my life I can confide in. Loneliness is a motherfucker, and it sneaks up on you when you least expect it.

You can be in a room full of people and, yet, feel more alone than ever before. My mind flits back to Nesrin, and what she said about love earlier.

"No. It has to do with me, Gen." I turn to Genevieve, pinning her with a stare that's fierce and confident. "Did you come here to ask me shit, so you can tell them all you've learned? Or did you come here because you wanted to get back in my bed?"

"Why are you such an asshole, Damien?" Gen bites back, her eyes glower with fury as she stares at me. Her long reddish-brown hair hangs to the middle of her back. The deep green of her eyes is black in the darkness. And her plump lips are pursed, but I no longer have any interest.

"Because that's how you like it." I shove by her, ignoring her frustrated hissy fit when I slip into the driver's seat of my Camaro. It's the only woman I love, the only woman who hasn't left me for something better.

"Fuck you," Gen bites out. She's angry now, but give it a couple of days, and she'll be begging to get back in my good graces.

"Already done that, Sweetheart, I'm done playing your games. And tell The Black Knights that I'm finished." I pull out onto the road, leaving her in the dark.

It doesn't take me long to reach home, and the moment I step foot in the house, I hear a guffaw coming from the living room. Stepping over the threshold of the large open-plan room, I find Finn and Nesrin giggling over something they're watching on his computer screen. They're on the sofa, almost snuggled up to each other. The sight itself brings rage to the forefront of my mind, burning through every vein in my body.

"Gen says to tell you that she wants your dick on Saturday," I tell Finn, who snaps his gaze to mine.

"Oh?" His dark brow arches, the smile on his face shows just how excited he is at the prospect. "Tell her I don't take sloppy seconds from my big brother, but I'll gladly feed her my dick if she's hungry."

I chuckle. And just as I thought, Nesrin's face falls when Finn's words sink in. Her eyes lock on mine, disappointment flits across her face for a second, before she schools her features.

I shrug and respond to Finn while keeping my eyes on the new girl, "I'm done with redheads, I think a brunette is next on the menu for me." With a cocky wink, I turn and leave them to ponder my words. A smile curls my lips as I make my way to my bedroom.

I look forward to hearing what the wild rose has to say about that tidbit of information tomorrow morning because I'm certainly not leaving the safety of my bedroom until then.

Even though I'm dying to know what she looks like while she's asleep.

Nesrin

The Past

"**W**HAT ARE YOU GOING TO DO IF IT DOESN'T work?" Jenny Shepherd asks. Her mother and mine work together, and since they've become friends, we've been thrown together. She's a sweet girl, innocent compared to others who I've met in the industry, but mostly, she doesn't care about the fame, just like me.

"I don't know. I mean, I like him, and I think I'm ready." I look at her, as I smooth down the material that hugs my every curve. It's been a while since I've been to a party, but this one is special. I'm about to meet up with Xavier, who's promised that tonight we're taking our relationship to the next level.

"But do you love him?" she asks.

Love. I don't know if that emotion is even worth thinking about. We've been seeing each other for four months, but I haven't said that word to him yet. I have seen the destruction love leaves in its path. It's not something I want to go through. But who knows, perhaps if we do finally take the next step, maybe then I'll feel it, or be able to say it.

"My v-card and love don't go hand in hand," I tell her, before glancing in the mirror again. She looks at me like I've lost my mind, and perhaps I have, but I can't focus on sappy emotions that I've seen as destructive. Watching my parents bicker and fight, even though they *loved* each other, has scared me.

Xavier wants me in *that* way. And even though I know my virginity is something to cherish, if Xavier can look past my scars, and be with me physically, then perhaps he is worthy of loving me.

Most girls think it's a rite of passage, I don't. My worry is that he'll see what I've done and hate me, but I can't tell my friend about that because nobody knows. Not even her.

Jenny looks at me with an arched brow, her brown eyes sparkling with amusement. "Sometimes, I worry about you."

"I worry about me too," I tell her with a laugh. "I'm serious, though. I don't see it as this big thing that we all have to talk about. It's just sex." Even as I shrug, I know in my heart, it's all fake.

"Your mother must've been great at the birds and bee's speech," she says, and I can't help but roll my eyes.

"You know what she's like," I tell my friend. Slipping my feet into the sleek, silver sandals, I turn and look at Jenny who's already dressed, waiting for me. "What do you think?"

"He's going to eat his heart out." She nods, pushing to her feet. With our heels on, we're both the same height. Both in black dresses, mine lower cut at the back, and Jenny's showing off her cleavage. I'm not as blessed in the front as she is, but I think we both look elegantly sexy.

"Let's go."

As we make our way through the house, I know my mother wouldn't give a shit where we're going. But Jenny's mom just might. We make it to the door before Laurel notices us sneaking out.

"Are you two off out on the town?" she asks, her words already slurring, so I know they'll be spending the night. One thing my mother's been good about is not driving when she's been drinking, and her friends are the same.

If they did need to leave, they'd have a driver collect them. Thankfully, I've learned to abide by the same set of rules, and tonight, I'm not drinking at all; but luckily, I have a driver who's waiting for us.

"Yes, Mom. I told you about the party," Jenny tells her, with a roll of her eyes. Most kids like us would rather stick forks in their eyes than to listen to their parents. They enjoy the rebellious side of being a child star, and this time, it's no different.

"Just don't get killed or pregnant," Laurel says.

I'm about to walk out when my mom pipes up, "Nesrin knows that if she walks in here pregnant, she'll be out on her ass."

"That's exactly what will happen to you as well, Missy," Laurel waves her finger in the air, pointing at her daughter.

"See you later," I call out, needing to leave before this scene turns into a session from a psychologist's worst nightmare. I can't deal with mind games from my mother tonight.

By the time we're in the car, I'm buzzing with excitement. The thought of finally losing my v-card, plus the party, has my stomach flip-flopping.

It doesn't take us long to pull up to the three-story house that looks like it's been coated in pure gold. Shimmering fairy lights, along with tiki torches, line the entrance and garden.

Inside, the house is already a mess from the party

that's in full swing. Kids ranging from sixteen upwards fill the garden, along with the living room which is overflowing with bodies gyrating and spilling beer on the wooden floors. Some of the older college kids are playing beer pong on the long dining room table, with cigarettes hanging from their lips.

Loud music screams from the speakers as the heavy bass vibrates through my chest and we try to weave our way through the bodies. As Jenny and I enter the kitchen which has a countertop filled with bottles of alcohol, I find Xavier talking to a couple of his friends, a Solo cup in hand. When his gaze lands on me, I can't help but notice the hunger that burns in his eyes.

"There she is," he says out loud, pulling me under the crook of his arm. "I missed you." His whisper is only for me to hear before he presses a kiss to my cheek.

Moments later, his two friends leave, along with Jenny, and we're alone. My heart thuds wildly against my chest at the thought of what's going to happen.

"Are you ready?" Xavier asks, lacing his fingers through mine. I nod, too nervous to even find the words to respond. He leads me through the house, up the stairs, and it's almost as if I can feel all eyes on us.

In the bedroom, he shuts the door and slowly pulls his shirt off. His toned chest is against me, pressing me between him and the door, and I'm shivering by the time his hands reach under my dress.

"I have been waiting for this for so long," he whispers, lifting me in his arms and setting me on the plush mattress. But the moment my skirt rides up my thighs, I see it in his eyes—pity.

Embarrassment blooms on my face, the heat of it surely making my cheeks bright red. He doesn't say anything for a long while, then looks up at me.

"Sorry, darling, I don't fuck freaks." He chuckles so loudly that it seems to be in surround sound, booming around me, like the music did downstairs. My cheeks burn, my eyes sting with tears as shame fills me. Xavier grabs his shirt and saunters from the room, leaving me curled on the bed, as tears spill from my eyes.

I don't know how long I lie there, but when I finally find myself in a bathroom, I close my eyes as I find my release of the shame with a blade I found, conveniently waiting for me in one of the cabinets. The cut is deeper than normal, but it helps with the knot in my stomach.

Once I'm feeling *normal* again, I chuck the blade into the trash and clean myself up. All I want to do is go home. Racing through the house, I make it outside, call the driver, and wait, alone, as the tears threaten me once more.

I can't do this.

I'm so fucking broken.

I can never show myself to anyone again.

Damien

Present day

THE HOUSE IS NOTHING LIKE I EXPECTED. GRANTED, I knew it was a mansion, but this is nothing short of a dark fairy tale. Black bricks make up the exterior, with turrets that reach up into the sky.

The three floors are exquisitely furnished, with dark wood and glass. The windows overlook a garden so vast, you can't tell where the property line ends.

My bedroom looks like something out of a home improvement show. A king-sized bed sits against one wall, with soft pink bedding and white sheets. The mattress is so soft, I don't think I can make it down to the party. But I know I'll need to, just to show my face since I *am* meant to be the guest of honor. I can't believe Cassian wanted to throw a party, just for me.

I haven't seen every part of the house yet, but what I have managed to venture into has left me breathless. Upon entering the main door, you're taken into an entrance hall that looks like it's part of a castle: with dark marble tiles and a rug that spans most of the open-plan space.

The staircase leads up to the second floor, where all our bedrooms are situated, and mine is right across the hall from Damien's. On the other end of the house, are Finn and Cassian's bedrooms. All of which I haven't yet seen.

As I make my way down the steps, I take a left, instead of right, and find myself in a hallway that leads me into a home gym, with an indoor swimming pool.

Two other doors sit on this side, but they're both locked. If I had to hazard a guess, I would say one was an office and the other, perhaps, a second guest room.

I can hear the party in full swing, so I turn back and make my way toward the living room, which is furnished with comfortable charcoal-colored sofas and two large wingback chairs, the same shade as the red wine that my mother loves to drink.

I don't know why I'm even going to this party. I should've told Cassian not to bother with something so big. A dinner would be great, with just me and the brothers. But he doesn't know just how much crowds affect me.

The words that Damien uttered the other night come back full-force when I think about which brunette he's interested in. I can't deny I wish he was talking about me, even though we can never be together.

By the time I reach the living room, I take in a much smaller group of people than I was expecting. Thankfully, it's nothing like the city parties; there's far less chaos.

I don't feel out of place here. Not yet. Finn and Cassian have been welcoming, but Damien... well, he's another story. I don't know why we haven't spoken much, but his aloofness makes me wonder if he hates the fact that my mother married his dad.

Outer appearances confirm we're nothing alike.

But I have a feeling, under his veneer, we're exactly the same.

And that's why, the moment I laid eyes on Damien Thorne, I knew my life would never be the same again. His aura is darker than that of his brothers, as if he's seen pain and heartache, felt it deeper than most.

"Little Sister!" Finn's already drunk. The past few days we've been preparing for the party, and as much as I want to hide in my room, I've come out just to see who these people are, who live in the town I now call home.

I look around as Finn pulls me through the throng of bodies. The warm evening is only heated further, with the large fire pit that Finn and Cassian have set up. My eyes rake over the partygoers, looking for one in particular, but I can't see him.

"Where are we going?" I ask Finn as he leads me into another small circle of people. There are three girls and four guys, one being Cassian.

"These are the coolest people here, you need to meet them, get to know them, and you'll be fine," Finn tells me, but when I meet Cassian's gaze, he's rolling his eyes, which makes me laugh.

"Hi, I'm Mali." One of the girls comes up to me. She's blonde, with big green eyes that shine in the dancing flames.

"Hi. It's good to meet you."

She wraps her arms around me, holding me for a few moments, before releasing me. "That's Holly," she tells me, pointing at a beautiful dark-haired girl with dark eyes. From here, I think they're brown, but I can't be sure. Holly smiles, waving at me, but she doesn't leave Cassian's side.

"I'm Keirin, that's Creed and Brody," one of the guys tells me. He looks to be about the same age as Damien, with jet-black hair and wide eyes that look like a silver lake.

"Nice to meet you," I mumble, feeling far too out of place. I'm nothing like any of these guys and girls. I grew up in the city, and being here with people who've known each other their whole lives feels strange.

"Don't be shy, we're all friends here," Mali says, but her gaze lands on Finn with a longing I feel right down to my gut. Because it's in that moment, I realize that's possibly how I look at Damien. As much as I try to deny my feelings, I know I can't. I do want him, even though he's far too old for me.

"Why don't you two go grab some wine," Cass tells me. "Mali knows where to go." He winks at her, mischievously, and I wonder what that meant. I'll ask her on the way inside.

"Oh, let me go to the restroom, just head into the kitchen, and right at the back, close to the cooker, is a door that leads down to the cellar. Grab any wine you'd like," she tells me with a smile, before racing down the hallway. I thought most people would be steered toward the pool house, but it seems like the plans have changed.

I still haven't seen Damien, and even though I shouldn't care, I do. And there's no way I would miss him. When he enters a room, it's almost as if people fall at his feet because he graced them with his presence.

And it seems like I'm turning into one of those admirers. I don't want to show him that I'm affected by him, but when he's near, I'm sure it's obvious to everyone around us.

As I make my way down the stairs, I feel around the smooth walls, hoping for a light switch, since I can't see anything in front of me. But by the time I reach the bottom, I still haven't found anything.

Something crashes behind me, causing me to startle and fall backward. "Hello?" I call out, but there's no response. My mind must be playing tricks on me. I've never liked being in the dark like this. I enjoy nighttime, when I'm lying in the dark, safe in my bedroom, but this is just plain scary.

I hold my hands out in front of me, wondering if there's one of those hanging tight strings that dangle from the ceiling, but I'm sure that being so wealthy, they'd have something more expensive than an old yellow lamp.

Suddenly, the bulb flickers on and I'm met with Damien's blue eyes, shining with sinister flames in front of me. A scream lodges itself in my throat, but his hand lands on my mouth, keeping me quiet.

"Shh," he tells me, murmuring in my ear, "It's only me."

As much as I don't want to think about Damien's hand on my mouth or his other hand on my hip, I can't think of anything else. It's almost as if he's all around me, consuming my every thought, as he holds onto me. His touch is firm, commanding, and I find myself staring into blue eyes.

He is the epitome of every girl's perfect fantasy.

"I like having a girl in the dark," he tells me, with a smirk that makes my heart thrum between my legs. "It's more fun when you can't see what's about to get you."

"Let go of me," I bite out when he finally lifts his hand from my mouth. I don't miss the fact that he doesn't release my hip. "Why are you hiding in the dark?"

"I wasn't hiding," he tells me, before taking his hand off my hip and stepping back. "I was grabbing some wine for the party."

The darkness seems to surround him, like it knows him well. I don't believe a word he says, but there's no proof for me to argue with him, so I break our eye contact and look around at the now dimly lit space. It's actually bigger than I thought it was.

It's not at all cold and dank like I expected it to be. It's the complete opposite. Expensively furnished with two dark blue velvet wingback chairs, which has a centerpiece table that looks like it had been carved from a tree trunk, with a heavy glass top between them.

Along the walls are rows of wine bottles which I'm sure cost more than the clothes I'm wearing. I pull one out, noting the date—nineteen eighty-two—and place it back in the shelf.

"The older the wine, the more expensive, and the better

the flavors," Damien says, waving his arm toward the wine, "why don't you pick something?" He's still close to me. Very close. The scent of his cologne clings to my nostrils, and I can't deny that I find him attractive. Even though I'm not supposed to.

Shaking my head, I focus on the shelves of bottles. A cold prickle races down my spine, and I find myself spinning around to Damien's deep gaze on me.

I don't want this anxiety to start again, those nights of fear that used to hold me hostage. Closing my eyes, I focus on my breaths, counting slowly from one, up to ten. It's what my therapist told me to do when I was a teenager, and I struggled with anxiety.

At times, I feel so broken, so ravaged by the anxious feelings, it seems to overwhelm me. There's only one thing I found that works, but right now, I need to keep calm and seem normal.

Facing the bottles again, I pick out four that I think sound good, but I'm not a great judge of alcohol. I haven't had a chance to drink very much, even though I've attended parties with my mother in the past. I turn around too quickly, slamming into Damien's body, which is hard and rigid.

My gaze darts up to find his familiar smooth jawline. Higher still, I locate the cold, shrewd, cerulean stare that makes my knees weak.

"Why are you still here?" My voice comes out breathy, like a stupid girl with a crush. Only, I don't have a crush on him, I shouldn't, but I can't fight this strange pull I have toward him. And I have a feeling he's noticed it because there's something between us. Even though I'm not used to guys flirting, I've picked up on his nuances.

"I was going to keep you company, you looked so lonely all alone in the dark," he tells me in a low, gravely tone. "What did you think I was going to do to you, wild rose?" He leans in, his mouth nearly brushing along my cheek, but he doesn't touch me.

"I don't like being down here," I bite out the words, frustrated by his nearness. "Can you get out of my way?" I question, my voice still a mere whisper, but I know he can hear me; he can probably hear every breath that's whooshing through my lungs. "Please?" I tack on afterward, hoping my manners will allow me freedom.

"Are you ready for the party tonight?" Damien asks, stepping back, and I can finally pull in a long deep breath, but the moment I do, it's all him I can smell.

The thick cologne, which reminds me of cinnamon and chocolate, along with the distinct smell of weed. I didn't know he smoked, but I guess the more time I spend with him, I'll learn.

"Yes. I'm not at all used to parties, though. I guess you could call me uptight," I tell him, squaring my shoulders and looking directly into those endless pools of blue.

"Mm," he murmurs to himself, as the corner of his mouth kicks up into a dark grin. His gaze turns away from me, glancing up the stairs at the door, before he turns and makes his way up the steps, leaving me gaping at his retreating form.

When I'm finally able to breathe, I realize my heart is kicking wildly against my ribs. My stomach is in turmoil, and my whole body is trembling. Thankfully, the grip I have on the wine bottles is so tight, I don't drop them. But my knuckles are, now, painfully white, and my fingers feel as if they're glued to the glass.

I hate the way he makes me feel. Scared, but also turned on. I've never had someone who made me feel an inkling of what Damien does; but all it is, is stupid hormones. At least, that's what I tell myself.

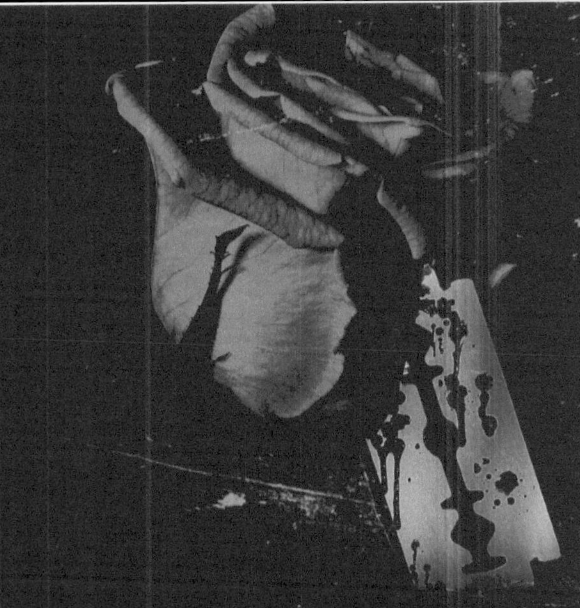

Nesrin

T HE DARK NEED THAT NORMALLY DRIVES ME TO DO shit like that is instinctive. The fear in Nesrin's eyes makes every nerve in my body spark to life. The party is in full swing when I reach the living room. I don't see any sign of Genevieve yet, but I know she'll be here. I spotted the Havens earlier, and where they are, she'll be.

Moving to the bar, I grab the bourbon and lock the cabinet, before I head out into the garden. Finn is with Mali, and Cass has his arm slung over Holly's shoulders.

Cassian's gaze meets mine, and he offers a wink, to which I grin. His plan had worked perfectly. The timing was just right for me to find my wild rose hidden in the cellar. Her scent is still clinging to my nostrils when

I make my way through the garden and down to the brand-new greenhouse that Bradford built for Nesrin's mother.

It's darker down here. It was one of my favorite places to hide, but now that this glass monstrosity is here, I figure I'll hide inside it. Pushing open the door, I head inside. Leaving the door ajar, I make my way to the back, where Dad had the roses set up. A variety of color greets me—pink, red, white, even a slightly blood-stained shade—and I pick up the darker one.

It's beautiful. With thorns that poke out of the stem, I smile, thinking of how feisty Nesrin is when I'm near her.

Fire burns in her eyes when our gazes lock, and my cock hardens at the thought. My heart thuds against my ribs, a warning that I'm going to get lost in the darkness along with her.

Perhaps my little sister would like to play hide and seek with me. I know this place like the back of my hand, and there are many shadowed corners to do dirty things.

My father trusted me with something precious, but he knows that I'm destructive. I've broken far too many fragile things in my life. And, this time, it will be no different because I will break Nesrin Ellington.

She'll never be a Thorne.

"I thought I'd find you in the shadows of the garden,"

Gen says, from behind me. I don't turn to her. I don't like that she's invaded my privacy. I open the bourbon and take a long gulp from the bottle.

"What are you doing in here?"

"I wanted to see if you would introduce me to your new sister. I hear she's quite the looker."

Her words have me spinning on my heel, my gaze boring into her. "Oh? And who would tell you that?"

She shrugs. I wonder if she notices how tightly my knuckles have wrapped around the bottleneck. The images of wrapping my hand around her delicate throat, just like this, makes me even harder. But it's not her face in my mind. It's someone far more forbidden.

"Get out. Go play with your boys, I don't have time for games." I sway the bottle toward her, gesturing for her to leave, but Gen's stubborn; she merely stares at me with a grin on her face.

"Are you turned on for her, Damien?" Gen glides forward, her black boots crunching over the ground, the sound seems louder than it is. "Does her innocence make your dick hard?" When she reaches me, her hand finds my crotch, and she palms me slowly. As much as I try to simmer the rage inside, I can't, because she knows I like it rough; I love it dirty, and I crave it violent.

"I said. Get. The. Fuck. Out." Even as I enunciate each word, a groan rumbles in my chest. There's a hand on my dick, and as much as I'd love to give Gen a hard pounding for being an insolent little bitch, I smirk before ripping her hand from my body. "When I tell you something, you obey. This is my fucking house, now get the fuck away from me, Gen."

The small, sinister smile that graces her lips makes my heart beat hard against my chest. "I'll leave, but don't think this is over." She turns on her heel and walks out of the greenhouse. The party is louder now, and I watch her moving toward the Havens, who are standing in a circle around the fire pit.

They were my biggest mistake.

"Hello?" A soft, familiar voice comes from the darkness, but I don't respond to it. "Is anyone down here?" she asks, and still, I remain silent. I want her here. I realize that my need wasn't for Gen or any other girl at this party. It's for the girl who steps over the threshold.

I slink into the shadows and watch her move deeper into the greenhouse. She's treading lightly. And I wait. Like a predator in the darkness, I watch my prey.

"Oh, wow," she gasps, the sound making my dick stand to attention. I shouldn't feel this need for her, but I do. She doesn't notice me, but if she turned her head an inch to the left, she would. Instead, she reaches for the blood-red rose and tenderly touches the petals. "You're beautiful."

Tipping my head to the side, I watch her. I wonder what that smooth skin would look like bruised. Marked by me. If I did that, it would mean I laid claim to her.

"I miss you, Dad," she suddenly mumbles. For one split second, I see a sad little girl instead of the woman who's making every drop of blood in my body burn for her. I see a girl who lost someone she loved. I don't know what happened to him, her father, but I can tell his absence has hurt her by the way she wipes the tears from her cheeks. She's adamant not to show emotion.

"In the dark, many secrets come to light." My voice startles her, causing her to gasp and leap backward. Her body hits the glass wall, her hand shoots to her heart, holding her chest.

"What are you doing in here?"

"I figured I could find peace from the chaos of the party my brother's insisted on hosting," I tell her. I think briefly that I should offer her something in return. I learned about her heartache.

"Spying on me isn't finding peace." Her fire is back, which makes me grin.

"I came in here to be alone, my father had this made for Marcia, since your mother is such a lover of plants. But I came in here to think."

"I thought you'd be with one of the girls at the party," she tells me, but there's a question hidden in her statement. Once again, I wonder if she's jealous.

"Fitting that you and I would find ourselves in here," I tell her, stepping out of the shadows and closer to her. "Since a greenhouse was our first meeting place." Her eyes widen, then narrow, as I know she's recalling watching me and the redhead at our parents' reception.

I hand her the bottle, offering her a drink. Slowly, she reaches for it, taking it from me. Her fingers brush along mine and sparks shoot through me. There's something utterly forbidden between us: lust, need, and something darker.

My gaze doesn't leave her mouth, as she takes a swallow of the burning liquid, which makes her cough. "This is gross."

"It helps with the pain," I tell her, causing her eyes to lock on mine. Her brows furrow, her expression filled with confusion.

"What pain? Are you hurt?"

I lean in, somehow knowing she'll understand when I say, "the pain inside." Nesrin tips her head back, our faces inches apart, as we stare into each other's eyes. I can feel her short, warm breaths on my lips. I want to feel her mouth on mine. I should take it, take her. I move closer, stepping toward her. She attempts to step back, but she's flush against the cool glass. A shiver wracks her body, and I harden against my zipper.

"What are you doing?" Her breathy whisper is enough to have me ready to sink into her. Steal into the warmth of her body.

"I'm testing your self-control."

"Mine or yours?" she challenges. Her mouth beckons, and I lean in even further, my lips whispering along hers. A whimper falls free from her mouth, and I want nothing more than to steal it from her.

"Both." I offer her only one word in response. Her lashes flutter against the apples of her cheeks. A gasp falls free when her mouth opens for me as if she's waiting for me to take the kiss I so desperately want.

Moments pass in the dark. I don't take it. I don't move forward, and neither does she. It's not the right time. I step back and hear the whoosh of breath from Nesrin.

"I have to get back to the house," I tell her. "Don't leave with anyone tonight." The warning is clear. I'm concerned that one of The Black Knights will want to take her home. I don't doubt those guys are only here to fuck with me. But they're not getting me or any of my family.

"I won't." Is all I hear when I leave her in the greenhouse. My body still feels as if there's a current racing through it, trickling into every nerve ending. I should never have done that. Never have had her pinned against the fucking wall like that.

But it was too easy to lose myself in her.

Too easy to crave her mouth on mine.

And I know that my self-control can only withstand so much.

Damien

THE PARTY IS SLOWLY SIMMERING DOWN AS I MAKE my way to my bedroom. But the moment I hit the landing, I feel a hand twist against my arm, and I'm spun around. Creed.

"I wanted to chat with you," he tells me. Deep green eyes hold me hostage, and something in my gut twists. Not in a good way. There's something about him that makes me nervous. I don't like it.

"About what?"

"I'm Creed Haven," he tells me. "We met earlier, I'm a friend of Damien's." His gaze flashes as he takes me in from head to toe. "He didn't tell me his sister was so gorgeous."

"I'm not his sister."

"Oh? I thought your mommy married Bradford." There's an underlying anger in his words, and I wonder what or why he would care.

"What do you want?" I counter, not wanting to play this game. I wish Damien would come out of his bedroom. I saw him disappear in there earlier, but he hasn't come out again. I want to scream, that would alert him that I'm not feeling comfortable, but I'm certain it would only anger Creed even more, and that's definitely not what I need or want.

"I wanted to see if I could come pick you up, take you on a tour of the town." He offers me a charming smile, and his eyes shimmer, as he regards me. If I wasn't so nervous, I'd think he's handsome. But it's in his eyes, they remind me of a snake's, so luminous, the green almost glowing.

"I don't think that's a good idea."

"I think it's a great idea," he tells me, before pulling me closer, causing me to stumble into his arms. I'm there for a split second before I'm suddenly ripped away from him and shoved behind a bare back of tensing muscles, as they tighten with rage.

"Get the fuck out of my house, Creed," Damien's voice is animalistic; the growl of possessiveness makes my stomach flip.

Creed grins as if he's happy he's angered Damien. It's clear they have a history, something that I'm not privy to, but I intend on getting answers from Damien the moment his *friend* is gone.

Green eyes land on me, before Creed says, "Soon, little one." He winks at me, then turns to walk down the stairs toward the door. All I can hear is my heart thudding in my ears. My stomach is in knots, and my breathing is labored as my lungs struggle to pull in air. I can't believe that just happened.

Damien spins around, and I'm met full force with his beauty. His slim yet chiseled body is smooth. His abs look like they've been carved from porcelain, with hips that taper into a pair of black sweatpants. His V line teases its way toward the waistband of his pants, and the dark trail of hair that leads from his belly button, disappearing below his clothes, has my body pulsing wildly.

"Are you done staring?" he challenges, the anger and rage that fueled him moments ago gone, in its place is a seductive grin that promises filthy things.

I snap my gaze up to his, my cheeks heating because I've been caught checking him out. "What was that?" I find my voice, trying to keep it calm, but trying not to look at Damien's body is a feat in itself.

"Stay away from him," Damien tells me, stalking down the hallway, but I'm hot on his heels. I want more answers than that.

"You have to tell me what the fuck that was, Damien." He stops suddenly, spinning on his heel, which causes me to crash into his body. My hands land on his pecs, and the heat coming off him is searing. But I don't let go, I don't move away, because his hands find my hips, his fingers digging into the flesh.

"Don't ever talk to me like that," he whispers, but there's no anger left in his tone or his blue eyes. They dance with desire, the pupils dilating, the color turning darker than they normally are. The corner of his mouth tilts sideways, the dimples forming in his cheeks.

"Or what?" I know I'm poking the beast, teasing the animal that he hides inside. But I don't care because I need him to do something. To kiss me or kill me. This heat that sizzles between us is unbearable.

He spins us both around, slamming me against the wall, knocking the breath from me, and seconds later, his mouth crashes on mine. His lips steal my whimper, his tongue darts against mine, tangling and dancing. He rolls his hips, pressing his erection against my stomach.

He consumes me. Taking all of my breaths and mingling them with his. But his hands don't move from my hips, if anything, they only seem to tighten their hold on me. I don't know if he's trying to restrain himself from touching me anywhere else, but I don't care. My hands wind around his neck, and I hold on as I'm kissed within an inch of my life.

A low rumbling growl vibrates through Damien's chest, and I feel every movement on my palms, as I lower them from his neck, feeling his hot flesh under my touch.

When he finally breaks the kiss, I'm breathless. The pulse between my legs is thrumming wildly, needing more, wanting him to do so much more, but he steps back, finally releasing me from his hold that I know will leave bruises.

"That is the first and last time." His words are void of any emotion, cold and aloof. His eyes change color before my gaze, from the darker shade to the usual glass-like blue that they always are.

He pushes by me, into his bedroom, and shuts the door behind him with a resounding thud. I'm still trying to catch my breath, trying to not fall to the ground. My knees are wobbly, as I make my way across the hall to my own bedroom that beckons with safety.

There's no use denying I crave him. It's fierce and hot. Even though my lips are still tingling from the contact with his, I can't stop wondering just what pain he's hiding deep inside.

I lean against the closed door, needing to collect my myriad of thoughts that are only of him. My panties are wet, but my heart aches at his promise, *this is the first and the last time*. There's darkness that follows Damien, pain he hides so well, and it felt like he was pouring all his agony into me with a single, heart-stopping, all-consuming kiss.

As forbidden as it is, I want another one. I want so many more breath-stealing kisses. Shaking my head, I make my way into the bathroom and pull out the box. For a long time, it's been my only solace in this world of judgments and ridicule because I'm not like everyone else. Not like my mother. I struggle to vocalize my emotions, what I'm feeling in the depths of my soul, and over the years, this has been the escape. It's been the answer I wanted and needed.

Cutting has been my screaming admission as to how I'm feeling. It's been an outlet of all those emotions that bubbled inside me, struggling to be set free. But only I could hear.

The shiny metal inside that reminds me I can breathe, when it steals my anxiousness and leaves me calm and serene. But the moment I flick open the lid and pick up the blade, I find myself consumed by thoughts of him. Instead of wanting to release the pent-up frustration, I find myself on the mattress, moments later, with my hand between my legs, as I replay the kiss in my mind.

It doesn't make sense that Damien's presence is so strong in my mind. I want to think about the tumultuous emotions I'm feeling, to ponder why he's affected me so much, but I can't think of anything but the warmth of his tongue, how his lips molded against mine.

I've never allowed myself to *feel* like this about anyone before. And as lust courses in my veins, I realize it's no longer pain that I seek out for release, it's pleasure. My eyes prick with tears when I realize Damien has fully consumed me, and I don't know how long it will last.

But I allow the moment to replay in my mind. It's as if it's a movie on a loop, and I can't stop it. My fingers dance over my slick entrance, and I call out his name as I find my orgasm racing through me. My limbs tremble, my body shudders, and I'm utterly consumed by him. The image of him in those low-slung sweatpants, the feel of his hardness against me. Everything about Damien Thorne is dangerous, but what he doesn't know is that I love danger. I love to do things I'm not meant to.

My body suddenly shakes, and I cry out as I leap over the edge of pleasure, leaving the pain behind while the tightening in my chest eases, and the usual anxiety releases me from its feral grip. And it's all because of him. Not a blade. Not the blood. No longer a cut.

And as I roll over on the bed, I cry because confusion has taken hold of me. I'm tipping over, falling, and I'm scared. So, fucking scared.

Even though he promised that would be the last time, I

wonder if he was trying to convince me or himself. Deep down, I pray that his restraint isn't as strong as he makes it out to be, because I do want more.

Nesrin

THE SUN IS RISING JUST ABOVE THE TREES. I'M not focused on the beautiful scenery, though; I'm thinking about Nesrin. I shouldn't have kissed her at the party, but I couldn't stop myself. It's been a handful of hours, and I can't stop replaying the moment in my mind.

My self-restraint unraveled when I had her close to me. The scent of her perfume and her body molding to mine broke me. And the echo of her whimpers and moans have been a soundtrack for me; I don't know how long I can fight this attraction. It's as if she's slowly burrowing her way inside me, into the marrow of my bones. I don't know what it is about her, but she's got a grip on me.

It's as if she's challenging the very restraint I hold dear. The control I've always prided myself on is slipping away, inch by torturous fucking inch. I fight, yet it feels like a losing battle.

It's almost as if she and I suffer from the same affliction. In the darkness, we're the same, but in the light, we're vastly different. She's too innocent for me and my world. But having her so close has me struggling to push these thoughts away.

The crunch behind me doesn't startle me; I felt him before he closed the distance. My brother has a way of sneaking into my private thoughts, and I know he's going to question me about her.

"Creed had a lot to say about you as he left," Cassian says. My brother knows about my formative years when I got up to shit with The Black Knights, shit that was considered wrong. But Creed is the man who will hide in the shadows, wanting to feast on your fear. A rogue under the tailored suits and friendly smiles.

Beneath the cool, confident exterior, is a man who is bad right down to the very marrow of his bones. Perhaps one day he'll find his match, the girl who will finally bring him to his knees. Someone who won't be afraid of the real Creed Haven and fight back, showing him he's found his equal.

Our town, Thorne Haven, was founded by two men

back in the day. Us, the Thornes and them, the Havens. The three of them, Creed, Brody, and Keirin, aren't blood brothers like we are, but they're close enough to act like it.

The Havens adopted them when they were young. We grew up together, our friendships grew over time, but when they decided to start shit in this town to spice up our meager teenage existence, I was at a place in my life where I was pulled into their twisted games.

"He can say anything he wants, he's a fucking asshole," I bite out, as my anger simmers just below the surface. I want to drive out into Haven territory and call Creed out. I want to drag him over the invisible line and give him a taste of his own medicine. But I don't. I know if I do it, I'll only start a war.

And that's not what Nesrin needs to see.

"You know she's caught his eye," Cass warns, his tone turning darker. I nod. Last night was just the first of what I can assume would be many chances that Creed would take. Even though we've kept the peace, ensuring appearances come across to others as peaceful, as if we're still all friends, we're not.

It's been a long time since we could have called ourselves friends.

"He won't fuck with her. I'll make sure of it."

"What about *La Ball Masqué*?" Cassian's question

causes my body to lock in fury. My hands fist at my sides, and I know I'm going to have to take her there. The town would've already heard about my father's wedding, and they would now know that I have Nesrin at the house. News travels fast in this town.

If I take her, I'm making a statement to the Havens. They'll read into it, and I don't know if I can follow through with what's needed. Creed will throw out a challenge if Nesrin is at my side at the dance.

I internally war with myself for a long moment. Silence hangs between us. It's a reminder that I'm not a man she can be with. This thing between us is not permanent, and whatever I'm feeling for her will bring about destruction to our family.

"She'll go with me."

I can almost feel Cassian's smile at my admission. He knows she's captured my attention. As much as I want to fight it, I'm losing the battle. I've already broken down and kissed her, but then told her it would never happen again, which was a blatant lie, because I don't know how to keep it platonic between us.

"Are you sure that's a good idea?" My brother questions slowly, but there's a warning in his tone, which causes me to look at him for the first time.

"Probably not," I answer, honestly, because I don't think it's a good idea for me to be anywhere near her. Not when she brings out such a ferocious need inside me.

Cassian and I stare at each other for a long time, before he tells me, "I have to get back to the house and help clean up."

"I'll be there shortly."

He nods and leaves me to my thoughts. The Masked Dance is an event that's held in the old castle that sits on the hill of our town. Every attendee is under thirty, men go to this to find a partner, a woman for the night, and perhaps longer.

The tradition started so long ago that I've lost track of how many of these things there have been. Over the years, it's morphed into something far more sinister than it was originally created to be.

Every attendee will be masked; it's the unknown that brings out the darkness of each act that happens in the town. It's like a sensually erotic version of Cirque Du Soleil. The show takes place in the majestic ballroom that will be decorated in black, gold, and silver.

Once the show comes to an end, music starts, drinks flow, and people disappear into corners of the castle to enjoy the night. I've been to a few, I've had my experience, and each one has been more malevolent than the last.

By the time I walk into the house again, it's quiet, indicating that nobody's home. A loud crash comes from the back of the house, though, forcing my feet into action as I race through the foyer and kitchen to find Nesrin standing over a tray of broken glasses.

Finn and Cassian also make their way in from outside. "What the hell?" Finn chuckles.

"I'm so sorry. I slipped; the floor was wet." Nesrin looks like she's close to tears, and I find myself at her side in seconds. Her body shakes, and I pull her into my arms, without thinking. Her body, once more, molds to mine, and when I meet Cassian's arched, questioning brow, I know I'm fucked.

"It's fine," I tell her, pulling her toward the door, gesturing with my chin toward the shards. "Clean that up, Finn." I lead Nesrin toward the bathroom. Inside, I lift her onto the counter, and I'm surprised she allows me to do so.

It's only then that I notice she's wearing shorts that ride up her slender legs. But it's not her clothing choice that captures my attention, it's the small red lines that mar her perfectly tanned flesh.

She jerks the material of her shorts down, covering her upper thighs, but she can't hide what I've already seen. When I lock my gaze on hers, I see the guilt flashing in those perfectly shiny golden eyes.

"What the fuck was that?" The growl that leaves my mouth is thunder, a storm brewing in my chest, the swirling of rage taking hold of me.

"Nothing." She pushes me away, scooting off the counter before I have time to react. She rushes for the door, but I find my wits, making me quicker. My hand slams it closed and shuts us inside.

"Don't fucking lie to me," I bite out, clenching my teeth so hard that my jaw aches painfully. "What the fuck was that, Nesrin?" I ask again, the fury in my voice is evident. When she looks up at me, under those dark lashes, defiance flashes in her stare. She isn't going to tell me.

Her hands ball into fists before they slam against my chest, and as much as she tries to push me away, she can't. I'm stronger, taller, and I'm far more solid than the wild rose that's trying to fight me away.

"Let me go, Damien." Her voice cracks, which only seems to make a gash right in the center of my chest.

I shake my head before I tell her, "You're not leaving here until you explain yourself."

"You are nothing to me! I'm not here to answer to you!" she screams at me, her voice breaking with emotion. Her eyes that are normally filled with fire are glistening with tears.

I slap the door on either side of her head, shocking her out of whatever fucking hysterical fit she was about to throw, and I lean my head down, so we're eye to eye.

"Listen to me, I've seen a lot of shit in my life," I tell her. "And that bullshit on your legs is not something I'll allow."

"You'll allow?" she spits out as if I've offended her. Perhaps I have. I don't care. She's mine. The thought shoots through me without barriers, the knowledge that I want her has settled in my veins. "You have no fucking clue who I am. I am not a possession you can own."

"Like fuck you aren't," I bite out. The air in the room is thick, heavy with the promise that I'm taking and claiming her, and I don't give a shit who says what about it.

"Damien, I'm not yours. I can't be. Don't act like you give a shit about me." Even though she attempts to square her shoulders to show off her confidence, the emotion falters in the tone of her voice.

"You want this bullshit?" I grab her thigh, squeezing it hard. Her eyes widen, shock sparks in her expression, in those pretty fucking eyes. "You want to get hurt? I'll hurt you so fucking badly, you'll never want to pick up a blade again." My voice lowers to a hushed whisper, and my lips feather along hers. "The only person who'll ever hurt you is me. And when I do, you'll beg me for more."

"You're a fucking asshole." Her words are ice, but her eyes dance with flames. "Let me—"

My mouth crashes down on hers, and I feel the tears she'd been holding back spill down her cheeks. I told her last night that this wouldn't happen again, but I can't stop myself.

Nesrin punches my chest as she wriggles beneath me, her body pinned between mine and the door. But the more she fights, the darker my need grows, and the harder my cock gets. My hands grip her thighs, squeezing hard until she mewls into my mouth. I lift her up, forcing her legs to wrap around my waist, as her hands continue to pummel me.

Our mouths fuse violently, my tongue darts deep in to taste her. We duel for long moments before I allow my tongue to slide out and taste her mouth. She bites down on my lower lip, tugging the flesh until she earns herself a feral growl.

I'm tempted to pull her clothes off, to inspect her body closely, to taste and lick those scars and see if they bear any resemblance to my own. But I don't. I force back the growing desire that's building inside me, and I break the kiss.

Her lips are swollen, her eyes glassy, and her cheeks shimmer with the tears she shed. Nesrin looks up at me as the air, that's now thick with sexual tension, hangs over us like a cloud of forbidden yearning.

"It's the only way I can feel. I'm so numb, so empty,

and I don't know why," she finally tells me, in a broken whisper, and my heart shatters alongside hers.

Damien

HE LOOKS AT ME FOR A LONG TIME. HIS EYES FLASH for a moment, and I think he's going to kiss me again, but then he sets me to my feet and looks down at the blood that came from the cut on my hand. I've messed up his shirt, the red staining it.

"You don't do it anymore!" He's not asking me; he's commanding me. Pain laces his voice, the husky baritone sending shivers through me. Those blue eyes pierce me as if he can see my soul. The stare that he pins on me makes me believe he can feel how torn and broken I am on the inside. Damien's hands move to the hem of his shirt, and he pulls the material over his head.

Once again, I'm assaulted by just how beautiful he

is. But also, under the harsh light of the bathroom, I see what he's showing me. Not the chiseled peaks and valleys of his body, not even the V muscles that sink beneath the waistband of his pants. And not the dusting of dark hair that sneaks from his navel down below the belt he's wearing.

It's what's lacing his smooth, tanned skin. I see them. My first night here, when I first saw him shirtless, the dim lighting didn't show them off. They weren't as prominent, but now that the harsh white glare is on him, the scars become visible.

When he starts unzipping his jeans, my mouth falls open in shock.

"What are you doing?" I'm stunned. I want to see more of him, but I also want to turn my gaze away. I'm not sure what he's doing, but the moment he pushes his pants down, my gaze finds the scars that were hidden behind the black material of his jeans.

Thick, angry lines of red, nothing like mine, mar his left thigh. They're not hidden, it's as if he's proud of them. There are only three thick angry lines, but they're prominent. I've never seen him in merely a pair of tight black boxer briefs, but now I see everything.

"Being the eldest Thorne in The Black Knights, I became something of a king for them. It's stupid, but they saw me as their leader. Until Creed and I fell out.

The six of us were always close. But the power that comes with running this town got to Creed. We fought in the forest to the cheers of the rest of the *gang*. Every young person who lives in this town watched us shed skin. I'll never forget the violence of that night. It will always stay with me."

He pulls his jeans back up, leaving them unzipped, but they still hug his hips, teasing me. Through the violence, through his scars, I see him. Broken and torn, just like me.

"I'm sorry."

"Don't fucking pity me," he spits, and I can't help but smile, to which he growls, "What?"

I step closer to him, my fingertips dancing along the small lines that adorn his skin. "You're beautiful." My voice is barely a whisper, but I know he heard me. "And I can never pity someone. I know how it feels to be looked at with such sorrowful eyes that it makes you want to slice open your flesh and bleed out."

"I meant what I said, wild rose," Damien says. "Never again." I know what he means, but I don't know if I can promise that to him. It's been my solace for so long. Damien cups my face in his hands, the softness of his thumb sweeping along the apples of my cheeks. "I mean it. If you want to hurt, I'll do it. I'll make you ache so badly; nothing will ever compare to how I make you feel."

His promise sends heat pooling between my legs.

"Tell me how?" My husky voice causes a smirk to appear on his face. The way his dimples deepen, as only one corner of his mouth tilts upward, making my skin prickle with awareness.

"I have something in mind, but I'll need you to trust me." His eyes simmer with something feral. There's pure animalistic need driving him because his expression holds lust and hunger.

"Can I trust you?"

"I'm meant to be here as your guardian, your older stepbrother, the person who's meant to keep you safe, and I've already broken the rules. I've kissed you, craved you, and now I'm about to make you do something stupid in the darkness of the forest," he speaks. His voice turns me molten with the thought of all those kisses, every touch and whisper.

"I don't like playing by the rules," I tell him confidently, squaring my shoulders, but even in my show of confidence, I'm trembling. I know we shouldn't be doing this, but I can't stop myself from being attracted to him.

"I noticed," he quips. "But then again, I've always liked a bad girl." More huskiness laces his voice, the gentle roughness of it running over my skin, making me shiver.

"How many—"

"Don't." The one word holds more weight than I ever

thought words could. He doesn't want to talk about his past, which only means he's had a lot of girls.

"I'm sorry. I didn't mean to sound like a jealous girlfriend." The moment the word leaves my lips, I know it's a mistake. Damien's blue eyes bore into me, drilling deep, finding the parts of me that I try to hide.

"Don't you ever apologize to me," he tells me. "I don't know what this is between us," he says. "But I know that as wrong as it is, I can't stop it."

"Aren't you meant to be the levelheaded adult here?"

This causes him to chuckle. "Oh, wild rose, if you only knew. I'm so far from sensible. That's why my father thinks of me as the black sheep."

"I thought Finn would be the black sheep," I counter. From what I've seen of the three Thorne sons, Cassian would probably be the most reliable, Damien second, and Finn would, most definitely, be last.

Damien grins, his eyes crinkling at the corners, the white-hot flame dancing in the blue. "We all hold a certain level of darkness within us," he tells me. "It's only a matter of time before you let yours shine through. So far, you've only seen mine." He winks at me, and my stomach flips wildly.

"So, what are our plans for tonight? You said you had an idea."

He leans in until his mouth is at my ear. "You'll learn

the truth behind Finders Keepers." He steps back, leaving me cold, as he opens the tap. I watch him get a cloth, soak it, and twist it before he turns to me and starts cleaning me up. Once he's taken care of me, he leads me to my bedroom and says, "Get some rest. You'll need it for tonight." And then leaves me staring at his back.

Nesrin

W**HEN** I **TOLD** C**ASS** **AND** F**INN** **ABOUT** **MY** **IDEA**, they were on board. I told Nesrin on her first night that she should be careful of the garden out back, but I didn't tell her why. And tonight, I'll gladly show her.

The thought of her cutting herself turns my blood hot with rage. Seeing her scars, earlier, was too much, and if she truly wants to feel a release, she'll find it with me. And only me.

"There's a storm coming," Cassian tells me, as we watch the stars flicker in the dark sky. The moon is merely a sliver of silver. The trees break through the glittering pinpricks, and I shiver with excitement at what's to come.

"There is a storm brewing in the distance," I agree. "I have a feeling that our annual dance is going to be explosive," I tell my brother.

"The Havens will want her," he tells me. "They're not going to stop until they claim something we have."

"They can't have her." My biting tone catches in my throat, the words hang heavy with promise, with rage. I'm barely keeping it together, and I know Creed will notice it the moment he's around Nesrin and me at the dance.

"If I didn't know better, I'd say you're marking your territory," Cassian muses beside me, and I can't stop the frustration at the situation from getting a hold of me.

I bite out, "I didn't piss on her."

"You may as well have," he tells me, causing my muscles to tense. If everyone else can see it, I'm sure she can as well.

I cast a quick glance at Cass. "Not into golden showers, brother," I retort when he crinkles his nose at the thought. "Besides, I don't need to piss on her to show him she's mine. All you have to do is see how she looks at me."

"Oh?" He quips. "Has she been undressing you with her eyes?"

"I don't blame the girl, I mean look at me, of course she has," I joke, but the thought of being naked in front of her, of seeing her bared to me, plays in my mind, and I have to shake it off. "Tonight, she'll either run or hide."

"Are you sure about this?" Cassian's worried. We haven't played this game in a couple of years. Not since the night Creed and I had a fight, and I know it's dangerous. But I think it's exactly what Nesrin needs.

"Not entirely, but if she finds solace in it, I'll do it."

My brother stares at me, I can feel his questioning eyes on me. Cassian and I have always had a strange connection. It's almost as if he can read my mind. "You're falling for her."

Snapping my gaze to my brother, I furrow my brows and find him looking at the garden, instead of me. "What the fuck do you mean?"

"You are. I can see it when you talk about her." He doesn't turn to me because he knows if he looks at me, I'll punch him right in the gut.

I don't love.

I've seen how destructive loving someone can be. I vowed never to fall for someone the way my father loved my mother. He got hurt, burned because he trusted her, he believed she was *the one*. All that fate bullshit is a farce.

"Don't deny it, Damien. I know you better than you know yourself. Even though I'm a year younger, at times, I feel a lot older."

"I'm ready," Finn says, as he enters the room,

interrupting our heated conversation. He's dressed all in black, just like me and Cass. We're all three wearing our hoodies. The first time I did this, I never felt so free, and I hope that I can give Nesrin that same experience. Nothing can ever compare to the exhilaration that flows through me when I race through the darkness. *Except for her kiss.* The thought comes to me quickly, but I push it back, hiding it in the shadows of my mind. I shouldn't want her so much. The moment our parents return, we'll need to stop this… thing we've started.

"Man, I'm so fucking excited for this. You know it's been too long since we let loose," Finn says, as he nears us. My youngest brother is the one who would walk back into The Black Knights and ask them to make him a part of their group. He's always loved rebelling against everything I've told him, including befriending the Havens.

When he was much younger, I cared far too much. I wanted him safe, and I didn't want him to end up like I did, with war wounds that will never heal.

Finders Keepers was a game that Creed and I invented after we turned sixteen. It was meant to be our way of choosing the girls we wanted. Being a teenager in this town meant that we could run amok, and nobody would flutter an eyelash, and Creed and I took advantage of that.

Leaving a burnt rose on the doorstep of the girl we wanted to take became well-known within the town, and we did it for a couple of years before it turned into something far darker than I anticipated. The rose was the signal that she was mine, or if he left the rose, the girl was his. I would leave red roses while he would leave pink.

It was a game of cat and mouse in the dark; while we were the hunters, the girls became our prey. We labeled it an adult version of hide and seek, even though we weren't nearly old enough to do the shit we did.

The thrill of chasing down a pretty girl in the darkness was intoxicating. Over the years, it became more and more exhilarating, and that's when we tried to one-up each other. I would do something, and Creed would add more danger, more thrill to it. But the moment Creed took it too far, I watched how dangerous his actions became, and I knew I had to walk away before this game turned fatal.

But tonight, I'm going to do it again.

I'm going to give Nesrin what she needs.

"Nesrin wants to experience our game, and we're going to show her how Thornes play Finders Keepers," I tell Finn, then glance at Cassian. His gaze narrows. The words he uttered to me earlier, ringing true.

I do like her.

More than I should.

If I were a good person, a moral person, I would walk away and allow her to meet someone who can offer her a happy life. She's eighteen, old enough to have a boyfriend, but the thought of any guy touching her sends the poisonous emotion—jealousy—racing through my veins.

I know I can never let her go. Not now that I've tasted her mouth, felt her body mold to mine. As much as I should make sure this is nothing more than a short fling, while our folks aren't home, I have a feeling it's nothing near the one night stands I used to crave.

She's mine.

And I know I can't walk away from her.

Damien

W HEN I REACH THE LIVING ROOM, ALL THREE brothers are staring at me as I walk through the doorway. I'm dressed in black, just like Damien asked me to be, with sneakers and a hoodie.

"What are we doing?"

Three sets of eyes pin me to the spot. But it's Damien who speaks, "We're playing a game of hunting the prey. Finders Keepers." His voice is deep. A baritone that sneaks through my veins and slides all the way over me, until it settles between my legs in a pulse of desire.

"Hunt?"

"Do you remember what I told you about going into the garden at night?" he asks, his dark brow arching and the corner of his mouth kicking into a familiar smirk that deepens his dimples.

"I do," I croak, the memory sending heat to my cheeks.

"You have a count of ten, after that, you're prey. We'll come after you." He crosses his arms, his gaze boring into me in challenge. Perhaps he's expecting me to refuse, to stop this stupidity because that's what it is. But what Damien Thorne doesn't bank on is me racing by him and out the door into the dark garden.

There's only a sliver of moon that illuminates my way, but other than that, I'm on my own. By the time I see the property line, I know I'm fucked because I can hear the soft footfalls behind me.

Their voices, grunts, are so close, it's as if I can feel the warmth of their breath in my neck causing goose bumps to dot my skin. I'm not a great runner, but the thought of them catching me has my feet moving quickly. I don't know how this is meant to stop my self-harm addiction, but for some unknown reason, I trust Damien to know what he's doing.

My breath is coming in short spurts, my eyes try to adjust to the darker surroundings, as I race through the too tall trees. Under the shroud, I can't see the moon anymore. Every now and then, there's a sliver of light that escapes.

"I'm coming for you, wild rose," Damien's shout

bounces off the trunks, reaching me in a dark promise that makes my heart slam against my ribs. Usually, the pain of cutting myself releases the anxious feelings, the darkness that swirls in my mind, but right now, those emotions are no longer here.

My focus is on the race, on the game, rather than the thoughts in my mind. It's freeing not having voices telling me I'm not good enough, or that I'm broken, damaged goods.

I'm not sure where I'm going, but I can hear the crack of branches, every now and then, as they start closing the distance. I take a left, rushing through the thick trunks. With every step, I feel another scrape as the branches attack my legs, but I've never felt such a rush.

Having Damien understand what I need has shocked me. As I move in the darkness, I find myself forgetting the stress of my life and focusing solely on the euphoria snaking through me.

"I'm coming for you, little sis," a voice startles me, causing my legs to move even quicker. Finn is close, so damn close. His footsteps crunch behind me, and I turn left, hoping he'll go right.

"You can't hide in here," Cassian's words trickle over me. Both brothers are moving fast, they're closing the distance between us, and if I don't do something quickly, they'll catch me. I turn right, then left. My mind free of the worries of everyday life, of my mother, and school. The only thing that matters is the darkness that's swallowing me as I move through the trees.

I find myself drenched in darkness and sweat. Stopping against one of the thicker trunks, I lean my head back, inhaling deeply, trying to catch my breath that the night has stolen.

My heart is racing faster than it ever has before, and my legs are shaky from the exertion, but I've never felt more myself than I do right now. A smile appears on my lips, and I look up at the murkiness above me. A splash of water echoes through the trees from somewhere in the darkness, and I push away from the trunk, my feet carrying me forward.

I don't know where Cass and Finn have gone, but they're no longer breathing down my neck. Thankfully, I'm able to catch a breath. My lungs are pulling in air, deeply, and as I exhale, the white puff of smoke from my lips is an indication of how chilly it is out here. But I don't feel it. I'm hot, sweating, and my mind is clear.

It doesn't take me long to pass by a break in the trees. I stop when the view before me changes from thick blackness to charcoal. There's a silver-topped lake in front of me, and I gasp in shock when I see it sparkling in the moonlight.

On the other side of the bank of water, I notice red

glowing. My gaze narrows, as I try to make out what it is. Suddenly, arms wrap around me, causing a piercing scream to tumble from my lips.

A hand snakes around my mouth, covering my lips. I can't call out, but I can certainly fight. My body wriggles in the tight hold of the person behind me. Hot breath fans over my neck, which is trickling with sweat.

"If you keep fighting, I'll only get hard, and then I'm going to have to ask you to help me with it," his voice threatens in the dark, causing heat to race down my spine, and pool between my thighs.

Even though I'm trying to speak, his hand is still covering my mouth. I cease all movement, and a dark, animalistic chuckle vibrates through his chest, into my back.

Damien is nothing short of a savage. A hunter who seems to enjoy the chase. He slowly releases me, his body still warming me, but the moment I spin on my heel, I'm met with those luminous eyes.

"You scared me," I tell him.

"It was all part of the plan, wild rose," he murmurs, the words feathering over my mouth, and I find myself leaning into him. I'm still shaking when he snakes his arm around my body, pulling me against his chest.

"That was…" I whisper, but I can't find the words to describe just what I'm feeling. The experience was otherworldly, and even though there are scratches all over my legs and hands, I would do it again.

Damien's gaze sneaks over my shoulder, momentarily, before he turns, tugging me with him. A quick glance over my shoulder shows me that the fire I noticed there earlier is gone.

"What's going on?"

"We need to get out of here," he speaks, but the tone of his voice belies the calmness of his body. Something is wrong.

"I'm not going anywhere until you—"

He cuts me off by spinning on his heel, sneaking his shoulder into my stomach, and hoisting me over his shoulder. And then we're moving.

I'm bumping against him, up and down, the breath from my lungs whooshing, each time I land stomach first on his shoulder.

"Put me the fuck down, Damien!" My voice carries in the darkness, bouncing off the trees, as we make our way back to the house. But I don't know if we are headed in the right direction since I'm upside down, and I'm lost.

I hear a branch crack in the distance, and Damien slows down. His feet squishing on the mulch beneath his shoes, and then, I'm sliding down his body. Every hard inch of him, flush with mine.

"I thought you weren't playing games anymore." A deep

voice comes from the shadows. I recognize it instantly—Creed.

"What do you want, Haven?" Damien pushes me behind him, shielding me from whatever is about to go down.

"I noticed your girl, and I thought I'd come to see if she's okay," Creed says. He's nothing like Damien, with short brown hair and luminous green eyes that shine with malicious intent. He's inked, from what I can tell when he closes the distance between us. I didn't notice his tattoos the night of the party, because I wasn't paying attention, but his neck is a canvas.

"She's fine." Damien's voice holds an edge of challenge. The men seem so engrossed in the fight that's brewing, which only annoys me because I'm not some toy for them to fight over.

Pushing past Damien, I step up to Creed. A smirk curls his full lips, and the piercing in the middle of his lower lip glints under the silver light of the moon.

"A pretty mouse captured by the big bad hunter," Creed says, his gaze flicking between Damien and me. "You know, Damien, when you walked away from The Dark Knights, I gave you the benefit of the doubt. I truly believed you had changed." Creed crosses his arms in front of his chest while he tips his head to the side. "But I think you're just as fucking tortured as the rest of us."

"I may be tortured, but I'm nothing like you." The venom in Damien's voice is ice, pouring between us, causing the large rift between the Thornes and the Havens to crack further.

"Does she know about the town? Does she know the secrets that broke us apart in the first place?" The look on Creed's face tells me there are more secrets between them than I've heard and more that I should have learned about.

"If you want to talk, you're more than welcome to come to me directly, other than that, Nesrin has no bearing on this world."

"Your little sister needs to learn, Damien."

"I'm not his sister," I bite out, anger surging through me, but it only causes Creed to stare at me. There's a hint of confusion that paints his expression, for a moment, before he smiles. But it's not friendly, there's a knowing to his face that makes me shiver with fear.

"You know, Thorne," he says, looking at Damien. "I never once pegged you for such a bad boy. Breaking all the rules and doing it with a straight face." This time, the laugh that comes from Creed is almost inhumane. "I'll see you both at the dance. And I'm sure that it's going to be a night to never forget."

He spins on his heel, leaving us in the darkness; me shaking with anxiety and Damien shuddering with rage.

His arms snake across my middle, and he holds me to his warmth.

"What did he mean?"

"He's seen me claim you," Damien murmurs in my ear.

Shock shakes me for a moment before I ask, "How?"

"The need for me to protect you overtook me, and I couldn't hide the fact that having him near you fucked with my head. He saw me. One thing you'll learn about Creed is that he's intuitive. He can read situations easily, and because he knows me, he's seen right through my possessive nature."

I turn around, his arms still holding me close. When I'm finally facing him, I look up into cerulean eyes. "He knows that we're..." The words filter off into the silence that hangs between us, but he doesn't have to respond because I know the truth.

Creed knows that Damien and I are more than we should be.

"He won't have you," Damien tells me. "You're mine. And I'm not losing that, not now, not ever."

"Don't say things that could change in an instant." My voice cracks, but he sees the pain that seems to haunt me. Damien cups my face in his strong hands, holding me close. "Please, Damien, take me home."

"If you say that in your seductive voice, I'm going to do more than take you home," he promises in the darkness.

"Then do it."

"On one condition," he practically growls the words, which only seems to send heat shooting through me.

"Anything."

A dark brow arches at my response. "Promise me you're mine."

"I can't—"

"I'm not asking for love, or any of that bullshit. I want to do things to you that should be illegal."

"I thought it would be since your father is married to my mother," I tease, the challenge hanging between us in the night sky.

"Oh, wild rose, you're just barely eighteen, and there are so many more illicit things that I can imagine doing to you all day, every day." Damien leans in close, his mouth brushing along mine. His lips hot, breath warm, and his thumbs swiping along my cheeks, ever so gently, but I know that Damien Thorne is not a gentleman, he's animalistic.

"I want it to hurt, I want all the pain, all the agony." I look up at him, as I say this, and I swear I see fire dancing in his gaze. The corner of his mouth tilts into one of those seductive smirks that make every inch of me tremble with need.

"No more cutting and I'll give you anything you want," he tells me, with the promise clear as day in his voice. I nod. "Good girl." His hands drop to mine, and he laces our fingers, as we make our way back to the house.

I don't know what's going to happen now, but what I do know is that Damien Thorne is slowly stealing me piece by piece, and the day he gets all of me is the day I know my heart is in his hands.

He has a power over me, an all-consuming command that takes hold of me and I can't fight it. And losing *that* control is what makes my heart skip a beat while my stomach churns with nervous energy. No matter how much I try to deny how I feel about him, I can't because Damien Thorne has engraved himself in my bones. And there's no cut deep enough to extricate him.

But when I think about it, I realize I don't want to.

I ache for him to be there. Inside me. Within me.

And that's what scares me the most.

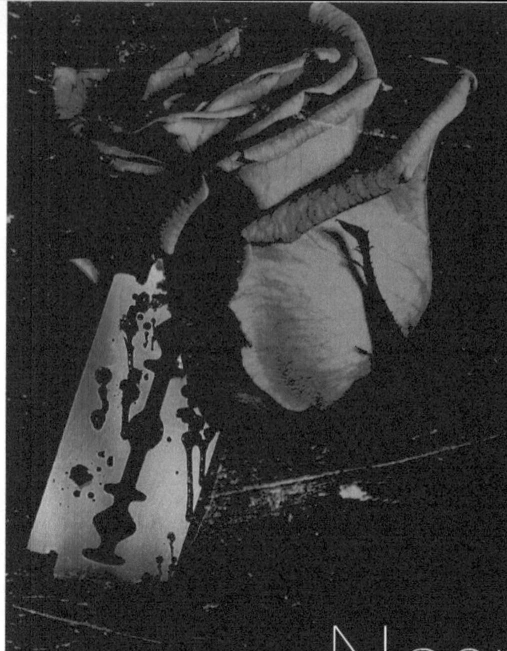

Nesrin

The night is coming to an end, and dawn is peeking on the horizon. I can't sleep, I've spent most of the night on my balcony, looking out over the garden.

Thorne Manor offers each bedroom a private wrought-iron balcony, with views of the town that are usually hidden amongst the trees of our property perimeter.

I spent my childhood looking through those trees, seeing the murkiness that hides amongst the thick trunks. I knew that one day when I was old enough, I'd venture into them, but I never thought I'd play the games we did.

The memory of my last burning rose comes to mind.

She must've seen it. The directions were clear as day. Creed is hidden somewhere to my left, along with Brody and Cassian. The younger boys—Finn and Keirin—are at home, prepping for the party.

My body is alert, my ears prick at the faintest sound. I inhale a deep breath, trying to still both my thudding heartbeat and the hardening of my dick. I guess being a horny teenager, I have to put up with it.

I know, as soon as I start the chase, I'll calm my erection down and focus on the trees that will be whipping by me.

Seconds later, I see it. The swooping lights from a car pulling into the lot. It won't be long now, until she walks into our line of sight, and then we'll sound the whistle that normally startles them into a frantic race for survival.

"Damien!" Her voice is drenched in fear, which only seems to make me harder, ready to feel her pulsing around me, as I make her come. Shaking my head, I attempt to focus, but it's been off for a few of our runs now.

Creed blows the whistle, and like clockwork, we watch as the pretty blonde spins on her heels, but she doesn't run toward the car, that's not part of the rules. I can't help but smile.

None of them ever run for their cars because they know what lies at the end of the cat and mouse game. We wait the five seconds, and then we move. The rustling of bush has my head turning to see Creed and Cassian, along with Keirin, making their way out onto the path. Only we know where it is.

"You want the blonde?" Creed arches his brow, looking at me, and I nod.

"Yeah. She's mine." I've laid my claim, now I need to make good on my promise. I allow my feet to carry me. Listening to the broken twigs echoing in the darkness, I follow the sound, moving swiftly through the trees.

We've done this so many times, I know where I'm going, without looking. In this darkness, you can't see much in front of you, but the white skirt of my prey is right in front of me. I don't catch her; instead, I allow her to think she's getting away.

A howl comes from behind me. Creed. The asshole loves to scare them more than I ever do. But I can't help chuckling at him. We've been friends for most of my life, growing up together, learning about each other, we've all become like a band of brothers.

Brother-in-arms.

Another long, pained howl bounces against the trees, and it's as if the sound is following me and blondie. I can't even remember her name. My legs work quickly, as I decide to make my move.

I'm in pouncing distance, but I watch in awe, as she races through the trees. Her breathing is panicked, and my dick gets hard. I bet her pupils have dilated, I wonder, briefly, if her pussy is wet. Because my dick is ready to find out.

It doesn't take long for us to reach the clearing, and that's when I grab her arm, spinning her around and pinning her *against one of the last trees in front of us.*

A squeal escapes her lips, which I quickly steal with my mouth. The kiss is frantic and sharp, short breaths mingled with the trembling of her body. I'm so fucking hard; I probably wouldn't last long the moment I felt her slick heat around me.

"Damien," she mumbles through the kiss.

"That's all me, Baby," I chuckle, leaning in to inhale her scent. A soft, strawberry fragrance mingled with the light scent of sweat. My hands travel down her body, gripping her ass, I pull her up and nestle myself between her thighs.

Time to collect my prize.

Shaking my head to clear the memory, I try not to think about what happened next. How my friends and my brother watched me claim her in the darkness.

She had no idea, while we were fucking, that they were there; it was only as she was screaming my name, did she notice them. But girls who came to the forest to play our game didn't care about morals, or how they were seen by the rest of the town.

No. These girls enjoyed being watched. Just like I did. And even though I walked out of the group and left The Black Knights behind, I still crave it so badly.

The voyeuristic tendencies still have a way of sneaking through the confines I've locked them in. They escape and take hold of me. And even though I haven't seen

Nesrin coming apart, yet, I know I will. And to watch that will be euphoric.

Usually, Creed and I would share her, we would take turns, sitting back and allowing the other to have his wicked way. But with her, it's different. I can't share her. Even the thought of someone else's hands on her makes me livid. Rage, jealousy, and anger take hold of me, and in its feral grip, I'm lost to the need of having her all to myself.

I have never been obsessive, that's Creed, which is why these emotions she's stirred within me are fucking with my head. I can't focus on anything else, besides her.

But I also know how wrong it is to want her.

I know I'll only hurt her in the end.

I turn toward my room and grab my leather jacket. Shrugging it on, I make my way to the door and down toward the living room, where I notice Cassian drinking bourbon.

"What the fuck are you doing?" I ask, moving deeper into the room.

He looks up at me, his gaze is far away. "I'm thinking."

"About?"

"The dance, if Creed knows you claimed her, since you did it in front of him last night..." Cass's words disappear into the heaviness that hangs in the air above us.

"I'm going to the cabin. I'll be back tomorrow." I don't

answer him about Creed, and I don't talk about what I did with Nesrin, how I showed the possessiveness in the forest last night.

"So, you're just leaving her?"

"Cass, please don't give me shit for this, I need to think."

He stares at me, lifting the tumbler to his lips and taking a long sip. I know I should stay. I should talk to Nesrin and tell her that I only said those things to get Creed away from her. But even as I think it, I know it's a lie; I said it because I *do* want her.

"Go. I'll watch over her," Cass tells me, waving his now empty glass toward the door. "We have three days to get her ready," he warns me. "I'll start showing her the dance, but I'm not leading her onto that dancefloor."

I nod. "Thanks, brother."

I turn to leave. Knowing that when I return, everything needs to change.

Nesrin

THE NIGHT OF THE FOREST RUN HAS COME AND GONE, and my body aches in ways I never thought it would. The sun is streaming through the window, forcing me to scoot up in bed.

My phone buzzes on the nightstand, and I grab it, reminding myself that I walked away from friends in LA. Even though we weren't close, there was still a hint of a connection, especially with Jenny. But the name on the screen is none of those, it's my mother's.

I've tried not to think about her because I knew the moment I did, the attraction I have to Damien would make me feel guilty, or worse than I already seem to have it.

I open the message and scan it while my heart sinks to my stomach.

I hope you're behaving. God knows we don't need to return to any of your antics again. Choose a college and make sure you've got your major sorted out. Mom.

She doesn't ask me how I am. She doesn't even show that she cares from the way she's worded her message. Perhaps I'm reading into it, but I know Marcia Ellington, now Thorne, and affection is certainly not her strong suit.

I don't know how to respond to her. How to tell her that I haven't given college a second thought. I'm not even sure what it is I want to study. Perhaps I can take a gap year, travel, and then decide.

Sighing, I push the blankets from my body and swing my legs over the edge of the bed. I sit there for a long while, trying to decide what I'm meant to tell my mother.

The phone buzzes again. This time, it's a call. I knew she'd do this if I didn't respond in time. She's always been manic about shit like that, whereas I need time to think.

I watch the call flashing, but I don't make a move to pick it up. Once it goes to the messaging service, I sigh, breathing deeply, as I think about my future.

I can't say that Damien will be a part of it; I don't even

know what all this means. Everything he's done for me can't continue when our folks get back. *Our folks.* We're meant to be a family, and all I can think about is his kiss, his touch, and seeing him in those tight black boxer briefs again.

I should stop it before I find myself falling, but if I'm honest, he's the first boy, man, who's ever shown me who I really am. He understands what bothers me inside, and he's given me an out. He's shown me there's more to life than the blades that I found solace in for seven long years.

But the moment he's gone, because he *will* leave, I don't know if I'm going to be strong enough to survive without him. The thought scares me, and I push off the bed and head into the bathroom.

Once I'm freshened up, I grab my phone and make my way down to the kitchen, where I find Joy making pancakes. She glances up, her smile brightening when she sees me.

"Good morning, Darling," she greets, before handing me an empty mug, which I gratefully accept.

"How are you?" I ask her while I pour some java. I feel tired, exhausted, actually.

"I'm doing really well," Joy says. She turns, holding a plate with a stack of fluffy goodness, which makes my stomach growl. "I think someone needs her breakfast," she muses, with a grin.

I follow her out to the dining room to find Finn already seated at the table. It's strange how they are always here for meals. Back home, I would eat alone, while my mother would be out with friends. We never had *family* time, even when Dad was around.

"Hey, little sis," Finn says, with a wave. "I didn't think you'd be up early today," he observes, his gaze taking in every inch of me. His dark hair is pointing in all directions, as those eyes lock on mine.

"I didn't think I would either, but I'm starving," I respond, settling in beside him at the large table. It makes no sense for them to have a table, which seats sixteen when there are only four of them in the house on a normal day.

"My kinda girl." Finn winks. We load our plates, but before I can tuck into my food, I feel his stare on me. When I look up, I find cocoa eyes on me. "You have your eye on my bro. Don't you?" Finn asks suddenly, sending heat to my cheeks.

My mouth falls open when I gasp. "What?"

"You have a crush on Damien," Finn tells me. It's definitely not posed as a question, so I don't respond. "You're both so easy to read."

"I'm not easy to read at all," I tell him, feeling the tension in my muscles tighten. If my feelings for Damien are so easy to see... can they all see it?

"Oh?" Finn pushes to his feet, his hands sliding into the front pockets of his jeans. The dark strands of his hair hang into those gentle, playful eyes, and he grins at me. His smile hasn't got the same effect on me that Damien's does, but it's just as intriguing.

"Yeah."

"I call liar, liar," Finn taunts, circling me before he stops right behind me, and I'm frozen to the spot.

"You can believe what you'd like to, but I know what I feel and what I think," I tell Finn, but the way he's looking at me, he knows I'm bullshitting him.

"Hey, I don't give a shit if you want to bounce on my brother's dick," he says, with a shrug. "Just don't let Dad find out, he'll lose his shit. Perhaps, you can even make Damien feel something other than that stick that's been shoved up his ass all these years."

I can't help but laugh at Finn. "He's just not a party animal."

"Oh, Darling. Damien is so much more than that. I'm guessing if you two are getting freaky, he's told you about The Black Knights?"

"We are *not* getting freaky." The words fall from my lips in a gasp at his words. "And he's mentioned a little about Creed and The Black Knights."

Finn shakes his head, as he reaches for the juice, which

he could've asked me to hand him, but I have a feeling he wanted to get under my skin by standing behind me. Once he's seated, he fills a glass, before looking at me. "Like I said, don't care."

"What about The Black Knights?" I have a feeling Damien may not want to give me the whole story, so if Finn is willing to talk about it, I'm not going to stop him. The more I can find out about the brothers I'm living with, the better.

"They're bad news, and even though my brothers have both been part of their group, I haven't gotten myself involved. They do stupid shit to keep themselves entertained."

Now I'm intrigued, and I can't focus on the food on my plate; instead, I'm staring at Finn. "Like?"

"Oh no, little sis, I ain't getting involved in this. If you want to know, ask D, he'll tell you. But just listen when he tells you to do something when we're around Creed and the rest of the guys."

"What about those girls?" I ask, still wondering about Mali and Holly. I remember the night of the party, Finn and Cassian were hanging around with them.

"Those are the Haven bunnies, they're like groupies. If they can get dicked down by one of The Black Knights, they'll do anything they're told." With a cocky wink, he pops a bite of pancake into his mouth.

"You mean any of the Havens or Thornes," I say, realizing my voice is tinged with jealousy when I voice my response.

Finn watches me for a moment, leaning back in his chair as he sips the juice with a grin on his face. He's noticed the inflection in my voice. The corner of his mouth curls slowly, just like his brother's.

"I think—"

The footsteps that sound behind us interrupt Finn's appraisal of me, and I'm thankful for that. When Cassian saunters in, I offer him a smile to which he tips his head in greeting.

"Family," he says, with a swagger that belies the almost innocent expression on his face. He doesn't strike me as a playboy type, not like Finn or Damien, but I have a feeling Cassian hides a lot of emotions under his pretty boy exterior.

Finn is outspoken, voicing whatever is on his mind.

Damien does hide certain things, but it doesn't stop him from making his feelings known. But Cassian, he's the silent brother, stoic and poised, but there's also a darkness to him that lingers under the pristine surface.

"What are we talking about?" he asks, while plating pancakes.

"Nesrin bouncing on Damien's dick," Finn says, nonchalantly, causing me to choke on my orange juice.

A chuckle rumbles from Cassian, as he shakes his head. I'm sure he's heard a lot from his youngest brother's mouth before, but the fact that Finn came right out and said that has my mind spinning.

"I think Damien may lose his temper with you saying something like that about our little sister," Cassian tells Finn, but the grin on his face belies the chastising of the youngest Thorne.

"If he can't deal with the truth, that ain't my problem," Finn shrugs, pushing his chair away from the table. I watch him pull a joint from his pocket and place it between his full lips. "I'm going for a smoke," he tells us. "Don't talk about anything important, I don't like missing the news."

He leaves us alone, and I turn to Cassian who's eating his breakfast in silence. I don't know what to say after Finn's blurting out about me and Damien having sex, so I fill my glass and drink down a mouthful of the cool, refreshing juice.

"You know," Cass speaks, "my brother doesn't really come with a filter, but if you're going to spend time around us, you'll get used to it."

"I just didn't think he'd talk about..." I wave my hand in the air, unsure of what to say, but Cass shakes his head.

"Don't worry about that, I know Damien has a thing for you," he says, shocking me speechless. "He's away for a couple of days, so you're going to spend time with me. I'm supposed to teach you the welcome dance that takes place at the ball."

"Welcome dance?"

"Yeah, it's all for show. Basically, it's some form of waltz," Cassian says, but his focus is on the plate in front of him. He seems so at ease with this, while I'm nervous, and the anxiety that's slowly twisting in my gut has me on edge.

"I am not great at dancing," I tell him, honestly.

He stops eating, piercing me with those blueish-green eyes, as he holds onto the silver knife and fork, and grins, before saying, "You haven't been taught by a Thorne." Then he continues wolfing down his food.

Guess I'm dancing today.

Damien

I HAVEN'T NEEDED TO TOUCH THE BOX I KEEP HIDDEN in my bathroom. Damien was right, our night run had given me a feeling of freedom from the anxiety. I can't describe the lightness in my chest from not being able to think about anything other than making it out of the forest alive and unscathed. Even with the scrapes from the branches, I would do it again.

The moment I step foot into the bedroom, my phone buzzes. When I glance at the screen, my mother's name glares at me condescendingly. Sighing, I answer, "Hi, Mom."

"I've been waiting for you to respond all morning. It's almost lunchtime, and I haven't heard a peep from you."

Her voice is abnormally shrill.

"I'm sorry, I've been working with Cassian to learn this stupid dance," I tell her, but if I had to be honest, I loved it. He's fun, nothing like Damien, and I enjoyed spending time with him.

"Have you decided on college?" she asks, not bothering to check if I'm okay or what dance I'm talking about. Even if she knew what it was, I would've liked her to show interest.

"Not yet, Mother," I respond, but the annoyance is evident in my voice. I know she's going to be angry with me, but at this stage, I no longer care.

"I was talking to Bradford, he's such a lovely man. He suggested you could look at applying to Oxford," she says, with a squeal in her voice, which is new. My mother's never been the squeaky type, not like her friends.

"Like... the one in England?" Confusion causes my brows to crease. I wasn't expecting her to say this, to even suggest me traveling on my own to another country, without her constant advice being whispered in my ear.

"Yes, England. Since Damien will be heading out there to set up the Thorne Corporation in London, you'll have someone you know to be there for you. Having family close by will be nice."

Of course, she has no clue to just what Damien is becoming to me because she's still away. I can't even explain what he means to me. But the thought of being in another country, away from his dad and my mom, sounds like heaven. Perhaps we'll be able to find our solace there.

Hope springs in my chest, but I tamp it down immediately. I can't think about the future *with* him when I don't know what he's thinking.

We haven't had time alone since that night, but I need to sit him down and talk about feelings. Emotions. The exact things I've noticed he doesn't like talking about.

"I'd like that," I finally answer, realizing my mother's probably waiting for me to respond. "I mean, yes, I'll look at Oxford. Thanks, Mom."

"Of course." She's silent for a moment and for the first time in a long while, I realize she's being nice. She's showing affection, even though it's over the phone. And that's new.

"I hope you're having fun."

"I am. Listen, when I get back, there's something I need to tell you," she says, in a hushed whisper. "It's important, and now that you're old enough, I think it's best you know."

"What is it?"

"You'll have to wait until we get back," she says. "I hope you enjoy your time with the boys. And behave yourself, don't give them too much trouble." Her admonishment comes after her affection, and if I had to be honest, it hurts.

For once, I'd just like my mother to tell me she's proud of me. Or that she loves me. But that's not who Marcia Ellington is. And a new last name clearly hasn't changed the cold, aloof woman who's my mother.

The line dies, and I blink back the tears. I'm old enough to know that people don't change. They grow up in a certain way and allow whatever happens to them to mold who they become.

And my mother is nothing but a cold-hearted woman who never wanted a child. I know this because I heard her and my dad fighting one night before he died.

And I realize nothing is going to change her.

Not now.

Not ever.

Having Cass and Finn around yesterday was nice, but I miss Damien. I've thought about him non-stop since my mother's call. Even though I'm anxious about what she wants to tell me, I'm focusing on going to Oxford. I need to get my application in and read up on the university, but I'm excited.

Sitting at my desk, I open my laptop and log in.

Opening the browser, I pull up the websites I need and scroll through the information. I open another tab and check the travel time between London and Oxford.

Not bad.

If he agrees to allow me to travel with him, I don't know what that would mean for us, but as soon as he gets back, I'm going to try to talk to him about it. I don't want to come across as needy, but this is my future.

If that doesn't involve him, I'd want to know sooner, rather than later.

Damien is different than any of the other guys I knew back home, and he's vastly different from his brothers. I know he's hiding his own pain, and even though he told me about the fight between him and Creed, I have a feeling there's more that he's hiding.

A knock on my door startles me. Pushing off the chair, I pad over to the door and pull it open to find Damien leaning against the opposite wall. He could've easily pushed his way into my bedroom, but he didn't.

"Hi."

"Hey," he greets with his dark brow arched and those dimples peeking at me playfully. "Busy?" His blue eyes trail over me, from my messy bun all the way down to my black painted toenails. When he locks those baby blues on me and gifts me his sinful smirk, heat trickles its way over me like warmth from a blazing fire on a cold day.

"Not really."

"Are you feeling better after the run?"

"Yeah, I... I enjoyed it." I look at him, really look at him, and take note of every inch of him. His teeth bite down on his lower lip when he nods.

"Meet me in the greenhouse tonight." He pushes off the wall and saunters toward the staircase. I watch him walk away; his back covered in a black tee that's a little too tight. His ass is hugged in a pair of jeans that make me lick my lips at the sight. He's too beautiful. My time with him, this month of not having our folks around will soon be over, and we'll have to face the truth. We may not be able to be together when they're back.

When our parents return from their honeymoon, Damien and I are going to need to talk. And just the thought of it has me worried.

It's still a few hours before tonight, and now that I know he wants to meet, I can't sit still. Pulling on a pair of sneakers, I head out of my room and make my way down the steps and toward the living room. The patio doors are open, and Finn is sitting on one of the chairs, smoking. The joint hangs from his full lips, his hair hanging over his forehead, as he looks down at his phone screen.

I can't tell what he's doing, but the moment I appear, he shoves it into his pocket and looks up at me. "Hey, little sis," he grins, with a playful expression making him look younger than his twenty-four years.

"What are you up to?" I ask, allowing my gaze to sweep across the garden, then I bring it back to Finn.

"Not much, just getting high and enjoying the sunshine before tonight."

I settle across from him before asking, "What's happening tonight?"

"Bonfire," he tells me. "The Black Knights and the Thornes always have a bonfire before the big dance in a week."

"The big dance?"

"You're going with me," Damien says, appearing at the door. "Finn, don't you have something to do?" He asks his brother, his eyes glowering down at the youngest Thorne.

"Nah," Finn winks at him, and I can feel the animosity in the air. I'm not sure what they're hiding, but I'll find out. "I've just been chatting to Gen."

"Leave her the fuck alone. She's bad news. You know she runs with the Havens." There's poison in Damien's words when he spits the last word. He told me briefly about them, but I don't know the full story. And I have a feeling it's quite a story.

"Are you going to the bonfire tonight?" I ask Damien, trying to calm the brothers down and to eliminate some of the animosity that seems to be brewing between them.

"No. And neither are you."

I shoot to my feet, crossing my arms over my chest, and question him, "What? Why?"

One thing I've come to learn about Damien Thorne over the past week, he doesn't say something because he wants a reaction. He tells me, Cass, and Finn something, so we can obey, but this time, I'm fighting back.

"Because I fucking said so," he tells me, with those flame-blue eyes boring through me. I expect him to close the distance between us, but I can also feel Finn's intrigued stare on me. Damien shakes his head before turning to leave. I'm starting to get used to watching Damien walk away from me.

"Just ignore him, he'll get over himself," Finn tells me. "Damien is the eldest, so he takes it upon himself to exert his power, but Cass will talk to him and get him to back down. You have to be at the bonfire, it's one of the most epic events, besides the actual dance."

"I'm not great in crowds," I tell Finn honestly. "I have anxiety. It starts slowly, taking hold of my muscles and twists in my stomach."

"You'll be fine. You'll have me, Cass, and the asshole to look after you. And if Damien tells you he's your date, I know he won't leave your side."

My heart stutters at Finn's words, but I don't reply, because I don't know how to tell him that I've done things with his brother. Granted, it was just intense making out, but I'm meant to be their family now. Even if we're not related.

"And I know my big brother wants to see if those petals of yours will wilt under his thorny exterior," Finn whispers when he walks away, chuckling at his unamusing comment.

Time to talk to Damien.

I may be young, but I'm not his property. He can't just tell me what to do and expect me to obey.

Damien

F INN IS PISSING ME OFF. THE FACT THAT HE'S GOT GEN on his radar has me extra cautious. She's trying to wiggle her way into our lives again. She's one mistake I'm not making again, and my brothers should steer clear as well.

Nesrin's face was a picture when I told her she's not going to the bonfire tonight. I knew she'd have something to say about it, especially with my brother acting like a teenager vying for attention.

I know she's angry. And I don't blame her, she should be. I'm an asshole who's not worthy of her, and my father's suggestion that she travels to England with me is preposterous.

She should be running away *from* me, not away *with* me. But I've not been forthcoming with her. I've only offered her the bare minimum, and she deserves more than that. I don't know why I give a shit, but I do.

Shaking my head, I run my fingers through my hair. Bradford is going to return in a couple of weeks, and he will more than likely find me balls deep in my stepsister because, each time I'm near her, I can't fight this need to have her.

Chuckling, I picture his face at the sight.

My father's been absent more times than I can count, and I wonder if seeing me with Nesrin will actually get him to *see* us. Finn, Cass, and I grew up with each other. I took the lead because I was older, but I never felt like I was a good role model.

When I realized they would be looking up to me, I walked away from The Black Knights. I never wanted my brothers to do the shit I did. Even though Cass was part of the group, for a short while, he didn't go through with initiation. And Finn has never shown interest in following that path. Which I'm thankful for.

It's almost time. This will be our second night in the greenhouse, the second meeting between us, and I can't stop thinking about what I want to propose. The bullshit I've witnessed over the years is nothing compared to Nesrin hurting herself. I know that the distractions I've given her won't last.

I know she'll want to go to the fucking bonfire tonight, which only sets the unease coiling in my gut. Having her around Creed is not what I planned for us tonight, but if she asks, I may indulge her.

But there will be rules.

And if she doesn't obey them, I'll punish her. The thought of having her on her knees in my bedroom has my zipper tightening. I make my way down the stairs, finding the house silent. Finn and Cass must've left already, so I head toward the patio. Time to find my wild rose.

When I finally reach the greenhouse, I'm tense. But the moment I step over the threshold, I find her waiting for me. She's dressed in black, a tight pair of pants that seem to be painted on her slender legs. Her hips flare beautifully, and my gaze drinks in the pretty curves of Nesrin Ellington.

She turns when she hears my feet crunch on the ground. Her eyes are shining, and I glance down at her hands to find her with a small, silver blade. She doesn't appear to be bleeding, but I race to her.

"What have you done?"

"You need to tell me what happened the night you and Creed fought." Her voice seems barren of emotion. She looks empty, as if she's lost in a world that I can't enter.

"Listen to me," I tell her, pulling her closer, my hands on her shoulders, holding her. "What happened? Why are you holding a blade?" Even though I'm asking her, I have a feeling I know what she's going to tell me.

"I didn't do anything, Damien," she bites out, frustration lacing her tone, but I don't believe her. I don't know why.

"Please, tell me."

"I needed to hold it. It's a safety net." Finally, she locks her gaze on mine, as if she's woken from a dream. "It's how I feel safe in my own mind."

"You are safe," I tell her. "I'm here, you're safe." Even though I'm confident in my words, her next question slams into me like a freight train, trying to take me down. "Like the games you used to play?"

"Those games have nothing to do with you, wild rose," I tell her. My frustration at Finn is taking on a whole new level. He had no right to tell her anything about my past. That's my story to tell.

"I want to know you," she finally says, setting the fucking blade down. "Share something of you with me." Those eyes, they cut me so deep, right down to my soul. She looks right through me, and I know she sees the darkness I hide inside.

"The way you feel holding a blade is the same way I feel holding my stories close to my chest. It's a safety net.

When I was younger, I felt like I needed those twisted games to survive this shit hole."

"If you hate it so much here, why do you stay?"

"Why do you want to delve into my mind so much?" I ask her, the pain in my voice is clear, and I know she'll hear it. I step closer to where she's standing. We're inches apart. The scent of her perfume invades my senses, turning my blood hot, my need for her growing at a rapid pace. "Do you like seeing what monsters lurk in the dark?"

"Monsters don't scare me." Her voice breaks, her eyes shimmer, and I fight the urge to smile at her glistening emotion. I'm a fucking monster.

I reach for her, swiping my thumb along her plump lower lip before I lean in farther and whisper, "they should."

"Why?" she challenges, tipping her chin up, her eyes locking on mine. "At least with a monster, he doesn't hide his true face. It's the people who show off their angelic nature that should scare you."

"Fake, polished, and pristine." I nod in understanding. The moonlight slowly disappears behind a heavy cloud, and soon enough, we're thrust into darkness. The pinpricks of the stars offer no illumination, and I find it easier to breathe her in.

"What are you doing?" Nesrin whispers when my hand trails up her thigh. I want so badly to open her legs, to lap at her pussy, to taste her sweetness. My cock hardens at the thought of all the things I would love to do to her, but the moment we cross the line, we'll never be able to go back.

"There are secrets in this town I hope you never learn about," I tell her. "This house, the darkness that resides here, has infected each and every person."

"Including you?" Nesrin looks up at me, the moment my fingertips reach her stomach. The top she's wearing rides up, and I continue my trail up to her breast. A gasp falls free from her mouth, and I'm so hungry to taste it. To once again devour her lips, but I watch her, as I reach her nipple, tugging the hardened bud between my fingers.

Another mewl tumbles free, and I lean in to whisper my lips along hers. "I'm the worst of all, wild rose." The promise and confession, wrapped in one, feathers over her. Her long, dark lashes flutter at my nearness, and I don't know how I'm going to quit her.

"I don't think you're bad." Her confidence is apparent in her words. I twist her nipple hard, tugging it until she cries out. "That's not a sign of you being a bad person, Damien."

The corner of my mouth kicks up. My other hand reaches for the back of her neck, my fingers tangling in her long dark hair, and I tug her head back, earning myself another dick-hardening moan.

"I never said I was a bad person, wild rose," I tell her. "I'm the fucking monster under your bed. The creature that will leave you broken and bleeding on the floor. I'll smile while you ask me for mercy." With every sentence I utter, I watch her tongue dart out, licking her lips. Even in the dark, I can see how affected she is by me.

"Show me." Her gaze snaps to mine in a confident challenge.

I step back, pulling her with me. Spinning us around, I push her against the cool glass wall. My hard cock presses against the globes of her ass. She cries out, as I grip her hips and hold her steady.

"You feel that?" My voice is inhumane, the monster inside me baring its teeth, ready to sink into the beauty before me.

She tries to nod, her voice not even audible, as she whimpers when I push against her again, pinning her between me and the cold glass. "Is that what you want?"

I crave her taste more than I do my next breath, but I know the moment I do, I'll never ever let her go. It wouldn't matter if her mother and my father were to threaten my life, I'd never leave her.

The thought of being hers, of her being mine, is like a shot of fucking adrenalin straight through my veins. It's as if I've stuck my fingers in an electric socket, and I'm being shocked back to life.

That's what this girl does to me.

She sees me.

Not the pristine exterior that most girls do; Nesrin sees my darkness, and yet, she's still here.

"Yes." Her hiss sends me into the darkness. My eyes close, and pleasure sparks through me. I want to drive myself into her, I want to feel her slick heat. I want to know how tight she is when she finds release, but I can't. I know it's wrong, on so many fucking levels, that I push away from her.

This back and forth is driving me insane.

She spins around, her wide eyes on me. "Don't tease me, I don't like playing games." I watch her race from the greenhouse and into the main house. My feet are frozen to the spot when I think about what I almost did. My control is hanging on by a thread, and I have a feeling, tonight, it's going to snap.

Nesrin

I SWALLOW BACK THE BOURBON BEFORE I SIGH AT THE thought of watching Nesrin run from me. I fucked up, but I'm not a man who apologizes. I've never allowed anyone to believe I'm anything but an asshole.

She ran inside, and even though I haven't gone up to her bedroom, I know I have to. Apologizing doesn't come easily to me. But with her, I feel the need to do it anyway.

Making my way up the stairs, I walk down the hall and stop outside her bedroom door. I knock twice and wait. Moments pass, and I knock once more.

"If you don't open this door, I'll break it down, Nesrin," I tell her through the thick wood. I know she can hear me. A couple of minutes pass before I twist the doorknob to find it unlocked. Pushing the door open, I step inside. The room is so tidy, you'd think that nobody lives here.

I move through the room into the bathroom to find it empty. A growl rumbles in my chest, as frustration takes hold of me. She must've gone to the party, but what's got me even more concerned is that I don't know how she would've got there.

Pulling my cell phone from my pocket, I unlock it and scroll down to one of my brother's names. I know it's easier to call Cassian because Finn will be off with one of the girls already.

My focus is on getting Cassian to find Nesrin and keep her away from Creed. Hitting dial, I put the device to my ear and listen. The incessant ring only seems to set my body on edge. If he's drunk, he'll never hear the fucking thing. My nerves bristle with annoyance. I'm about to hang up when I hear his voice.

"What's up, bro?"

"Where are you?" I ask Cass.

The background noise breaks through the line, and I hear laughter and girls giggling. A loud guttural shout from one of the partygoers comes from the speakers before I can hear Cassian's response, "The lake."

"Is she there?" I wonder if he can hear the concern in my tone, but, right now, I don't give a shit.

"Yeah, Nesrin and Mali just walked up," he tells me.

"See you soon," I hang up before he can say anything more. I race down the hall, leaving her bedroom door open. In a matter of seconds, I'm in the garage and in the driver's seat of my Camaro, before I have time to rethink the shit that's about to go down.

The engine roars to life, and I put my foot on the gas. The speakers vibrate with Echos singing about Saints, and I can't help but chuckle. A saint is far from what I am.

The drive won't take me long, but it gives me time to think. The town is built on a hill, giving off the illusion of being sunk down in a forest, with the lake at the bottom. Surrounded by thick trees, Thorne Haven has been cited as one of the most haunted towns in America.

The beauty of it is indescribable, with tourists frequenting it every year, while we have our summer months. But by the time winter hits and the snow comes down, we're locked away from the rest of the country, as if we were on our own island.

Hidden within the trees, we've played our games. Toyed with the girls who wanted to take a chance on The Black Knights, but over the years, I've seen the destructive behavior it brought about. That's why I don't want Nesrin anywhere near them.

If something happens to her, Dad will kill me. Even though I know I shouldn't play these games with her, show her what they're like, I can't deny that my curiosity for this girl has taken the forefront of my thoughts.

My attention has been caught, like a fly in a web. I'm drawn to the tormented girl who has just as many scars as I do. Who would've thought a princess from the glittering lights of stardom would be so broken?

Even her name gives away her hidden depths—my wild rose.

When I pull up to the lake, I find almost all the town's teenagers standing around drinking, smoking, and making out against the tall trees that surround the body of water. This party is going to get out of control, just like every other one we've had here for years.

At twenty-seven, I'm used to seeing the newbies puking their guts out after Cassian makes his infamous punch. The blue liquid is nothing more than far too much vodka mixed with some other shit I would rather not know about.

But because it tastes like candy with the syrupy sweet mixers, the kids, who visit from out of town, think they can handle it. The difference between some of the kids here and us is that we grew up drinking this shit, while Daddy Dearest went out to find us a new mother. And each time he brought someone home, we would send her packing not long after.

"Hey, Brother." Cassian smiles at me when I stalk

toward the tables that are set up with red cups and jugs of alcohol. "You still looking for Nesrin? Seems our little sister has made some friends."

"I don't want her with those fucking girls," I tell him, as I pick up one of the cups. I fill it to the brim and swallow down a mouthful before I have time to reconsider drinking this shit. I shouldn't be drinking tonight, but I can't calm down after my encounter with Nesrin.

"What the fuck is up your ass?" Cass questions, shoving me in the shoulder, playfully. But when he takes note of my expression, he stills.

"I kissed her. I touched her, more than I should as her stepbrother," I tell him. "I shouldn't have fucking gone there with her, but I couldn't help myself." Cassian understands the darkness that I fight daily. He saw how much control I'd lost when I was a Knight. Even he walked out after the first few times.

The games.

The burning roses.

And the thorns.

"And?" He nudges, knowing I won't just offer up information if he doesn't want it. That's how we've always been—keep things to ourselves, until we need an outlet. Mine being rather violent compared to my brothers, but they're just as dangerous as I am.

"I don't know. This isn't going to go anywhere. I mean,

as soon as Dad gets back, I'm heading out to the offices in London. He won't allow me to keep Nesrin for my own. No matter how I feel," I tell him.

"What about her finding out about The Black Knights? She could be one of the girls they toy with." He's right, but I never wanted to consider it. Even though we had a run out in the forest, she's not ready to hear about my past.

"Creed will not have her." My tone is adamant, but even so, I know what my former best friend is like. Since Brody and Keirin have joined the ranks, they've only gotten worse. It doesn't help that our neighboring town's students keep coming through here. Each semester, new girls pop up, and each year, more roses are scorched.

"Will you tell her the truth about...?" Cassian knows it's not an option. Not right now, anyway. She needs time, and that's something I'll happily give her, but that doesn't mean I can't toy with her.

"Soon," I tell him, and swallow down another mouthful of his secret concoction. "Right now, I need to party." I leave my brother and move deeper into the crowd. The song playing is loud, echoing through the woods. The water is silver under the moon's light, and I take a path deeper into the forest to find myself alone. No doubt Gen will find me, she always does, but for now, I can breathe, as the alcohol courses through my veins.

From here, I can see Creed with Brody and Keirin. They're laughing, smoking, and hanging on every word some pretty blonde tells them.

Girls are squealing from behind me, and when I turn to look at them, my chest tightens, when I see my wild rose walking with Mali, and they're headed right for Creed and his pack. She doesn't see me, at first, it takes a second for her eyes to lock on mine, and it's as if time stops.

I lift my cup, tipping it toward her. My eyes don't leave hers for a long moment. I can feel her glare on me, which makes me smile. I'm not here to encroach on her, but I'll be watching.

"Hey, handsome," a gentle whisper comes from beside me, and I turn to find the bottle blonde that I haven't seen in a few months. She's one of those curvy girls with pouty lips that look good wrapped around my dick.

"What's up, Brittany?" I ask, but keep my gaze on the dark-haired beauty who's now shooting bullets at me with those pretty golden eyes.

"I missed you." Brittany grins happily, and her eyes spark with desire like I knew they would. All these women are the same; they see a Thorne, and they drop their fucking panties, lightning-fast. "I didn't think you'd be here," she tells me.

"Why not?"

She steps up to me, her body flush with mine, when she leans up to my ear and whispers, "Because you're a lone wolf." Her words bring back a memory of the night I fucked her in the woods. It was so dark. It was also dangerous, which is why she's back for more.

She was one of my first burnt roses. One of the first girls I took into the woods as part of my initiation. And even though it was just high school games, at the time, she thought it was love.

I didn't think Brittany saw it the way I did. She was too young for me to toy with her, and I made that mistake far too many times to count. Girls became a distraction from the bullshit I had to deal with at home.

Being the eldest, I needed to prove something to my father, even though I know he'd never let me rule over the corporation; I still wanted him to see me for who I was. A man. But Bradford didn't like that.

"Being alone is part of my charm," I inform her. "But tonight, perhaps company would be nice." I finish my drink and head to a table to fill up my empty cup. Brittany follows me like a lost puppy, just like I knew she would.

I perch myself on one of the tables, my feet on the bench seat, as I take in the party. I find Nesrin talking to Creed, and it looks friendly enough, but when he leans in to whisper something in her ear, every muscle in my body tenses. She laughs when he finally steps back, and he does as well.

His gaze locks on mine, for a moment, before he releases his hold on her arm and hands her a Solo cup, with what I can only assume is filled with his cocktail. She takes a sip, tentative in her movements, then smiles up at him.

"Damien," Brittany calls to me, dragging my attention away from my nemesis and the girl who is surely going to bring me to my knees. I glance at Brittany, taking her in for a moment, and I wonder what the fuck I'm doing. "Are you listening to me?"

"Want to do something for me?" I ask her. I know she'll obey me. She's a groupie, she wants a dick—Thorne or Haven—and she'll do anything to get it. Granted, she has had mine, but that was years ago. When I fucked her, I had no clue what the hell I was doing.

"Yeah." She bops her head happily, and I bite my lip to keep from smiling.

"Go to Creed, tell him you're ready for him to finally take you into the forest," I tell her in a whisper, not allowing my gaze to leave Nesrin and Creed. "And if he refuses, tell him you'll do anything he'd like."

I smile at her quickly, offering a nod, before she notices my attention is nowhere near her. She drops her hand to my thigh, slowly moving it up toward my crotch, but my dick has no intention of fucking her tonight.

I wanted to release tension using a body, but, right now, all I can think of is taking Nesrin deep into the woods and showing her just how violent I can be. I want to hear her scream. At that thought, my dick decides it's time to wake up, and Brittany smiles, thinking she's the one doing that to me.

"Did you not fucking hear me?" I ask, arching a brow when I look at the blonde. She gasps at my rudeness, but when I tip my head to the side and offer her my smirk, she blushes and nods.

I watch her ass bounce all the way to Creed, who seems taken with her the moment she sidles up to him. He wraps an arm around her waist after she whispers in his ear, and I can't help but laugh.

Nesrin's gaze locks on mine, and I gesture with my head for her to follow me, as I get up and move toward the forest. I don't turn to see if she's following me, because I know she is.

Call it overconfidence, but girls do as I say, when I say. When I hear the grass under her steps, I turn to find those golden eyes on me.

"What are you doing?"

"Get on your knees," I tell her, as I pull at my zipper. My eyes are locked on the woman I really want as the blonde takes Creed into the darkness with Keirin and Brody following behind.

"I'm not one of your groupies," Nesrin bites out, crossing her arms over her chest, as she looks up at me with fire burning bright.

"Let me make something clear, you're mine." My voice may be low, but she hears every fucking syllable. "Now, when I tell you I want you on your knees, you drop down for me. If you want this, want me, this is what you get."

"Let me make something clear—"

"Once you're done swallowing my dick," I tell her, with a growl, "I'm going to feast on your pretty pussy until you're crying. I want to see tears streaming down your cheeks when you come. And you know why you're going to cry?"

Her mouth opens, then closes, and I can't help but chuckle at her sweet innocence. Sometimes, she seems so grown up, but I know she can't have much experience because of the blush on her cheeks.

"Because you'll feel like the holy fucking spirit has entered you," I bite out, and she obeys, slowly dropping to her knees. Soon, I'm fisting my cock and painting Nesrin's lips with the arousal that's seeping from the tip.

I'm not ready for the moment her lips wrap around my dick. It's as if fireworks are taking flight behind my eyelids because all I see are sparks.

She works me like a fucking pro. Back and forth, taking me deeper with every suck and teasing me with the tip of her tongue with every pull. When she finally takes me into her throat, I see the edge of euphoria teasing me.

It's at that very second, Cassian's gaze falters, as it lands on me and Nesrin. He watches with a grin, shaking his head when he realizes my hips are thrusting toward Nesrin's mouth.

I fuck her faster, as I feel my balls draw up, and my fingers tangle in her hair, holding her steady. Her movements are nothing short of expert level, as the alcohol and music take hold, spinning us in the darkness. My desire burns hot and electric for her.

I glance down and smile at her, tipping my drink, as I take a gulp. She blinks a few times, as her lips slide down my shaft and the vision of her taking me like this is too much; I can't stop the feral growl from vibrating through my chest, as I empty my seed down her throat.

Moments later, I watch her wipe those swollen lips. She rises slowly, before I mouth, *your turn next.*

"You're an asshole," Nesrin tells me, "I'm not a fucking toy you can use when you need release." Her biting tone belies the way her pupils are dilated, and her lips are wet and inviting.

"No, you're not," I agree. "But I needed to make sure everyone knows who you belong to." Even though I expect her to tell me she's not a possession, I'm shocked when she doesn't say anything. Instead, she smiles and laces her fingers with my outstretched hand. I lean in to plant a kiss on her lips. "Now I'm going to take you home and make you come on my face until you're seeing God in Heaven."

And I always make good on my promises.

Damien

I'M BEING DRAGGED THROUGH THE CROWD. IT FEELS like everyone is watching me. As if they know what I just did, but they couldn't. We were hidden behind the trees. By the time we reach the car, Damien stills, and I stumble into his back.

"What the hell are you doing?" I bite out in frustration. I didn't expect him to be the cuddling type, but he seems angry. As if what just happened was a mistake. And if he feels that way, perhaps I should just leave. I wanted my answer about what is going on between us, and now, I have it. He's not interested. Which hurts, but I'd rather know now than to fall in love with him and then deal with this bullshit.

I'm still reeling from the taste of him—saltiness mixed with him, just a masculinity that's slowly seeping through me. I shiver at the thought and bite my lip to keep from giggling. I think that punch was stronger than I anticipated.

He opens the door, gesturing for me to get inside, but I'm not obeying him like one of his groupies. Folding my arms across my chest, I arch a brow, looking directly into those luminous blue eyes.

"Get in the fucking car, Nesrin," Damien bites out through gritted teeth. He's apprehensive. Surely, he should be calmer since he's just come in my mouth. But he seems even more anxious than before.

"Why? I'm not one of your—"

He shuts me up with a kiss. His lips mold to mine, searing every inch of me, with a swipe of his tongue. He doesn't touch me, he doesn't press his body against mine, he merely consumes every thought I have with a single touch of his mouth to mine.

Our tongues dance against each other, the flavor of the alcohol mingles between us, and I can't stop myself from lacing my hands around his neck. My fingers tangle in his jet-black hair, and I tug the strands, earning me a growl that has my thighs squeezing together.

When he finally breaks the kiss, I'm breathless and still angry at him. But then he lifts his gaze, locks it on mine and smirks.

"If you don't get in the car, I'm going to go back to the party, and I'm going to have Brittany, or any of those other groupies spread their legs for me. And you know what will happen then? I'm going to enjoy fucking the frustration of not being able to have you, out on them."

My mouth falls open in shock, and my hand has a mind of its own when I lift it, slapping Damien across the face. He stumbles backward, and I make my escape. Anger surges through me, which has my feet racing from the party.

I can hear him call for me, but I ignore it. I know he'll follow. The darkness swallows me, and I blink back the tears. The salty emotion is streaming down my cheeks, and I taste the flavor of my sadness. But I don't know why I'm sad. I knew Damien wasn't mine. I should've expected him to want other girls.

I don't know why I'm angry, but I am. I'm halfway through the thick crop of trees when I hear it. A howl, so deep and pained that I stop dead in my tracks. I spin around, but I'm lost in the night, and there's no light, not even from the party I just left behind.

I turn back to the way I was heading and start running. I don't know what's out there, but I don't feel like being prey tonight. My lungs ache. My legs burn. And my chest is tight with my erratic heartbeat slamming against my ribs by the time I reach the lake. From here, I can see the silver bed of water, and I move forward, finding a pathway around the water, and to the other side. I'm guessing that's how Creed found us when we had our night run.

Once I reach the other side, I run once more. My feet have a mind of their own, and I trust my instinct. It doesn't take me long to see the mansion before me.

In the darkness, there's a foreboding sense of awareness that takes hold of me. But I ignore it and head inside. Thankfully, I'm able to get to my bedroom before I hear the front door open, and Damien's voice bounces off the walls.

"Nesrin fucking Ellington!" I ignore him, locking myself inside.

I'm not sure what mood he'll be in when he comes through there, but I don't want to see him. I head into the bathroom and turn on the shower, before stripping off my clothes.

Sweat drips from me. My gaze finds my reflection in the mirror, and I take in my bright rosy cheeks and my plump lips that are still shimmery from the kiss.

Shaking my head, I step under the spray and stand there for a moment, trying to clear my mind of the image of Damien and another girl doing things that I want him to do with me. But no matter how much I try to ignore it, to not feel jealousy raging through me, I can't.

Picking up my razor, I stare, for a long while, at the silver blades. I have to decide if it's worth it. *Is it?* I nod. Unclipping the blades, I take one in hand and lean against the cold tiles. Under the spray, I slide down until my ass hits the ground. I spread my legs, taking in the scars that are already there.

With a deep breath, I slip the blade across my skin, watching in awe at the crimson trickling from the cut. Biting pain shoots through me. My lungs finally feel as if they're working as they pull in enough air to offer serenity. And my mind is cleared of the memory that has been haunting me since I first saw Damien Thorne.

I don't want to admit his words hurt. But I'm here because this is how I deal with the emotional war that's raging inside me. Even though I know it's not only about him, my cuts run deeper than I've ever admitted. And I just don't know how to find relief anyway else.

As much as I don't want to admit it, I'm still a little girl who wants her mother to be proud of her. It only hurts for a second, before I need one more just to clear the tension in my muscles. The water steals my evidence, and it rushes down the drain, along with my guilty tears.

I drop my head back against the wall, and I close my eyes. Those blue eyes haunt me. They remind me of what I can never have. The moment he has to admit his feelings to the world, he'll realize I'm too young, and he's my stepbrother.

Suddenly, the door bursts open, breaking on the hinges, and Damien stands there, looking like he'd just fought through an army to get to me. My heart surges, coming to life and thudding wildly against my chest. The lump in my throat thickens when his gaze lands on the blade in my hand, and more guilt washes over me.

He doesn't wait. He races toward me, where I'm drenched. With one shove, he pushes the glass door so hard, I'm surprised it didn't shatter. But that's just Damien, a controlled storm.

When he enters a room, people fall at his feet simply because he graced them with his presence. And I am the one who keeps fighting the need to be one of those admirers.

He glowers, the rage that's simmering through him right now is reaching boiling point as he looks at me. The blue igniting to the true shade of an open flame. They say that pure hydrocarbons burn with a blue flame, and that's what his eyes look like right now, searing me.

"Get out of the shower." His words are stern, filled with frustration. Slowly, I push up, still holding onto the small, silver blade. "Get. Out. Of. The. Shower." The hint of barely restrained rage drips from every word. When I step out onto the rug, Damien rushes forward and wraps me in a fluffy towel. I expect him to shout at me. To curse and scream, but all he does is lean in, so his mouth is at my ear. "Get on the bed and wait for me," he orders, in a gruff voice that I've come to recognize as Damien not needing me to argue.

The no-nonsense tone sends sparks of awareness through me. I'm in trouble. His fists clench, and his expression is wrought with frustration and anger at my actions. I don't blame him. If the tables were turned, I'd feel the same, and guilt slowly morphs into a heavy weight in my stomach.

My heart is kicking against my ribs, needing an escape because, with every interaction with Damien, it wants him more and more.

He releases me, and I pad slowly into the bedroom, which is warmer than I anticipated. I slide up onto the mattress and lie back. I'm not sure if I should put clothes on, but for some reason, I just want to obey Damien.

It doesn't take him long to join me. He's still in boxers, as he walks to the foot of the bed. Silence hangs overhead, heavy and resounding. Guilt grips me, and so do his hands. He takes hold of my ankles and spreads my legs lewdly. The towel falls away, and all that's left is me. Bared. Not only my body, but my heart and soul.

The glare he rakes over me makes me blush, as embarrassment burns my cheeks. He looks furious. It seems his two default settings when he's around me are angry and horny—but I wouldn't have it any other way.

He tugs me down the mattress, earning him a squeak of surprise. And then my legs are hanging over the edge, while my top half is still on the soft mattress. I expect him to spank me or shout at me, but that's not what happens next.

His knee comes up between my thighs, pressing against my core. A whimper falls free from my lips, and I watch as his mouth tilts into a satisfied smirk, as he finds pleasure in making me feel things for him.

"You're being punished tonight," he tells me, as he rubs his knee against me, up and down, the slow motion turning my body hot and needy. My toes curl as pleasure zips down my spine and over every inch of my skin.

Goosebumps appear on my exposed flesh. His taunting makes me angry and vengeful, but if I slap him again, I might get more punishment than is already in the cards.

"Fuck you, Damien," I bite out, trying to buck him off me, but he doesn't move. His hands come down on either side of my head. I've never been so exposed to anyone before. Not even the night I thought I was going to lose my virginity.

His one hand strokes my neck, gently at first, but then he wraps his fingers around the column of my throat. He holds me still but doesn't squeeze. His other hand snakes down to my inner thigh, where it comes back with crimson on his fingertips.

I watch him wide-eyed when he presses the pads of his fingers to his tongue and licks the blood with a grin that's filled with feral lust. He hums, eyes fluttering, as he takes me in.

"If you ever," he starts speaking in a low, threatening tone. Slow and steady. "Ever do that again..." The words come to a halt when his other hand tightens around my throat. The air I was so freely inhaling is stolen, and I lock my gaze on his. It's a challenge, how far can he take it.

His leg starts moving again. A whimper escapes me when he chuckles darkly at the sound. When his thigh stills, my hips involuntarily buck, needing the friction on my clit that's throbbing from the attention. I need a release. The coiling desire in my stomach is tightening, twisting, and I chase the high of an orgasm until Damien pulls his leg away.

A pained cry tumbles from my lips, and another laugh comes from him. This isn't punishment; it's fucking torture.

The look in his eyes is pure evil when he leans in closer to my mouth. I almost expect him to kiss me, but that wouldn't be punishment. His tongue darts out, licking my lips. "Do you want it, little sis?" he questions, using the nickname Finn gave me. "Do you want to come all over my leg?"

His query makes my cheeks heat. We shouldn't be like this. I know it's wrong, but I no longer care. I nod. It's honest, it's true, and I can't shy away from my desire that seems to stem from the man before me.

His fingers glide down my naked body along with his gaze. His mouth finds my nipple, suckling it, before biting down on the hardened bud, which earns him another moan of pleasure.

But when his fingers find my core, my eyes snap open, locking on pools of blue. I could get lost in them. Perhaps I already have. His fingers tease my entrance, slowly at first, but when he dips a digit inside me, I cry out—the sound, husky, from not having sufficient oxygen.

He toys with me expertly. Again and again, swirling his fingers over my clit, making my toes curl into the carpet. I'm barely holding onto any semblance of focus because my body is a toy and Damien is playing me like a puppet on a string.

The climb to the edge is sweet, it's welcome, it's everything I want it to be. Suddenly, Damien pulls his hand away, and I can't help crying out for more, my eyes watering, as he smirks down at me.

And then, he slaps my pussy—once, twice, three times—before he starts teasing my clit. He pulls away, and another three swats come hard and fast. He continues this rhythm until I'm clawing his shoulders, my nails digging into his skin, and suddenly, he dips two fingers into me, causing an eruption so violent, I scream. My eyes shut so tight that I see the fucking starry sky burst with fireworks. I quake under him, and his fingers squeeze all the air from my lungs until I'm a wet shuddering mess.

I'm no longer here on earth. I'm not on this bed. I'm somewhere else, somewhere I've never been. I don't know how long it takes me to open my eyes again, but when I do, I'm lying with my head on the pillows, and Damien kneeling between my thighs.

"What…" I glance around, noticing I'm in my bedroom. I feel like I'm no longer in my body. It's a strange feeling.

"Nice to see you back with me," he says, as his hands roam my legs, up to my thighs. And then he's nestled between my legs. "I was going to fuck you tonight, but you were a bad girl."

"I… I got jealous."

"I know. I did it to get a reaction out of you," he tells me. He doesn't make a move to tease me, but I can feel his hardness pressing against my core.

"What are you going to do now?"

He doesn't look at me, he's lying on me, but his head is facing the window. I reach up, tangling my fingers in his silky hair. I watch his long lashes flutter, and I wonder if he's going to fall asleep like this.

"I'm not someone who's vulnerable," he speaks after a long silence. "I don't allow people to see that side of me. I don't break, I don't fall, and I certainly don't care for people besides my brothers."

"Okay."

I'm sure he can hear the confusion in my voice, but he doesn't look at me, even now. I don't know what else to tell him. I've never felt so vulnerable, myself. But, actually, telling him so would make it real. And if I'm merely a fun time for him, while he's here looking after me, then I don't want him to know how I feel.

"You make me vulnerable, Nesrin. You've fucking broken through walls I've had up for years." The honesty in his voice is raw, brutal almost, and it steals my breath. "I don't like this feeling of not being in control, of me, of you, of my fucking feelings."

"Are you saying you have feelings for me?" I ask, but I can't stop the stupid smile from appearing on my face. Damien finally glances up at me, and my stomach flutters because him being so close, looking directly at me, feels as if he's boring a hole right to my very soul.

"That's exactly what I'm saying."

Nesrin

Heat sears me. Smooth, silky skin envelops me, and I smile when I open my eyes. Every inch of tanned, caramel flesh is exposed, but it's the heat from between her thighs that has me hardening.

I didn't fuck her like I wanted to. Seeing her hurt herself broke me last night. I opened up; I ripped my chest wide, so she could see what she's doing to me. As much as I tried to deny it, I have feelings. And they're nothing like I've experienced before.

She's still asleep when I reach for her mouth. The pad of my thumb swipes along the plump flesh. Her soft breaths come out faster. Snaking my hand down to her thighs, my fingers delve toward the prize, and I find her wet.

"Naughty girl," I murmur, and a small smile creeps up on her lips. "Are you lying there wanting to hump my thigh?" I ask as she curls herself around me.

"I'm sleeping." Her reply is drenched with sleep. But I don't stop my ministrations, pumping my fingers into her body. She's so fucking tight. I have no idea how she's going to take me inside her. And I want that, I crave it more than anything else on earth.

Nesrin mumbles something under her breath, but her hips seem to have a mind of their own. I allow her to find her pleasure on my fingers. My hand soaked in her slick, sweet juices. She trembles when her orgasm rocks through her, and I gently pull my fingers from her body and paint her lips with the scent of her. Leaning in, I kiss her, licking at the flavor that coats her lower lip.

"You taste good in the morning," I whisper. Large, golden eyes lock on mine. She holds my stare, the confidence in her expression making me smile. When she's fire, she burns me from the inside out, and I willingly accept it.

"I never expected to feel this," Nesrin says, her voice low, barely even a whisper. The redness on her cheeks blooms like a rose in spring. She's striking. Even sleepy, post-orgasm, she's more beautiful than anyone I've ever had the pleasure of waking up beside or falling asleep next to.

"Trust me, wild rose," I tell her. "Neither did I." I clean my fingers, lapping the remnants of her from both digits before I roll out of bed and pull on the boxer briefs that found their way to the carpet last night. "We need to talk."

Her mouth opens, then closes. She knows what I want to say. A slow nod is all she offers. I feel guilty for spouting shit that hurt her, and I'm not someone who allows my emotions to take hold of me, until last night, until her.

"You hurting yourself is wrong. I know it's something you needed in the past, but…" I settle on the bed beside her and, facing her, I take her hand in mine. "If you ever feel the need to do that, to pick up a blade, come to me." There's a plea that hangs on every syllable I utter, and I hope she sees it as so much more than me wanting to control her. It's about me *feeling* something.

"I was so hurt, so angry." Her eyes are shimmering, and I want to wipe away her pain.

Nodding, I say, "I get that. But never again. You come to me. Promise me that." The urgency in my voice is evidence that this girl is slowly undoing me. And I can't fight it anymore. She's young, but I no longer give a fuck. She's legal, eighteen, and nothing is going to stop me from having her for myself.

A small smile lights up her face, and she nods. "I promise, Damien." I give her a quick kiss before standing. Her eyes are crotch level with me, and they widen.

"Don't you... I mean..." Her words are stilted, nervous energy emanates from her, and I know she's trying to question my morning wood. It's cute that she's so brazen when she's turned on, but just talking about sex makes her a flustering goddess.

"We need to practice today. Dance, dance, dance," I tell her. "Perhaps later we'll play again, and then I'll make you scream my name over and over again," I promise her with a grin, expecting her to refuse, but she smiles and nods.

"Sounds like a plan." I would love to take her now, but I'm prolonging it for as long as possible. Not because I *don't* want her, but because all I can think of is feeling her pulse around me.

"Get dressed and meet me downstairs," I tell her, as I make my way to the door. I'm about to pull it open when I feel her hands on my skin. Her touch warming my back.

"You're not really the kiss and cuddle type," she muses from behind me. "But I'd like a kiss, please?" Her confidence is an aphrodisiac. If I wasn't hard before, I'm certainly solid steel now.

I turn to regard her, my hands cup her face, and I gently press my lips to hers. It's not desire-fueled, merely affectionate. And when I pull away, I see her smile.

"Happy now?"

"Yes," she tells me with a grin brightening her expression. "You should learn to do that more often. I like it."

"Who put you in charge? Remember, Sweetheart, I'm older, I'm wiser, and I'm far more in control." My voice dips lower. "Unless you'd like another punishment?" Her cheeks turn bright red at the reminder, and I nod with a grin. "See you downstairs."

Back in my bedroom, I shut myself in and breathe. Not once in my life have I felt so connected to another being. Yes, my brothers are my family; they're blood, but she's a girl who's come into my life by some strange feat, and she's broken down walls I had so carefully constructed over the years.

I don't know what Cass and Finn are going to make of this. Granted, my brothers have both noticed my possessiveness for her. So, it may only be me that's been trying to act as if Nesrin isn't mine. That she isn't burrowed in my heart, in my soul. Everything about her is woven into the fabric of who I am.

In the bathroom, I turn on the shower and step under the spray, before it has time to heat. My focus needs to be on the dance; in two days, we'll be attending the ball. I'm still hard as the warm spray attacks my shoulders, and I can't stop myself from fisting my erection, stroking slowly, as my other hand is flat against the cool tiles of the shower. My body shakes, trembling with need, as I close my eyes and picture her beautiful body.

I wanted nothing more than to sink into her, but that will come, and when the moment is right, I'm going to kiss every fucking inch of her. The caramel skin that taunted me last night was enough to have me rock hard; even through my sleep, I couldn't stop my desire for her.

I watch my release spill down the drain, and I wonder briefly if I'll be able to feel her without a condom. It's not something I've ever done before. I'm always sheathed, but with Nesrin, I want to connect with her on more than just a physical level, I want so much more, and I know I can't bank on it lasting forever.

I dry off quickly and dress in a pair of black jeans and a navy-blue shirt. Buttoned up, I slip a belt through the loops of my pants. Once my boots are on, I'm out the door and walking down the hallway when I walk into Gen, as she exits Finn's bedroom.

Her fiery red hair is messy, her lips look like they've been kissed all night. But it's her eyes that have me halting. The shimmering tears that sparkle in her green eyes tell me my brother has done something to piss her off.

"What's going on?" I ask, nearing her, as we come to

the top of the staircase at the same time. I stop, leaning against the balustrade, I cross my arms in front of my chest.

"Nothing," she mumbles, pulling on her sandals, taking the steps two at a time. Instead of following her, I head to Finn's bedroom and shove the door open. He's naked, standing at the window smoking a joint.

My brother's been a rebel since he turned thirteen, and I walked in on him getting his first blowjob. When he was sixteen, we overheard a girl screaming in his bedroom, and when Cass and I walked in, we found them banging against the wall. She was definitely a loud one.

"What the fuck are you doing with Gen?"

Finn doesn't pay me any attention; he slowly finishes his smoke, then turns to the bed and flops down on the mattress. Having him at home has been good, I didn't think he'd stick around once he finished school, especially with how our father acts, as if we're a burden on him.

"Finn, I'm fucking serious. You should not be—"

"Like you didn't fuck Gen?" he challenges. "Listen, I'm having fun. Got my dick wet, time to move on."

"Gen isn't the kind of girl who lets go easily," I tell him. I thought she was a one-night-of-fun as well, and it turned into something I wasn't expecting. She wanted love, and all I had to offer were orgasms. I regret getting pulled in deep, but, at the time, it was what I needed.

"She walked out. Didn't she?"

"What did you tell her?"

Finn crosses his arms behind his head and peeks at me from under his dark lashes. There's a smirk of satisfaction on his face, but then I realize he's not looking at me. I turn to find Nesrin staring at him, her mouth an O of shock.

"Go wait downstairs," I bite out in frustration. She shouldn't have seen him like this. It's my fault for not closing the door, but I wasn't thinking straight when I saw Gen walking out of my youngest brother's bedroom.

"I think your girlfriend just realized she got the short end of the deal," Finn says, with a chuckle, and I'm tempted to throw something at him.

"Put some fucking clothes on," I grit, spinning on my heel. I head out into the hallway, before slamming the door behind me. He infuriates me at times, but he knows that even when I'm angry, I love the asshole.

I take the steps quickly and find Nesrin talking to Joy in the kitchen. The arch of Joy's golden brow tells me she heard things I'd rather she not know about.

"Good morning," I greet her, before grabbing my mug and filling it with coffee. I am going to need this injected straight into my veins today. I'm tired.

"Are you boys fighting?" Joy always hated when we

argued. I think she saw far too many nights with my mother and father at odds. Their fights could go down in history. Volatile and drenched in hate.

"No. Finn's being an asshole."

A swat of the dishtowel hits me right on the ribs. "Language."

Nesrin giggles when I apologize to Joy, but the moment my gaze lands on my girl, she notices the look I'm giving her which is a *don't you start* look.

"These boys are responsible for my gray hair," Joy tells Nesrin, who nods in understanding.

"I can only imagine." My girl decides to respond, but she knows the moment I have her alone, I'll be punishing her for that. Last night, she seemed to enjoy it. And so did I.

"Let's go, wild rose," I tell her, as I grab another mug, fill it, and head out the door and toward the gym. Our ground floor has two offices, one music room, and a gym, which my father put in at the request of the three of us when Finn turned sixteen. He didn't see the point in it but, after a while, agreed.

I set the mugs down and watch Nesrin walk into the room. She's dressed in a tight pair of yoga pants that will, most certainly, have me distracted for most of the session. Her tank top doesn't help either. It's tight, showing off the fact that she's not wearing a bra.

Fuck me.

Nesrin

"**W**HAT THE FUCK ARE YOU WEARING?" HE GRITS angrily, blue eyes sparking with annoyance, but my mouth tilts into a smile.

Glancing down, I shrug nonchalantly, because the desire to push him to admit his feelings has my stomach fluttering. "Clothes."

His glare pins me to the spot, the fire that dances in those endless pools scorch me. But he doesn't say anything more. Instead, he moves to the stereo that Cassian and I used and flicks it on. The speakers come to life and, soon enough, the large gym is filled with the melodic sounds of Dan Owen singing "Made to Love You."

The sound of the piano fills the large room. But the space seems so much smaller when Damien turns to regard me. He crooks his finger, calling me closer, and my feet obey, taking me along, as I close the distance between us. I stop inches from him, our bodies close, but not touching. Damien raises his hand, and I slip mine into his. The heat sears me, but I swallow back the desire and breathe.

His other arm snakes around my middle, and soon, we're practically floating across the soft flooring of the gym. The only sound, besides the song that's echoing around us, is our rhythmic breathing.

Damien leads with confidence, his hands warming me where they grasp. His eyes lock on mine, a smirk curling his lips perfectly. He's poised and confident, with squared shoulders and a spine that's strong and straight.

Everything this man does captures me. My attention is glued to him, as he sways through the room like he owns it. As if everything is merely in *his* way, instead of the other way around. And I know the night of the ball, it will be the same. He'll lead, and I'll follow.

When the song comes to an end, we stop. The stereo continues, the next song comes on, and I'm once more gripped in his arms, like I'm his lifeline, instead of him being mine.

Sara Phillips sings about "The Way You Move", and

that's exactly what I feel. His body and mine are a symphony, molding together, and moving like we're one, instead of two. My heart leaps into my throat when Damien spins me around, before catching me in a hold that dips me backward. I feel like I'm falling, but certainly not physically because he's holding onto me.

"You're beautiful," he says suddenly. When he pulls me back up, my hands land on his chest, my body flush with his, and I can feel the hardness of him prodding my stomach. Even though I'm barefoot, and I'm more than a head shorter than him, I feel like I'm on top of the world being in his arms.

"You're quite the dancer," I respond, unsure of what else to say to him. I can't move, because he's holding me so tight. But I find myself wanting to be there, in his grasp.

"I learned at a young age. Growing up in Thorne Haven, I needed to keep up appearances." There's sadness lacing his tone, which makes my heart ache. Even though I still have no clue what we are, I know that I'll always care about him.

"I like hearing about your life," I tell him honestly. Blue eyes pin themselves on mine. "I mean... I just don't know much about you and Cass and Finn."

"There's not much to know."

"I think there is a lot more that I don't know," I tell him, with our soundtrack playing in the background. A small smile curls his lips. The dimples I've come to love, appear, and I can't help myself from grinning.

"I don't know what you do to me," Damien tells me.

"I think we both make each other feel," I admit. I'm not saying I love him, and I'm not under the impression he could love me, but I know he cares for me.

"Feel," he tastes the word on his tongue. His voice rumbles through me like it always does. It's as if he and I are connected. "I know what I felt when I saw your scars." His gaze sweeps over my face: from my forehead, to my eyes, down to my mouth, then they snap back to my stare. "Rage, fury, frustration. Everything I couldn't explain with words."

"So you... so you punished me?" The air in the room shifts, it's stifling. I can't think straight with him so close. The song changes suddenly, which forces me to glance at the stereo.

Andrew Belle sings "In My Veins," as we move. And it truly feels as if Damien is inside me. It's the strangest feeling, this connection we have is all-consuming.

"I wanted to do so much more, I wanted to hurt you, to make you cry. I wanted to see you ache and hear you beg and plead." The words take on a husky tone. "I don't know how this will ever work."

"I know it can't."

"Why?"

"Because you're meant to be my stepbrother. My mother will never allow us to be like this. To be together."

"You'll have to be my favorite secret," he tells me, and

there's no hint of a joke in his voice. My mouth opens, then shuts, and I'm flustered at the thought of being with him in the future. I was prepared for this to end in a week. I believed the moment our parents walked in, we would become platonic, even though I had no clue how I'd be able to do that.

"Don't all secrets come out in the end?" I ask, curiosity lacing my words. His gaze flickers with knowing, we both know this could end tragically. I know I'd be broken, but Damien, he'd be okay because he's stronger than I am. I think.

"They do," he acquiesces, with a nod, as he turns us around. We move across the floor to the song. It's slow, but it's beautiful. Damien gifts me a smile; it's not so much sad, as it is worried. He does look like he's feeling more for me than I originally thought. "Let's enjoy our time together," he says, as the song comes to an end. "And when we reach the bridge of no return," he whispers, "I'll take you with me."

My heart skips a beat, and I want to tell him not to make promises he can't keep, but instead, I smile and press a kiss to his lips. It's chaste, but it lingers for a moment longer than normal.

I don't know how I'll say goodbye to him, but I know he'll be the one cut that's too deep to heal from.

Damien

WHEN I ASKED CASSIAN TO TAKE ME TO THE STORE to buy a dress, Damien almost lost his mind. But I did remind him that I needed to do this on my own. Even though I've shopped for fancy clothes before, this trip is special. I want to surprise Damien when he sees me in the dress.

He mentioned he'd be buying the masks, so that part is sorted. I glance up, taking in my reflection in all three mirrors that surround me. It's perfect. The deep royal blue shimmers like a million stars have been sewn into the material.

The back is non-existent, which I'm sure will have Damien telling me I'm not allowed to wear it, but this is my gown and my night. I want to feel beautiful. With most of the back cut out, the gentle material runs in an arch along the base of my spine and up along my sides, leaving my whole back visible. All that holds it together is a short zipper that snakes over my butt, and the long flowing floor-length gown feels as if it's painted against my hips.

My tanned, caramel skin looks amazing against the dark blue. The front is less revealing, and thankfully, I don't have to wear a bra. The V that dips between my cleavage is held together by five strips of material. And the halter neck hugs me tightly.

Opening the dressing room door, I step out, and Cassian glances up. His face is a picture; I wish I had a camera to capture his expression. Steel eyes shimmer with amusement.

"What?"

"Damien's probably never going to allow you out of the house looking like that," he tells me earnestly, and I don't doubt him. The possessive nature of the eldest Thorne is no secret. And if Cassian says it, I know I have a fight on my hands.

"I know. But he'll see things my way, I have my arguments ready," I tell him, spinning around, so he can look at the whole outfit. "

"Jesus," Cassian murmurs. "If you weren't into D, I'd

have to give you my best lines to get you in my bed.”

I stop twirling, staring at Cassian in shock.

“What?” Cass shrugs guiltily. “A man can only take so much. You look gorgeous,” he tells me.

“Thank you.” I look at my reflection, once more, before I change back into my jeans and tee. Once I find the right shoes, we pay, and we’re back in the car. I’m not one of those girls who takes hours to find the right outfit, but this had to have been the quickest shopping trip I’ve ever had. The moment I walked into the boutique, my eye caught the blue, and I knew I had to have it.

In the car, Cassian’s silent for a short while before he says, “My brother is falling for you.”

I snap my gaze at him in shock. “What?”

“I’ve seen him over the years, watched him with girls. The longest he’s ever spent with someone was Gen. The redhead. But you’re different.”

I turn toward him as my curiosity is piqued by what he’s just said. “How so?”

“I don’t know. I can’t explain it, but you challenge him, which no other girl has ever had the balls to do. You question him, you make him think and, more importantly, you make him feel.”

“I don’t know if feelings are a good thing. When our folks get back, it’s going to be hell if they know what we’ve been doing.”

"But does it *feel* wrong?" He emphasizes the word *feel*. It's something I've been pondering since the first time Damien's lips touched mine. And honestly, I have to say no.

"Not in the slightest. It feels right, it feels perfect when I'm with him. I'm only used to what my mother is like."

Cassian chuckles. "If you think your mother is bad, she has nothing on my dad. He's ruled this house with an iron first for years. When my mother walked out, she took his heart along with her, and we were left with the cold, aloof Bradford Thorne."

Sadness laces his words, and for a moment, I'm upset that they had to go through that. But, then again, they've grown into men who are strong and resilient. They don't need anyone to look after them. I see it as a good thing.

"My mother offered to allow me to go to Oxford next year. When the school year starts, I could be in England."

"You'll be near Damien," Cassian offers, with a sly grin. "I think you should go. My brother may not admit to a lot, but I can see how much he cares for you. I'm not sure he'll ever be able to love, though."

"What happened to him?" I've been curious to know about his past, and Cassian seems happy to give me some insight into Damien. "He's never spoken about anything other than The Black Knights. I don't know if he was ever with someone who, perhaps, broke his heart."

"It was my mother." Cassian's words sink into my chest, slicing right through my heart. "When he was fourteen, he witnessed my mother and father fighting. I was locked up in my room, so was Finn. Damien had sat on the top of the stairs, listening to them bicker, which turned into a full-blown argument."

"And now he believes love doesn't last?" I stare at Cass who glances my way as we pull up to the house. While the wrought-iron gates swing open, he nods. "I guess it makes sense."

"He believes that love is a lie. He always has. But what he doesn't realize is that it's an emotion that can't be stopped or thwarted by walls you put up. But Damien is convinced it's only a word people utter to get what they want."

"And if I said it to him, then he would think I'm being dishonest."

Cassian nods once more. "Not because he thinks you're only here for status or money, or anything like that. It's just how his mind portrayed love as a lie, and his beliefs turned all the good into something sinister. Knowing how my parents used each other stuck with him."

"I understand."

"Do you love him?" Cassian asks, as he kills the engine and turns to look at me. His eyes shimmer, more green than blue. It's a beautiful color. As endless as Damien's and Finn's.

"I think I do. It's not easy to say those words," I tell him, "I wasn't brought up in the most loving home either. My mother was more concerned with her latest award or the next movie deal. So, I understand why he's hesitant."

"Don't take how he is with you for granted. I've never seen him like this," Cassian tells me, before he pushes his door open, "but also, don't expect too much from him too soon."

"I won't."

That's the end of our heart to heart, and I'm thankful for it. Even though I knew that Damien wouldn't come to terms with the thought of loving someone, he's still allowing himself to care. And that's all I can ask for.

I follow Cass inside and make a beeline for my bedroom. Inside, I grab a hanger and drape the dress, hiding it in my closet. If Damien walks in here, I don't want him to see it before tomorrow night.

The moment my bedroom door whooshes open, I *feel* him. He steps inside, stopping beside my bed as I'm shutting the closet. His gaze narrows, sweeping over the room and notices the empty bag, the shoe box, but that's all he can find.

"Did you get a dress?"

"Yeah," I tell him, crossing my arms, to keep from showing him just how nervous I am.

Without a word, Damien closes the distance between us, and the air thickens with hunger. It's as if he can devour me with merely a glance. His hands grip my hips, and he holds me steady. One of his hands releases me, and with that, he tips my chin, so I'm looking into those cerulean orbs.

"Where is it?"

"You'll see it tomorrow." My voice is a failed attempt at sounding confident. I'm met with a smirk, dark and devious, just like he wants.

"If you're showing any skin tomorrow, I will punish you, and this time, it most certainly won't end with you coming all over my hand." His promise is laced with lust—rabid and feral.

"I don't doubt it," I tell him, attempting to sound calm, but my hands are shaking like a leaf in a summer breeze. I want to turn away, to sit down, but I'm suddenly hoisted up against Damien's rigid body, and he walks us over to the bed where he sets me down.

Seconds later, he's reaching behind him and pulling a small black velvet box from his pocket. He hands it to me before saying, "I got you something that I want you to wear."

My heart is thudding wildly, and I'm thankful he didn't drop to one knee when he pulled it out because I may have fainted from the sweetness of his gesture.

I flick open the lid. Inside, nestled on the darkest velvet, is a gold rose with small thorns adorning the stem. The shimmering ruby that sits in the center of the bud is beautifully carved, fitting strikingly in the setting. Attached to the rose is a sleek choker that I tug from the cushion.

"This is exquisite. But I don't know if I can wear it."

"Why?"

I glance up, meeting his questioning stare. "It's too much, Damien."

"You're a Thorne, but you're also a rose. My wild rose." He watches me intently, his eyes boring into me like they always do, but this time those flames that usually dance only with desire, now offer more.

Affection.

Caring.

And an emotion I'd rather not voice, even to myself.

But then he says, "My rose."

Nesrin

WITH A QUICK GLANCE AT THE CLOCK, I SIGH, knowing we'll be late if she doesn't come down the fucking stairs in the next few moments.

I didn't think Nesrin would be here for long. I figured she'd just turn around and head back to the city because that's what she grew up with. City lights and streets paved with dreams.

She has certainly changed my mind about her. Since the first day I saw her, I had an idea in mind as to what she was like. But she's not *only* offered me a calm and solace I never thought I'd have. Nesrin has also tormented my demons, dragging them to the forefront, calling them to come out and play.

Tonight is a test. She knows about the dance, but she doesn't realize that, afterward, if I really want to claim her as mine, this town doesn't like anything they deem forbidden. They don't like rules being broken. And Nesrin and I are going to make them talk.

Even though my plan is to head to England when Daddy Dearest returns, I want to ensure she's safe. Her being here alone doesn't sit well with me. But the thought of dragging her across the ocean, that might work.

I wanted to fight my feelings for her. I should've fought my attraction, but I knew the girl who watched me in the greenhouse the night of our parents' wedding reception would be mine.

She is everything I craved, and she gives me everything I need. I think back to the night of the party when she was talking to Creed. Her laugh echoed across to me, and even then, I knew I would kill him before I allowed him to have her.

But she doesn't know the truth. And I'm going to have to tell her everything. Perhaps not tonight. Maybe I can delay it till tomorrow.

Suddenly, Nesrin appears at the top of the staircase. Her hair has been curled around her shoulders, which are bare. The halter neck of the dress is bound, holding up the sleek material, which seems to be painted to every curve of her body.

The moment she takes a step, her left leg bares itself to me, as the slit opens from her ankle, all the way up to her smooth, slender thigh.

Jesus fucking Christ Almighty.

"You're not wearing that," I bite out, as raging jealousy courses through me. I take a step, but she lifts her hand and stops me as she reaches the bottom of the steps.

"I'm a grown woman, Damien. I am yours, but I also have my own mind. If you can't trust me," she says, squaring her shoulders, "then we may as well go separately." Her chin tips upward, and that familiar fire in her gaze dances wildly, challenging me to argue.

"You're going to be the death of me one day, wild rose," I tell her. "And it's not you I don't trust. It's all those men who'll be in attendance."

"They can't touch me without my permission," she bites out, and I have to agree. Because if they come anywhere near her with their filthy hands, I'll kill them all.

I lift the mask I'd been holding and offer it to her. The intricate silver design looks like lace, which will curve and mold to her face perfectly. She smiles, moving slowly toward me. The choker I gave her fits snugly around the delicate column of her neck, and I can't stop the grin that tilts my lips.

"You do look exquisite. Thankfully, you're all mine," I tell her, as I lean in to press my lips to hers. She's got a darker shade of lip color on; it's not shimmering or glossy, but the contrast of the deep red with her caramel skin looks like it was made just for her.

"Thank you. You scrub up well," she informs me, with a naughty grin on her pretty face. No, she's not just pretty. This woman is flawless.

"Tonight, you stay beside me. I don't want you alone with Creed. At all."

"What happened between the two of you?" she questions, and my heart stops for a short moment. My chest tightens, and I'm not sure how to answer her because, if I do, I'll have to tell her the truth. The reason she's here, the reason I chose her, and also, who she really is.

"Why don't we enjoy this evening, and when we get home, we can talk," I suggest, not wanting to spoil the ball for her. As much as I know she needs to learn what's been hidden from her, I can't bring myself to utter the words.

I pushed it to the back of my mind for weeks. And, before that, I knew the time would come when I would need to tell her everything, but not right now.

"Let's go."

We make our way to the car, and I open the door, allowing her to slip into the backseat. Our driver nods when I round the vehicle, giving him the gesture that we're ready.

Since Cass and Finn are gone already, we can have some privacy on our drive into town and then back out toward the castle. The darkness swallows us as the Thorne driver, Hank, takes us to the party.

"What happens at this event?" Nesrin asks, but her voice is low, whispered along the air between us. *Do I tell her?*

"Tonight, we will drink, dance, and then we'll watch the initiation into the town for newcomers." I didn't want to tell her about this part until we were at the castle, but I need her to be confident when she walks in there. If she knew what fear does to these assholes, she wouldn't want to be by my side tonight taking them head-on.

"What kind of initiation?"

I don't want to respond. I remain silent and pull out my cell phone. Scrolling through the names, I hit dial on Cassian's number and press the device to my ear.

"What's up, Brother?"

"Are you at the castle?" I ask quickly. I can feel Nesrin's gaze burning a hole through the side of my face.

"Yeah. The Havens are here. With the rest of The Black Knights." There's a warning lacing his words, and my stomach turns. "She's here, too."

"Fuck." The plan we've carefully constructed is slowly falling apart. The person I was hoping wouldn't make an appearance is there. Instead of panicking, I nod to myself.

"Keep her company. We'll be there in five," I tell him. "When we arrive, I want her gone." I hang up before Cassian can give me shit about the orders that I've just given him.

"What's going on?" Nesrin's curious nature is going to get her into trouble tonight. All I wanted was this godforsaken party to go off without a hitch. I got too close to Nesrin, when all I was meant to do is keep her in line. But now that I'm invested, I know I can't walk away.

"I hope you're ready for this," I tell her, keeping my tone cool. "Because tonight may be difficult for everyone involved." I can't meet her gaze, as I say this, because I'm guilty.

The lie that's been eating me up from inside is going to spill free and poison us both. I should've told her the truth when I first met her. But I couldn't. I didn't realize I'd feel like this about her, and now, I'm on the way to my own fucking reckoning.

"Are you okay?" Nesrin's hand lands on my thigh, which causes me to turn my attention on her. I finally lock eyes with her and see all the questions that are dancing in those pretty eyes.

"At the end of this, all I want you to do is not hate me." I reach for her, pulling her onto my lap and grip her hips.

"Promise me." I'm pleading like a fucking asshole.

"What are you talking about?" She tips her head to the side, regarding me with such confusion it steals my breath. "I can't hate you, Damien. Even if I tried." Her hands cup my face, her heat searing my crotch, and her sweet smile worsening my guilt.

"Nothing." I shake my head, attempting to calm the fuck down. I can work through this. Snaking my hand between her splayed thighs, I tease the silky material of her panties, feeling her wetness soak through. "Someone is thinking dirty thoughts." I attempt to distract her, but I have a feeling Nesrin won't be swayed easily.

"You touching me won't change the fact that you're worried about something." Her voice breaks and her breathing hitches when I press against her clit. "Damien." My name comes out a breathy murmur that only serves to make me hard beneath her.

"Like I said, tonight you will be mine. I'm going to dance with you, I'm going to drink champagne with you, and when I take you home, you're going straight into my bedroom, and I'm going to rip this poor fucking excuse for a dress off, and I'm going to fuck you."

Her eyes snap open, and her mouth parts into a perfectly formed O that would wrap perfectly around my dick. Her hips roll, her fingers dig into my shoulders, and her panties become slick with her arousal. One.

Two. Three. And then she's shaking above me, taking her pleasure, like I know she enjoys.

"Dirty fucking girl," I growl, leaning in to inhale her perfume that's been gently applied to her neck. "And don't you dare forget who owns that pretty pussy that's just soaked my fingers." The reminder sends another wave of trembling through her before I set her down and straighten my jacket.

We pull up to the entrance of the large, looming castle, and before Nesrin can move, I lift my fingers to my nose and inhale her scent. Her shock is clear, and I can't help but smile.

"All mine." With a wink, I push open my door, as Hank pulls open Nesrin's. We meet at the pathway toward the entrance, as she slides her arm through mine.

The perfect couple.

And a perfectly formed lie.

Damien

WHEN I HAVE A SECOND TO REALLY TAKE IN THE building before us, I'm astounded that it really does look like a castle. The windows are small; yet, they offer up yellow light that streams outward.

Each turret has a darkened hole where I can imagine you would get an impeccable view. Along the second floor are two long balconies that overlook the driveway, which I'm guessing come from a couple of bedrooms.

Built with dark brick, it reminds me of the historic castles in Scotland. Most of them are falling apart, merely ruins, but this one is immaculate. The door is a large archway drenched in golden light, as two butlers stand on either side receiving guests with a smile.

Damien and I adorn our masks; he helps me fasten a bow behind my head. He leans in, allowing the warmth of his breath to slide over me.

"I'm going to kill Cassian for allowing you to buy this dress," he whispers suddenly. "And then I'm going to punish you for wearing it." His promise has my stomach flip-flopping at the thought.

"You don't own me, Damien." I turn to smile at him, my mask firmly in place, but I know he can see the confidence in my eyes.

"We'll see about that," he hisses under his breath, but grins as if nothing is wrong. He places his fingers at the base of my spine, causing my skin to tingle at the contact, as we make our way through the entrance into a breathtaking foyer.

The floors are tiled with patterns better suited for a church. The ceiling is high, with a painting that would make Leonardo Da Vinci jealous. And a chandelier that reminds me of golden champagne flutes hanging above us.

Everything glitters. But doesn't the saying go, *all that glitters isn't gold.*

We're led through the house, out toward a dining hall that has been set up with a table that looks to seat at least twenty people, probably more, but my attention is captured by three young men standing on the patio, just outside the large glass doors.

Wealth drips from them. The Havens. The girls, who loiter just behind them, are drenched in priceless jewels. The men in expensive tailored suits and the women in designer-cut dresses.

Style.

Beauty.

Money.

"I think you're far more beautiful than any female in this place," Damien whispers, conspiratorially, in my ear. He looks like the epitome of a playboy. Perfectly styled black hair and ice-blue eyes. His charcoal suit fits him like a glove, with a crisp white shirt that doesn't have a single crease. The tie he's wearing is a striking blue that matches my dress, and I have a feeling that Cassian had a hand in picking it out.

"Only the females?" I challenge him with a grin.

"Don't get sassy with me," Damien murmurs, as he pulls two glasses of champagne from a tray. He hands me mine, and then we head toward the rest of the guests, who seem to be milling around; some talking in groups, others in couples.

"Where are Cass and Finn?" I ask, glancing at Damien, who looks handsome with the silver mask covering half his face. It reminds me of a *Phantom of the Opera* mask. He doesn't look at me. It's the same way he acted in the car, which has me on alert that something is wrong. One thing about him was that he was always forthcoming in either noticing me or talking to me. But there's been a shift, and I can't quite put my finger on what's going on.

Music filters from speakers that I can't see, as couples move toward a makeshift dancefloor in the middle of the garden. They get close, holding onto each other, and for a moment, I wish Damien would ask me to dance, but he's not even paying attention.

"Could I ask you for a dance, young lady?" The question comes from one of the guests dressed solely in black, including a mask.

"She's with me."

"I didn't think you'd mind, since you don't seem to be wanting to dance," the man tells Damien, and the prickly feeling I'm getting from beside me makes me nervous. I don't think he'll start a fight, but Damien and I haven't really been out, unless you count the bonfire.

"Sure," I finally respond, much to Damien's disdain. It flashes in his eyes, but all I do is offer a grin and follow the man onto the dancefloor. We move to the music, and thankfully, he keeps his distance friendly.

With every turn, my gaze lands on the blue fire that's burning a hole into the back of my dance partner's head.

"He doesn't like to share. Does he?"

"Not particularly," I smile back. "So, are you allowed to

tell me who you are? Or is this whole event completely anonymous?"

"This is your first dance?" When he tips his head to the side, regarding me curiously, a strange shift happens. But before I can figure out what exactly, I'm spun around and find myself in Damien's arms.

"She's dancing with me now," he tells the man, now behind me. Then he drops his gaze to me. "I told you, you're mine, you don't dance with anyone else."

"I wanted to dance, he offered. It wasn't like I was going to drop to my knees on the dancefloor in front of him." My biting tone causes Damien to chuckle, but his smile doesn't reach his eyes. It's the first tell I pick up on. When he grins, when he smirks, his smile always reaches his sparkling gaze; this time, there's tension in his expression. "Are you going to tell me what's wrong?"

He spins me on the dancefloor, our bodies moving to the song, but he doesn't respond. A couple walks out onto the dancefloor, and it's as if the air has thickened to scorching.

Everyone moves to the edge of the large tiled square, and the music stops. A gentle hum of whispers lingers, but it stills the moment the man picks up a microphone.

The woman beside him glances around, and Damien's body stiffens beside me, but I don't have time to look at him because the man speaks.

"Good evening to the young Thorne Haven elite," he greets to whoops and howls of excitement. "It is with great pleasure that I welcome you to the fiftieth annual Le Ball Masqué."

"I thought you said it's all the younger kids attending tonight?" My whisper feathers up toward Damien, and he tilts his head down to my ear. The warmth of his breath makes my skin tingle with awareness of his nearness.

"It is. They're the owners of The Castle."

"Who are they?" The moment I pose the question, the man's glance lands on me, and I look directly into his eyes for the first time since he walked into the crowd. A lead weight drops into my stomach, and bile rises up to my throat. "Is that...?"

"Yes." That's all Damien says, but his arm snakes around my middle, holding me up because my knees buckle. "I need you to keep calm so we can explain," he tells me in a lowered voice, but my heart thumps wildly in my ears, beating a rhythm that drowns out everything else.

Damien holds me up. He's a rock, and I feel like I'm flailing in the darkness, but the spicy scent of his cologne is calming. Breathing deeply, I watch her smile. Even under the bright red mask, I would know her anywhere. She's holding onto the man beside her, as if he's her lifeline.

How can she not tell me where she was?

Why is she living in Thorne Haven?

And why the hell didn't Damien tell me?

The man finishes his speech, but I'm still in shock when the crowd claps and whistles. I turn toward Damien, his blue eyes sparking with sadness and guilt.

"Talk to me Damien," I plead, tears filling my eyes. His hand latches onto mine, and he tugs me through the crowd and deeper into the darkness of the garden. My heels aren't made for the grass, so I stumble behind him. When we reach a beautifully carved fountain, with Cupid shooting an arrow down at us, I can't help the laugh that bubbles in my chest at the irony.

"Sit." Damien points at the smooth, marble seating bench that surrounds the fountain. I obey silently because I have a feeling, if I fight him on this, he'll only keep more secrets from me. My chest is tight with agony. She didn't even look at me. Surely, she knows I'm here.

"Damien, I don't know what's going on, but I need to know why the fuck my aunt is here. And why she's hanging onto the man making the speech."

"I know." He nods, as he runs his fingers through his hair, which only makes it look messily sexy. Shaking my head, I focus on the anger that's surging through me, along with confusion at my aunt's actions.

"Who is the man?" I whisper. Damien looks at me

before he sighs and settles beside me. I know something bad is coming. If he's being this quiet about it, this can't be good at all.

"The man is Creed's father."

I shoot to my feet. "What?" My voice comes out with a croak of shock. "That... I can't... She's... No."

"They got married last year. She moved to Thorne Haven, and as time passed, she became part of the community. When I met you at the reception, I couldn't bring myself to tell you because everything else didn't matter. Only your eyes on me. I was being selfish." His words falter off into the dark night. It feels like the world is closing in on me.

"I don't understand. Why wouldn't she tell me? What is actually going on?" Even though I have a million questions running through my mind, one comes to the forefront, and I voice it. "Did you and I happen because of that?" I point back to the castle behind us. "Did you make a move on me because you were trying to make Creed angry?"

"No!" Damien's on his feet, his hands on my hips. He holds me tenderly, but firmly. "I want you, Nesrin. When I first saw you at the reception, all I could think about was being beside you, inside you." Damien leans in close, his mouth feathering over mine. "You've burrowed your way into my life and into my heart."

He doesn't blink, keeping his gaze locked on mine. I believe him. He doesn't smile; he doesn't grin and play his admission off, so I know there's truth in his statement.

"I can't get my heart broken, Damien." My plea is clear. He knows I'm not strong. I may come across as such, but I'm so far from it, and this has hurt me more than I can explain.

"Wild rose," Damien whispers the nickname he's given me. "If I do ever hurt you, I'll be hurting myself ten times over. When you came into my life, I was..." He shakes his head. I've never seen Damien vulnerable. I have never witnessed him look so torn and broken. Not even when he showed me his scars.

"You were?" I urge, needing him to tell me the truth. I don't know why I'm so needy, so fucking childish, but I want his words, and nothing else will suffice. Not now.

"I don't trust myself around you."

"Why?"

"Isn't this cozy?" Creed's voice comes from behind me. Damien's gaze lifts to the man with a spark of annoyance.

"What the fuck do you want, Creed?"

"You know I'm allowed a dance with any new girls who've come to Thorne Haven. It's part of the rules." A shiver runs down my spine, and goosebumps rise on my bare skin.

"We'll rejoin the party shortly, Creed." Damien's voice is ice. The heat behind me is the only way I know that the other man has stepped closer to me. I'm sandwiched between the two, and the animosity is so thick, you could cut it with a knife.

"Don't disappoint me, Thorne," Creed says in a low, violent tone. "You of all people know I don't like being disappointed." He spins on his heel, and the cool air he leaves behind makes me shiver.

"Are you ever going to tell me what the hell is going on between the two of you?" I question, looking up at the man who's stolen my heart.

"Tonight. For now, we need to get back. And please don't be angry with your aunt."

"Why? She neglected to tell me about her being married to a man who practically owns a town. She didn't even mention knowing you when she stood in front of me at the reception. Does my mother know?"

"Let's get back to the party. I'll answer any questions later. I promise," he tells me, not meeting my questioning gaze, and I know there is so much more that's being kept from me.

"Fine," I bite out, as frustration shoots through me, heating my blood. I spin around and make my way back to the house, leaving Damien staring at my back.

If Creed wants to dance with me, I'll do it. Perhaps he'll be more forthcoming with information.

Nesrin

IDON'T RUN AFTER HER BECAUSE I KNOW SHE'LL ONLY push me away. I don't blame her for being angry, but there are reasons behind everything I've done. It was all to keep her safe, and I would do it again if I had another chance.

When I reach the house, I step into the ballroom and head straight for the bar. Cassian joins me, a smirk on his face, and I want nothing more than to punch him, but that wouldn't help matters.

"She saw Mallory?" he asks, and I nod. "You knew it would happen. It's not up to you to keep her safe from the truth. Her family should do it."

"I'm her..." I allow my confession to silence because I

can't admit shit right now.

"I know you're in love with her, Damien. It's time you stopped denying it." Cassian watches my reaction to his response. I gulp down the bourbon and gesture to the barman for another.

"You know what love did to our father, Cass," I bite out when I have another double shot of bourbon. Turning to the dancefloor, I watch her from afar, talking to and dancing with Creed. Her smile is bright, but I don't miss how her gaze finds me across the crowd.

Her hands snake around his neck, and my body burns with jealous rage. I know she's doing it to piss me off. The man who's wanted the legacy of Thorne Haven for himself is enjoying the dance. Creed has always wanted everything that's mine. Our fathers are one and the same, but, the difference is, Bradford Thorne would not happily leave Thorne Corporation to me. Whereas Octavius Haven would wrap his legacy in a bow, before leaving it to his eldest son.

He moves closer to her, and every instinct in my body hums with violence. I'm so close to tearing through him, ripping him to shreds and fucking her drenched in his blood.

Would I enjoy it? Of course.

The darkness that's always consumed me has a hold of me, and it's not letting go. Not until I can make Nesrin completely mine, without anything hanging over our heads.

But it's wrong.

Perhaps not to us.

But to my father, to her mother, her aunt. My feelings have grown; they've taken over, and all of this will ensure our lives are torn apart, left in shambles at the feet of the man who will gladly take everything from me—Creed Haven.

"Are you going to kill him?" Cassian's amused voice comes from beside me, but I don't look at my brother. I can't. Because if I do, I'll see the mirror image of my need dancing in his own eyes. We have experienced The Black Knights side by side. He knows how much I loved the games, the twisted runs in the darkness. Cassian also knows how deeply my body craves the fear in their eyes because I confessed my yearning to him.

Even though he's a year younger than me, Cassian also understands my hesitation. This party is not the time or place to act out. Especially since we're on Haven property.

"Perhaps I'll torture him, watch him beg for mercy, while I enjoy a drink and smile at his pleas," I mumble, unable to tear my gaze away from Nesrin, as she grins at him.

"I don't think your girl would enjoy that," Cass says with a shoulder bumping against mine as amusement laces his words. Even if I don't look at him to see it for myself, I know he's grinning. He's right. Nesrin's fighting her own demons, but when we're together, it's as if she forgets about her pain, her dark thoughts. She forgets to hurt herself.

And, for me, that's the only thing that matters.

Because I'm the only person, the only thing that can hurt her. Because, if I walk away, I'll break her worse than anything ever has.

"I want to show her the roof tonight," I tell him, then feel his heated stare on the side of my face, as I take a sip of my drink. The burning amber liquid trickles a hot path down my throat, warming my stomach moments later.

"Do you think she'll like it up there?" he asks, with amused curiosity. I'm not doing it for her. Even though I've ensured she's comfortable, that she's ready for what's coming, I have secretly been selfish with my needs. I won't apologize for it, and I certainly will never admit it to her, but my brother's question makes me consider just how much this girl has burrowed herself in my mind.

I'm aching to finally have her. To feel her pussy pulse around my cock. And that's the one place I know we'll have complete privacy. The lights dim and the blue spotlights illuminate the dancefloor. It's time for the couples to take the stage. I swallow back my drink and pat Cassian on the shoulder, not answering his previous question, but rather telling him, "Time to play."

With a wink, I turn and make a beeline directly for my girl and Creed. When I reach them, my hand captures her hip, causing her to gasp.

"Your dance is over," I say, looking directly at Creed who, for a moment, looks like he doesn't want to let go. But he tips his head in acknowledgment and steps back.

"Thank you for the dance, Nesrin," he tells her, before leaving me with my wild rose.

"What's happening?" she asks, looking around as if she's only now noticed the blue illumination that surrounds us.

"It's time for the dance we practiced. Afterward, there'll be a game," I tell her, as the music starts, and we move across the floor. The fluid motion of the couples is beautifully in sync. Nothing else matters to me in this moment, though, because her gaze is on me.

"Game?"

"Think of it as hide and seek," I say, leaning my face down to steal a kiss. But Nesrin turns her head, giving me her cheek, which causes my body to lock in anger. "What are you doing?"

"I'm trying to get a hold of everything that's been said tonight."

"What did Creed tell you?" My voice comes out laced

with anger, even though I try not to let it get to me. I should have known the asshole would've said something to make her feel like this.

She doesn't respond. We dance until the song ends, and the speakers come alive with the deep voice of Creed's father.

"Every female attendee will now find her hiding spot. Time to play," he says into the microphone, the booming baritone makes Nesrin shiver. "The person to find you first will be your partner at the upcoming year-end ball in December. It will be the person you're publicly professing as…" the words filter off, leaving anticipation hanging in the air, "the girl you're either in love with, or the girl you'd like to be with."

I cup her face, holding her, so she doesn't turn away from me because I feel like she's about to disappear. Keeping my gaze locked with hers, I don't blink, as I swipe my thumb along her lower lip. "I'll find you."

"What if you don't?" There's fear twined around her words, and it twists in my chest. There is no guarantee that I will be the first to find her, but I'll kill anyone who gets in my way.

"Don't be afraid. I'll always find you, even in the dark." The words are out of my mouth before I can swallow them back. My admission means more than she knows. Seconds later, she's racing through the doors, leaving me to watch her disappearing form. A childish game made for adults. If she only knew what's to come.

"She's a beauty," Creed says, from beside me. We stand in silence. I can't speak to him, if I do, I'll say something that could cause a war. "I didn't tell her all the secrets you're still hiding from her. And I definitely didn't tell her about Gen. Perhaps you can," he murmurs, with a chuckle.

"If you don't stop this bullshit, I will kill you," I promise. "I don't give a shit who you are."

"You're in love with her," he muses. "I can see the appeal. But have you taken her for a test drive yet?"

His question has rage burning through my veins. My hands fist, but a touch on my shoulder from Cassian, reminds me to keep calm. Creed enjoys taunting me and, as much as I want to hurt him, I know I can't. Not yet, anyway.

We're the same age, grew up together, but one event turned our loyalty into hate. There's a fine line between loving someone and hating them. And teetering on the barrier of those two emotions can be detrimental.

"Will you win tonight? Can the polished and perfect, Damien Thorne, ever cause a scandal in this town?"

"If you go near her tonight," I speak, keeping my voice low so only he can hear me, "I will come for you, and I'll make sure everyone knows what happened that night."

The moment the words are out, the buzzer sounds, and we're on the move. I grab a rose from the basket on the table which sits inside the dining hall and make my way into the bowels of the castle, praying with all I have that I find her.

I need to get to Nesrin before he does.

Or he'll steal her from me, just like he did with *her*.

Damien

THE HALLWAYS ARE LIKE A MAZE OF COOL BRICK AND dimly lit bulbs. The eeriness of the castle itself makes me shiver. I find a door, push it open, and step into a library that looks like heaven for a book lover. Books line three of the four walls, with colorful spines from floor to ceiling. I shut myself inside and move deeper into the room.

I'll find you, even in the dark.

Damien's words linger in my mind, as I find myself at the window overlooking the grounds that stretch into the distance. Even in the dark, I can make out just how large the property is.

Heavy velvet curtains hang on either side of the arched

window, and I smile, knowing I have my hiding spot if the door were to whoosh open. This night has taken on a sinister feeling, which has me shivering. Soon enough, the snow will arrive, and we'll be in the throes of winter, but for now, the mild weather seems to be holding out. I wonder if that's why they have this ball so early.

"Gotcha." A deep voice startles me, causing me to spin on my heels and come face to face with Creed Haven. In the darkness, he looks sinister as he approaches me. A salacious grin breaks on his ruggedly handsome face and a shiver races down my spine, making me tremble. My throat is thick with a lump of worry, and my stomach somersaults when his head tilts to the side, his eyes taking me in from head to toe.

"How?" I glance at the door; it's still shut. I didn't hear him enter. I didn't even notice him until he spoke.

He turns, gesturing to another door, which I didn't notice earlier. It's hidden in the corner of the room nestled between two bookshelves. "My bedroom is on the other side," he tells me when his dark gaze lands on me once more.

"So, you hide out here to scare girls?" I ask, trying to sound confident, but the slight squeak that escapes my lips when he closes the distance is unmistakable.

"I do. The fear that I see dancing in those pretty eyes makes my dick hard." He chuckles, and his hand grabs at his crotch as if he's proud of the admission.

"You're sick," I bite out. Damien was right; he's definitely nothing like Creed. I know they were friends for a while, but something tells me that Creed wouldn't think twice about taking what a girl isn't offering.

"I like to call it, determined," he tells me, before turning away. A breath, I had been holding, escapes in relief. I watch him move through the room toward the trolley, holding decanters of all colors. He pours himself a drink and glances at me over his shoulder. "Drink?"

I shake my head, unable to find words. When we're around others, he comes across as *normal*, but here in the dimly lit room, he definitely scares me.

"Why are you in here?"

"I sniffed out prey, and as a hunter, I wanted to peek at the pretty girl who entered my library." He speaks, but his focus is on his glass. Even though he's not looking at me, I feel his eyes roaming my frame. The silver light from the moon streams through the moment a cloud passes, allowing the illumination to cast a spell around us.

"Your library?"

"Yes, my father gifted it to me when I turned thirteen," he tells me. "I have a love of the written word." He swallows back the drink, before setting the empty glass down and turning his attention on me. "Are you in love with him?”

His question stills me for a short moment, before I realize he’s asking about Damien. I don’t know about love, but I do have feelings for him.

“Love is a wasted emotion,” I mimic Damien’s words from the first night I spent at Thorne Manor.

“I see my best friend has been rubbing off on you,” Creed murmurs. “It is wasted, but only on those who don’t offer it back. Damien is a special breed of male.”

“And you?”

“Oh, Darling, I’m nothing like him. You see, Damien may want to appear dangerous, feral, but he’s not. Down to his core, he’s a gentleman.”

“And you’re not?” I know the answer, but I ask it anyway. Creed is something else entirely, and now I see why Damien didn’t want me around him. He doesn’t seem apologetic when he glances at me. I watch him settle on a long black couch that faces the window. He crosses one ankle over the opposite knee and drapes his arm across the back.

“I don’t like not being obeyed.” His words drip with malice. “I don’t like being made a fool of, and I certainly don’t appreciate being lied to.” I’m not sure where he’s going with this. “I’m sure you’ve seen the redhead who follows Damien around like a puppy.”

Genevieve.

"I have."

"She'll bounce on any Thorne dick. After Damien broke it off with her, she made sure to befriend his brothers. Granted, Finn is a sucker for a woman with big tits, I know he's fucked her."

"Why are you telling me this?"

"Because you asked me what I'm like." He smiles, the corner of his mouth is the only thing that tilts upward, and in that single second, I notice how haunted his gaze is. "Gen is one of those girls who *crave* status. Damien offered it to her for a short while, because he thought she was decent. I, on the other hand, broke her down until there was nothing left. Your boyfriend tried to *fix* her."

"Is that why you two aren't friends anymore?" I ask, drawn into his words like a moth to the flame, and I wonder if his confession will burn me or if it will merely singe.

"Damien didn't agree with my methods, my need to control and claim. I wanted to test the limits of our games, and he got scared."

"What did you do?" I ask, my voice low, a whisper laced with fear. I have a feeling that I'm not going to like the answer, but I'm here now, so I may as well learn what happened.

"Let's just say that terrible things happen in the dark." Creed smiles, his eyes blazing with the threat of sinister actions. A shiver takes hold of me, and he notices my hands shaking. "Perhaps you should go find your boyfriend." He gestures to the door with his chin. "Unless you'd like to join me next door." This time, his eyes glance toward my left, to the door that he mentioned leads to his bedroom.

"Can I ask you one thing before I go?" I don't know why I'm still standing here, but my feet don't move. He lifts a hand, signaling for me to continue. "What happened to you to make you like this?" My question is also an answer. When I was trying to decide what I'd like to study, I never really knew where my passion lies. But it's in this moment, with Creed, that I realize what I'd like to major in. It may seem silly, but for the longest time I thought I should go with a *safe bet* like marketing or business, but as I study the man before me, I ponder people's actions because I'm curious as to why they do certain things. Like the satisfaction in Creed's gaze when he notices my nervous energy and fearful stance.

Even my own addiction to a blade comes to mind. I cut myself to ease the anxiety that twists inside me. To allow the emotions I can't voice to flow from me, to release me from the bindings of things that most people can easily talk about. I have never truly thought about the why, but watching Creed, I realize I need to know.

"Because I learned from a very young age that life

doesn't always give you what you want and need. That people will lie to your face, and when you turn your back, they'll stick the knife in so deep, that while you're writhing in pain, they'll twist it until you're nothing more than a broken mess. I vowed never to be that broken person again."

I regard him for a long while as I soak in his admission, knowing I shouldn't ask my next question, but also realizing he won't hurt me; not here and now, "So, you turned into a monster?"

Creed pushes to his feet, but he doesn't come near me. Thankfully, because I'm still trembling from our encounter. He offers a small smile before he shakes his head. Then he tells me, "I turned into the one holding the knife."

He takes a step toward me, which has me retreating. But the more I move, so does he, until my back hits the cool glass. Creed's hands cup my face, his thumbs resting on my cheeks, the heat of him searing me.

He is good looking, rugged, brutal, with ink on his hands and peeking out from the collar of his shirt, but he's not Damien. I want to scream, but when my mouth opens, his lips steal the sound, and he kisses me deeply.

The whoosh of the other door has Creed breaking our connection, and I turn to lock my gaze on blue eyes so volatile, I feel faint.

Nesrin

I WATCH HIM KISS HER THROUGH A CLOUD OF RAGE. I know I shouldn't be jealous because she wants me, but I can't stop the toxic emotion from racing like a poison through my veins.

My body moves, and without thinking, my fist connects with Creed's face before I have time to think. Nesrin's squeak of surprise bounces off the walls, but I don't even look at her.

"I told you, I will start a fucking war, Creed," I inform him. Anger takes hold of me, and I'm on him again, my hands slamming into his chest, his face, but he doesn't fight back.

"Damien," Nesrin calls to me, but her voice seems so

far away, as if she's on the other end of a tunnel, and I just can't get to her. "Damien stop." Her words break through the cloud surrounding me, her hand on my shoulder stills me for a moment.

Looking at my former best friend, I realize he's smiling. Blood drips from his lip and nose, and his left eye is already starting to swell. I told him not to come near her, but he didn't listen. He brought this on himself.

His gaze lands on Nesrin who's behind me, and I want to wipe the bloody smirk off his face. "I told you, Darling," he says. "We may not be the same in our needs, but our wants, they're exactly alike. The violence that simmers in this town runs in all of us."

"Get the fuck out of here." I grit out through clenched teeth, as I attempt to tamp down my anger. This is ridiculous. I don't *want* to fight, but he knows I'll do it if I'm pushed into a corner.

Creed tips his head, before retreating through the door that leads to his bedroom. We used to sneak in through there when we were younger, listening to his father when he had meetings in the library. It was our way of rebelling. Stupidly spying on the men of Thorne Haven, learning the secrets that run this town.

When we're alone, I turn to Nesrin, pulling her into my arms and holding her there. Like an animal, I want to bathe her in my scent, to mark her as mine. But after the spat with Creed, he now knows not to come near her again. He was testing me, seeing if I'd fight for her, and I did. And I'll do it again and again.

"Let's go," I pull her along, my fingers laced with hers. She doesn't fight me all the way to the car, as people stare at her holding the rose that I gave her. The gossiping will start the moment we're in the vehicle. Even as we drive home, Nesrin is silent, and I want to ask what Creed told her, but I don't.

I have a feeling I already know. By the time we reach the house, the tension in my muscles has eased, and I take Nesrin's hand, leading her up the stairs to the second floor, then down a small corridor that leads to the staircase that will deposit us onto the rooftop. I need her beside me tonight, more than ever. And this is my favorite place in the world.

When we get to the top, I allow her to step onto the landing first. Before us is a king-sized mattress, covered in a basic sheet and comforter, with a few pillows, along with a minibar fridge.

Nesrin stands behind me, as I tug my tie free and unbutton my shirt. She watches me, her eyes wide, as she takes me in. I turn to look at her, my body facing hers, and I reach for her, lifting her against me.

Her legs wrap around my waist, and every nerve in my body sparks to life as if I've been shocked by a live wire.

A buzz skitters through me because, tonight, I'm having her. Claiming her. She's fucking mine.

"I-I... I've never seen you so angry," she whispers, as I lower her onto the mattress. The rooftop was a place of refuge when I was growing up. I loved being up here, away from everyone—even my brothers.

"Having his hands on you, his mouth on yours, it made me crazy. I saw red." I settle beside her, needing her warmth and aching for her touch. Nesrin rolls over onto her side. Her eyes rake over me, burning every inch of me.

"I told you before, and I'll tell you again, I'm yours." Even though she says it, it didn't stop me from flying into a rage earlier when I saw her with him. She reaches for my face, her touch warming me from the inside out.

"I want to see you," I tell her, rolling onto my back as I crook my finger. With a narrowed gaze, she sits up, kneeling on the bed beside me. "Straddle me." The order is clear, concise. She doesn't argue, and I watch her climb over me as if she's about to ride me, which makes my cock jerk with approval.

"Now what?" she sasses, crossing her arms in front of her chest; she tips her head to the side, but rolls her hips to taunt me.

"Take that dress off." My voice is husky, my body is tense, craving to touch her, but I don't. Not yet. Slowly,

Nesrin reaches for the tie around her neck and unbuttons it. The material slips down her chest, toward her hips. Then, she slowly tugs the zipper down, the hiss of the metal teeth echoes in the night, which causes my blood to run hot through my veins as desire takes over.

I watch in awe, as she pulls the material over her body, and soon, she's only in a pair of panties that covers her pussy. The dress finds the floor, and I lick my lips at the thought of tasting her again. Her nipples are hardened pebbles, taunting me.

"And now?"

"Touch yourself, tug those nipples for me." A groan rumbles in my chest when she wiggles her ass on my crotch. Her hands move tentatively. I can see her tremble. Even though she squares her shoulders, attempting to show confidence, I can tell she's nervous. Her eyes dart between my mouth and my eyes.

"I'm…"

"Look at me," I command. "We're alone up here. And you're making me so fucking hard, I can't think straight. Just seeing your beautiful body has my muscles tense." Her eyes widen, shock dancing in those golden orbs. "In a very good way."

"It's new to me. Having someone watch me," she admits what I read in her demeanor. Nervous energy emanates from her with every shiver that passes through her frame.

"That's okay," I tell her, hoping to sound calm and not like a raging beast craving to devour her whole. I take her hands, guiding her fingers slowly up her sides, teasing a path to her tits. They're just over a handful, her nipples are a light brown, with pebbled buds that are calling to me to suck on. "Close your eyes and imagine you're alone. That you're in bed, and I'm not even here."

A slight nod is all I get, and she obeys. Her lashes flutter onto her cheeks, and she focuses on the task at hand. A soft moan falls from her lips as she tweaks them. Tugging gently, she whimpers when I grip her hips to keep her from moving on me. My cock is aching, and for a moment, I'm second-guessing this particular game.

I watch her for a long moment. She truly is spectacular. "If you keep that up, I'm going to make it hurt more than I already plan to," I warn. My jaw ticking as my teeth grind together in an attempt to calm down. But she only smiles, finding her rhythm, lost in the pleasure she's bestowing on herself, as well as me.

Another dick-jolting sigh comes from her plump lips as she taunts me with her heat flush against my crotch. Reaching up, I allow my fingertips to trail over the smooth, caramel skin of her chest, down between her breasts, and over her flat stomach. The panties she's wearing are tight against her mound, and the heat of her is searing on my crotch.

I lift her up, moving us, so I can stand. With my gaze locked on hers, I watch her expression change, as she takes in my body when I shrug out of my unbuttoned shirt, then my slacks. Soon, I'm standing before her in only my boxer briefs.

I take my place on the bed again, before gently tugging on the waistband of her panties, pulling it down, just so I can see the smoothness of her body before I find the small dark strip of hair.

Lying back, I pull her over me again. I love watching her in control above me. Glancing up, I take in her expression. Her eyes are closed, as she toys with her tits.

"Look at me now," I order from below her. Those golden eyes snap open, locking on my blue ones. "I want to see you, and I need you to see me." I slip a hand between us and find her smooth lips.

The slickness of her arousal coats my middle finger when I tease her clit, circling it slowly. I revel in the shiver that takes hold of her when I tease her opening, before dipping a finger into her tight heat.

"Oh god," Nesrin mumbles into the night sky. The stars twinkle above us, as she sits astride me, her body beautiful under the silver moonlight.

"That's my girl," I murmur. "Take your pleasure." My words filter up to her with every gentle stroke of my fingers, in and out. Her body pulses around the two digits I have inside her.

Her thighs shake as her hips start moving faster and faster. I want so much for her to come right now, but the need to be inside her has me at boiling point.

"Stop." I pull my fingers from her panties, causing a mewl of frustration to tumble from her lips. Her eyes are on mine, shimmering with desire and need.

"Why?" Nesrin whines, and I can't help smiling at her frustration. I shouldn't love it so much, but my control over her is intoxicating.

"Because when you do come, it will be on my cock," I tell her, before reaching up to her tits, my fingers twisting her nipples, tugging them harshly and causing her to whimper. Her hips move. Her pussy rubbing against my thick erection earns her a growl of pleasure that vibrates in my chest. "Behave yourself," I bite out, allowing my left hand to trail up to her neck.

My fingers wrap around the column of her throat, keeping her tit in my right hand. I squeeze her neck, stealing her breath for a moment, and I watch in the dim light how her eyes shine with challenge.

"Take my cock out." My voice is unrecognizable. Her hands move to my boxer briefs, and she slowly taunts the tip of my shaft, as she tugs the material to my thighs. I keep a hold of her neck, as her palm warms my throbbing shaft.

"Damien."

"Stroke me," I order, lost, as pleasure sparks in my veins. Every inch of my body feels like it's alight with flames licking my skin with every movement.

Nesrin's hand moves from base to tip, over and over again, her thumb snaking over the slick blunt head, using my arousal, as she jerks me off.

"Jesus."

"It's just me," she sasses, causing me to look into those golden eyes shining down at me. I pull her closer by her neck until her mouth is inches from mine.

"Suck me."

I release my hold on her and watch as she slides down my body until she's kneeling between my splayed thighs. Her mouth engulfs me easily, forcing a groan of animalistic need to rumble through me.

Nesrin licks and laves at me as if I were her favorite fucking lollipop, and I don't think I can be more turned on than I am right now. She sucks me into her mouth. Even though it's a tentative movement, the sparkle in her eyes has me wondering if my wild rose is enjoying herself.

Her throat closes around the tip of my cock, as I watch her take me deeper with every swallow. My orgasm nears, pushing me closer to the edge before I pull her off.

"Time for me to have some fun," I tell her, as I flip us over. I'm on top of her in seconds. My mouth trailing soft kisses over her mouth, cheeks, and down her neck. I move to her nipples, pulling each one between my lips, grazing my teeth around the hardened buds.

"Oh god, Damien, please," she pleads, her fingers tangling in my hair, but I'm not done yet. I kiss my way down her smooth stomach until I reach her mound, which I bypass, much to her annoyance. Instead, I push her thighs open, pressing gentle kisses to the scars that adorn her flesh.

"These are beautiful, they speak of pain," I tell her, as I worship her body, just like I've been wanting to since I first saw her. "But they also scream of survival." My mouth finds each small scar. My fingers trail over them, feeling the small ridges, knowing that even in her pain, even in her heartache, she's perfect in every way.

Glancing up from between her thighs, I meet her stare and smile, before my mouth lands on her pussy and my tongue darts between her slick folds. Her taste is like a drug. Like pure fucking heroin shot right into my veins.

I use my thumbs to open her to my gaze before I feast on her pussy. Glistening and wet, she's writhing with every kiss and suck. My tongue dips into her, deep inside the tightness that my cock is throbbing to enter.

"Damien, please, I'm so close," Nesrin pleads with me,

and I glance up to find her needy gaze on mine.

I shake my head and move up her body until our faces are inches apart. I reach to the floor, finding my slacks and pulling out my wallet. The foil wrapper is torn, and I'm sheathed without another word.

I nestle between her thighs, my cock nudging her entrance. The heat from her is taunting me, and I can't think about anything other than feeling her.

"It's..." Nesrin's gaze locks on mine, and I have a feeling I know what she's going to say. But I wait for it. "It's my first time."

"I'll be gentle," I promise something I'm not sure I can keep. She nods, and I inch myself into her tightness. The heat sears me, causing my eyes to roll back in my head.

"Oh," her whimper seems to echo through me. With every nudge of my hips, her nails dig farther into my shoulders. Her slickness accepting me, but her tightness practically choking me. I still for a moment, as soon as I hit the barrier of her innocence. "Move, Damien. Just do it," Nesrin grits, through clenched teeth. And I obey her. My hips thrust, my cock sinks into her, breaking through, claiming her as mine.

Nesrin's body arches into mine, her tits against my chest, her nipples hard, her mouth parted on a moan, as her head falls back. Leaning in, my mouth captures her neck, sucking the smooth flesh, tasting her as if I'm starved, and she's my only sustenance.

I've never been with a virgin before. I've never taken purity from a girl, but with Nesrin, it feels as if I was meant to. Her legs wrap around my waist, and her gaze snaps to mine.

"Fuck me," she pleads, before lifting herself against me, taking me without my permission. I can't help but smile at her strength and bravery, at her claiming me, instead of the other way around.

Pulling out, I watch her face, as I sink back in, thrusting deep. My hips move quickly. With Nesrin's soft sighs taking precedence over my desire, I watch, as she winces, each time I slide into her. But she doesn't ask me to stop; instead, she digs her nails in and pulls me closer. Her lips part, her eyes lock on mine, and a slow smile curves on her face.

"You're beautiful," I tell her, honestly. My voice is husky. The words are raw with emotion that wrap themselves around my throat, tightening with each movement.

"I've wanted this since I first saw you," she whispers, as our bodies move. Even though I can see she's still in pain with every movement, she allows me to fuck her harshly.

I reach between us, circling her clit, teasing her with my fingers. Her body pulses around mine. I'm sure she won't find her release since it's her first time, but I slow my movements with every taunt of my thumb.

"Fuck, Damien," she begs when I pinch the hardened nub between my fingers. Her body clamps down on my shaft, sucking me into her heat.

"I can't hold out."

"Come," she orders me, but I don't think she realizes just what she's saying. "I want you. I want all of you."

I pull out suddenly, sitting back on my heels, I jerk the condom from my dick and fist myself. Nesrin's eyes widen at my movements before she locks her gaze on my cock. I stroke my shaft, back and forth—once, twice—on the third stroke, I shoot my release over her mound, coating her stomach and thighs.

I wanted to come inside her. To find pleasure in her body, but I couldn't do it when she was in pain. It's going to take her time to get used to my size, and I'll gladly practice with her every day until she finds her own release when I'm inside her.

But, for now, that was everything I ever wanted and more. Looking up, I stare at her expression, trying to make out what she's feeling, but Nesrin hides her emotions right when I need to read her.

"I'm sticky," she mumbles, gently swiping my arousal from her stomach, and doing something that only makes my cock jolt in appreciation. She presses her wet fingers to her tongue and licks my seed from both digits.

"Fuck."

"I like the taste of you," she whispers, with a shy smile on her face.

"I like watching you taste me," I tell her, with a grin that's not normally something I offer anyone. I haven't felt happy or at peace for a long time. Years have come and passed, and the heartbreak of seeing my family fall apart stole my teenage years from me. But as I settle beside Nesrin, pulling the comforter over us, I watch her nestle in the crook of my arm, and I'm not sure I can ever let her go now.

My father won't be happy. I know he'll lose his shit the moment he gets back, and I tell him what my plans are, but he'll have to live with it because she's mine.

And after tonight, I'm never letting her go.

"Thank you," Nesrin says softly, dragging me from the thoughts that have taken hold of me. "I like this."

"I told you, wild rose, you're mine." I want to tell her more, something so much more than just the words I've uttered previously, but it's not the right time. "Thank you for waiting for me."

She giggles, the sound melodic and heartwarming. "I didn't wait for you," she tells me confidently. "I was waiting for the right man."

"Are you trying to tell me I'm not the right man?"

Nesrin rolls her eyes in indignation, but the smile on her face makes everything right. I know we're meant to be. I can see it in the way we find our happiness with each other. She silences my demons when she needs to, but she also plays with them when they seek her out.

"Can I sleep now?" she sasses me. "Tomorrow is going to be a long day." She's right. I nod, pulling her into me, as we settle on the bed and look up at the stars. They twinkle down at us, reminding me just how insignificant we are. But our folks arrive home in a couple of days, so I need to make the most of the time I have with her before they return.

In the darkness, we find solace. She's my ocean—deep and endless—and I want to drown in her. Nothing compares to being beside her. And I know if she walks away, I'll break.

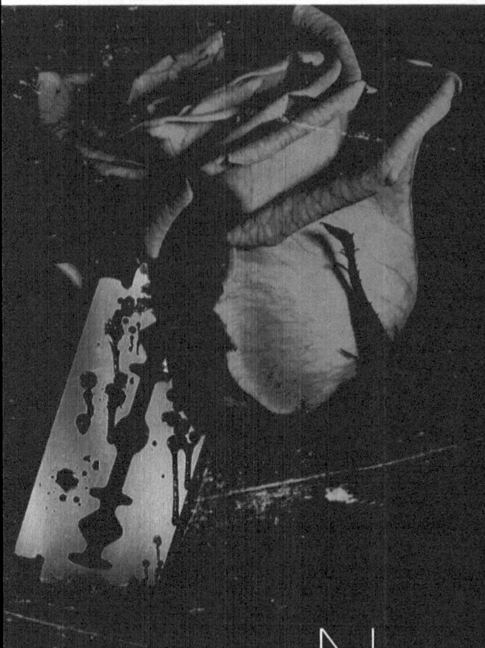

Nesrin

WHEN I ROLL OVER, I FIND MYSELF IN MY OWN BED. Last night, I distinctly remember falling asleep beside Damien on the roof. The discomfort between my thighs is no longer the cause of my stupidity from using a blade, but because I've leaped over the edge from girl to woman. I was honest with Damien last night; I never once found someone I wanted to give that part of me to. Yes, I almost lost it, almost gave it away to someone who didn't matter, but when he walked out with disgust on his face, I knew I needed my first time to be special.

And it was.

Reaching for the pillow beside me, I pull it to my nose

and inhale. Damien's cologne still saturates the material, and I enjoy it for a short while, before my door swings open.

"You're awake," Damien says, drawing my attention to him. Last night was filled with strange occurrences. My aunt disappeared after the hide and seek game, and I asked Damien if I could talk to her. He promised today would be the day, but when he settles on the bed, he offers me a guilty smile.

"What's wrong?" I ask, before scooting up in bed. My back is flush with the headboard, and I tug the sheet to cover my naked body.

Blue eyes drink me in slowly as if he's attempting to caress me with merely a glance.

"My father just called," he says, "they're arriving back tonight."

"What?" Shock laces my tone as my heartbeat kicks into overdrive. They can't be back so soon. I have so many questions for my aunt before my mother returns. "They... I need to speak to Mallory before my mother gets here."

Damien nods. "I know. I called, and she said we can come by today. I was going to come and wake you, so you can put some clothes on."

"Is that it?" I quip, as my chest tightens. After last night, I thought he'd be more affectionate. But Damien is cold this morning, different in the light of day.

He pushes to his feet, his eyes narrowing on me, and I'm sure he's going to walk out, but he turns to face me fully, pulling something from his back pocket.

"That wasn't it," he tells me, with an arch in his dark brow. "I want you to wear this." He hands me a small box. Without thinking, I shift toward him, causing the comforter to fall from my grip and those deep blue depths darken with need. "You're going to have to behave while our folks are around."

"Oh?" I take the box, flicking it open, ignoring his desire-filled stare on my naked breasts. "Damien." His name is a whisper that tumbles from my lips. "This is exquisite."

The thin golden choker has a rose hanging off it. But the gemstone in the center is a deep blue.

"Nothing can be as devastatingly beautiful as you are," he responds in a low murmur. "Let me put it on." I watch his slender fingers lift the delicate necklace from its velvet cushion. Within seconds, it's unclasped, and I'm kneeling before him with my hair pinned up. Once the cool pendant touches my skin, I can't stop the shiver that trickles through me.

His lips find my neck, pressing a heated kiss to the skin, leaving goosebumps in the wake of his warmth. "When they get back," Damien whispers. "We need to be careful. You're mine, always and forever, and I need you not to doubt me."

Twisting on the bed, I look up at him. His hands reach for my shoulders, massaging them gently, as he lowers his touch to my nipples, which peak at the feather-light whisper of his fingertips.

"Because we're forbidden," I say, my gaze locked on his.

"Yes. But I want to talk with my father," he tells me. "If he can understand my feelings, perhaps he'll allow me to make my own choices."

"What about me?"

"I'm not walking away from you. I'm not leaving here without you," he affirms. "When I get on that plane to London, you'll be by my side."

"As your sister."

"As my girlfriend," Damien says, shocking me silent. "Last night wasn't just sex for me, Nesrin. I haven't felt connected to anyone before. I've always been alone, not physically, but mentally, emotionally."

"And now?" I ask, unsure of where he's going. Even though Damien's given me strength in ways I have never imagined one person could do for another, I'm still scared. He could have any girl out there.

"Now," Damien whispers, as his hand reaches for my face, holding it gently, while his thumb swipes over my lips. His gaze burns with desire, regarding me thoughtfully. "Now I'm lost in you."

"And if our parents fight us on this?" It's a question I've been wanting to ask for days, since the first time he kissed me. Even though I didn't think it would go this far, I know I can't go back now. And I'm sure he can't either.

"We will have to cross that bridge when we come to it," he tells me. "Right now, I need you to get dressed. Mallory wants to see us before the folks get back." Damien settles on my bed, lying back, with his hands crossed behind his head.

"What are you doing?"

"Watching you get dressed," he informs me as if it's the most natural thing for him to do. "Once they're back, our time together will be limited. And I'm not passing up the chance to see your beautiful body naked, as you put your clothes on."

"And what makes you think I'd be willing to let you watch me get dressed?" I sass him as I cross my arms over my chest.

The hungry gaze of the predator burns me, as he takes in my body. "Because you enjoy taunting me, and you can't deny it, because I know the moment I look at you like this," he waves his hand toward his expression, "that pretty pussy gets soaking wet."

Rolling my eyes, I point at the door. "If you're not going to be quiet, then you can leave." A chuckle rumbles in his chest and the smirk he offers me does things to me, but we need to leave. I turn to focus on my clothing choices, instead of Damien's hungry stare.

I grab a pair of baby pink tights, along with my denim skirt. A long-sleeved top that matches the color of my leggings, and some underwear, which I hide from Damien's gaze.

I rush into the bathroom to get ready. After a quick shower, I moisturize my skin, taking extra care of the scars with some tissue oil, which has helped keep the redness at bay. When I first started doing it, I had spent time researching how to hide my mistakes. I never had anyone to talk to.

Now I wonder if Damien would be someone who I could confide in. He's made it clear he wants me, especially after last night. Also, he accepted me for who I am, what I've done. He didn't see my scars as me being a freak, like Xavier did.

Damien saw my inner turmoil, and he cared for me. He took me gently, giving me the affection I've craved for so long. But it's not only the physical part of it, it's the emotional freedom he's offered.

By the time I reach the bedroom again, Damien is standing at the window, looking out over the garden. He turns his head, his eyes sweeping over me appreciatively, as he takes in my outfit.

"Cute," he says, with the corner of his mouth ticking

up. "Like the pink on you, makes you look sweet and innocent."

"I *am* sweet and innocent," I bite out, causing him to chuckle at my retort. But all he does is shake his head in response. "Can we go?" I pick up my purse and spin on my heel, heading for the door.

Damien

Тhe drive to the Haven manor is silent. I'm not sure why I'm nervous, but I am. Although my mind is on my mother returning from her month-long honeymoon, my fear is that Damien is going to break things off.

The anxiety is winding in my stomach, and my breath comes out in short spurts as I try to calm myself. It's at times like this, I feel young. Like a stupid teenager with a crush on a man far too old for her.

He kills the engine, then turns to me. "Hey." Damien takes my hand, brings it to his lips, and presses a kiss to my knuckles. "It's all going to work out," he tells me, and as much as I want to believe him, I'm still fearful.

Nodding, I offer him a weak smile, and we both exit his Camaro. He doesn't take my hand as we walk up to the door, and I know he's trying to play the big brother role.

The moment it swings open, we're met with the maid who gives us a smile and steps aside to allow us in.

"There's my girl," Mallory coos, as she glides through the entrance foyer from where the kitchen and back of the house are hidden. Dressed in a long, flowery gown, I can't help but wonder who this woman is.

Most of my life, she's been the only person I could talk to when she was around. Flakey at best, my aunt wasn't always responsible, and I know that's why mom and her would fight non-stop when she visited.

"Mallory," I respond, as she pulls me into her arms. The scent of her perfume invades my senses. She's like a stranger to me. I don't know why on earth she'd be so different to how she normally is, but it's clear that living in a castle has taken hold of her and changed her.

"Come, let's sit down and catch up." She lifts her gaze behind me. "You too, Damien. It's nice to have you here."

We follow her through the house, and I notice just how different it looks in the light of day. When I was last here, it felt eerie, haunted, but now that the sun is streaming through, it's exquisite.

Seating ourselves in the dining room, I settle beside

Damien, as Mallory sits opposite us. She's had coffee put out as well as a plate with sweet treats, which I really want to try, but I don't reach for them; instead, I focus on her.

"Why didn't you tell me about this? When you were at the reception."

My question stills her, for a moment, before she waves her hand in the air as if it's nothing. "I didn't want to upstage your mother's perfect day." Guilt flashes in her gaze, but it's gone within a second, and I'm left more confused than ever.

"But you could have called. This is big news. And it's exciting." I try to sound light-hearted, but there's a hint of heartbreak in my voice when I speak.

She's been the one woman who's always given me every ounce of respect, treating me like an equal. But for her not to share something, as major as this, hurts.

"Listen to me, Poppet," she says, but she doesn't look me in the eye. "There are so many things that I've tried to live with, but your mother's judgement, over the years, has made me wary of sharing anything with her. Or you."

"I would never—"

"I know. I didn't mean you would judge me. We've been so close, but... I just needed something for me." This time, she does meet my gaze, and I notice the tears that shimmer in those familiar eyes. "You'll understand when you fall in love," she tells me, sweeping her gaze over Damien, for an instant, before looking back at me. "Anyway. Tell me how you're loving Thorne Haven. And let's have some coffee." The serious part of the conversation is over. And I know I'm not going to get anything more out of her now.

So, instead of pushing like my mother would, I smile and nod.

An hour later, we're back home, and I'm still not confident that Mallory was being honest about her living here, or even why she didn't feel the need to tell me.

Her excuse was weak. But the thought of what's going to happen tonight has my mind playing out scenarios that aren't helping my anxiety. My focus is on Damien, the moment we walk into the house. In the entrance foyer, we spy suitcases, shopping bags, and shoes, which seem to have been thrown haphazardly on the expensive marble tiles.

"Looks like they're back," Damien says, before pulling me back out onto the porch. "I need to do this before we go in there." Seconds later, his lips are on mine. Heated and hungry, he kisses me, swiping his tongue along mine, as his hands hold my face gently.

My body eases, as the tension melts away into the kiss. But it ends too soon, and I know we're going to have to face the music.

"Promise me something," I say, as we step inside once more.

"Anything."

"Don't leave me." The words are choked out, emotion dripping from them. Fear that he will break up with me, even though we're not officially together. We haven't spoken about it, but I feel as if I'm ready. I want this with him.

I just hope he wants it, too.

"Not a chance, wild rose, not a fucking chance."

"Damien," Bradford saunters in from the kitchen. "I'd like to talk to you in my office. Meet me there. Hello, Nesrin. I hope you're enjoying your time here." He seems aloof, different from what he was like at the reception dinner.

"Thank you, yes, it's a beautiful home you have." He nods at my assessment, before turning and leaving us in the entrance foyer.

"I better go see what the old man wants." Damien glances my way before saying, "I'm yours." And then he's gone.

I'm not sure where my mother is, but for now, I head to my bedroom to hide away from the judgment she'll offer me, the moment she lays eyes on me.

Just a few more moments before I have to deal with it.

That's all I need.

Nesrin

MY FATHER SITS BEHIND HIS DESK, LOOKING formidable. I know he's not going to be happy with what I have to say, so when I enter the room, I offer him a swift nod. Friendliness is reserved for others. Between Bradford and me, there's only cold aloofness that has no bearing on familial affection.

"Father."

"What is it, Damien?" he asks, sitting back in his chair to regard me. His fingers steeple, his gaze locked on mine, as I settle in the chair facing his desk. I have a feeling he already knows, but he wants me to utter the words, so he can shoot me down.

My father has always enjoyed breaking people's spirit.

Whether they're employees or family. He did it to my mother, and he's done it to all three of his sons. I wonder just how long it's going to take for him to do it to his new wife.

"I wanted to speak to you about London." Crossing my left ankle over my right knee, I ensure my posture is calm and relaxed, not wound tight like a spring that's about to snap.

One thing about my father is that he's tenacious when it comes to business, to negotiations, and if he saw an inkling of nervous energy in me, he'd shut this thing down. I promised Nesrin I wouldn't hurt her, but with Bradford Thorne, promises can't always be kept.

"What about it?"

"I'd like Nesrin to accompany me." Keeping my expression schooled, my voice calm, I meet his stare dead on. Deep down, I pray that he doesn't see how much she means to me because if he did, he'd deny my request.

"Why? She's got a good school the next town over, she will have Finn and Cassian here, if she needs them," he speaks. "And her mother and I are here." His words make no sense because I know Nesrin mentioned her mother said that Oxford was an option.

"Oxford would be a much better option for her." His eyes, which match mine, fill with sinister intent. I've watched my father break down his opponents in the boardroom countless times, without batting an eyelash, and now, I'm the person he's fighting against.

"Is there something you're not telling me, Son?" he asks, his dark brow arching, as he regards me. The man is nearing fifty-six, and yet, he still looks like he's in his forties.

"What could I be hiding?" I challenge him, painting a smirk on my face. The shrewd glare he's taught me since I was fourteen is what I offer him in return.

"I've spoken to Marcia, and she's agreed that, perhaps, Nesrin and Creed should attend the year-end ball together," he expresses suddenly. The words turn my blood cold with shock but heat my chest with jealousy.

"No."

Tilting his head to the side with mirth pasted over his expression, he asks, "Are you refusing me?"

"Yes. I am. She's not to go near Creed or any of the Havens."

"I'm the man of this house and what I say goes. I've spoken to Mallory and Octavius Haven. They're setting up a date for the two of them for this weekend. You'll be gone by then. Didn't you tell me you wanted to leave as soon as possible?" And there it is, the challenge. My father knows more than I've told him, more than he's letting on because he would never ask me that otherwise.

"I do. And I think in Nesrin's best interest, she should

leave with me." I push up from the chair and make my way over to Dad's liquor cabinet. Grabbing a tumbler, I pour a generous shot of bourbon. The amber liquid shimmers in the dim light of his office. The alcohol swills around the edge of the crystal, before I swallow it down in one gulp. The burn helps my focus. He's not going to relent until I tell him I want her.

"Damien, I've known you all your life. You can't lie to me and expect me to relinquish anything in your care."

"Why? Because everything I touch turns to shit?" I bite out, but I don't look at him. For years, my father blamed my teenage rage, as the reason my mother walked out, but he never looked in the mirror when he needed a reason.

"Because she's your sister."

Spinning on my heel, I pin him with a stare. "And?" My free hand fists at my side, but I know he can't see it. The tension in my shoulders has hardened, twisting my muscles tight. If he thinks I'm letting her go, he's sorely mistaken, because I will steal her from this house if I have to.

"I'll make you a deal," he tells me earnestly. Those blue eyes that remind me of mine hold more malice than mine ever could. I never trusted his deals; I've seen how he controlled those around him, using his power of influence. Perhaps that's where I learned it from.

"I was taught never to make a deal with the devil," I tell him, the biting words causing him to flinch, but it's the only reaction I get. It's miniscule, but I saw it.

"Are there feelings involved?" he asks suddenly. "Because she's your sister and I doubt anyone in this town would approve."

"You're more concerned with the approval of others than you are of your own family," I tell him. "Nesrin is mine." My admittance causes a sly grin to spread across his face. My father is nothing more than a bully, but I'm a grown man, and if I want something, I'll take it. "If I take your deal, I lose her. I'm not accepting that because, for the first time in my life, I want what makes me happy."

His response comes out resolute and firm. "She'll go to Creed this weekend. You'll leave for London as per our agreement, and she'll join you if she so chooses, after the ball. That's the only way I'll agree to it. If you fight me, you'll lose your place at Thorne Corporation, you'll lose everything, including her, I'll make sure of it." He rises in one fluid motion, stalking toward me, and picking up a tumbler to fill it with vodka. I watch him swallow back the alcohol in one gulp.

"She's not someone I'd trust Creed with."

"I thought you were best friends," my father says, and it just shows how long ago he's taken note of my life. I haven't been friends with Creed for such a long time.

"He's not someone I consider a friend. You do realize she's his cousin," I tell my father.

"And you do realize she's your sister."

"Stepsister, she's not related to me by blood." Even though I insist, he merely chuckles at me. It's stupid to fight this with him, since Creed and Nesrin are as far away from being family as she and I are, more so, since her mother is married to my father.

"Agree?" Dad says, lifting his glass, he waits for me to clink mine to the rim of his. I don't want to agree to this but it's, ultimately, up to Nesrin, and if she's learned anything from me, it's that Creed is not trustworthy.

"Fine. But you'll be the one to tell her," I inform him, before swallowing my drink and setting the glass down. By the time I leave his office, I'm angry and frustrated.

When I reach my bedroom door, I hear hers whoosh open behind me, but I don't turn to look at her. The scent of her perfume invades my senses.

"Hey," she greets me, her hand landing on my shoulder.

"My father wants to see you in his office. I need to pack," I tell her, without meeting her curious gaze, which is currently burning a hole in my back.

"What? Why? Are we leaving?"

"I'm leaving," I tell her. I have to give her a fair chance to decide. If I do say anything to her now, she'll only find a reason to deny my father's request to go on a date with

Creed. And if that happens, everyone will know about us, everyone who can shape our lives in ways I'd rather not think about.

Dad was right, this town has its beliefs, its secrets. And if they don't want something to take place, it won't. Nesrin and I are forbidden.

"Damien," her voice breaks on my name, and I close my eyes. "Please." Her plea almost breaks me. But I know my father will hurt us much more if I swayed her decision.

"I need you to trust me, Nesrin. He needs to speak with you. I suggest you go now before he loses patience." I push open the door and step inside my bedroom. And it's only when I turn to shut it, do I look into her eyes. With a silent plea, I close myself inside, leaving her outside.

Nesrin

WHEN I STEP INTO THE OFFICE, I FIND MY MOTHER and Bradford perched on the old brown leather sofa and chatting. The room is dark, but the yellow light from each of the lamps that sit on either side of his desk illuminate the space dimly.

"Damien said you wanted to see me," I tell Bradford. I haven't had a chance to talk to my mother since she got back from her honeymoon. After my conversation with my aunt, I need answers from the woman who I believe lied to me my whole life.

"Please sit," Bradford offers, gesturing with his hand to the armchair that matches the brown leather of the sofa. When I seat myself, the material of the chair creaks under my frame.

Both adults stare at me, and my heart kicks in my chest painfully. My mother sits back, submissively silent, as she twists her hands in her lap. It's Bradford who takes the lead and speaks. "I've been talking to your mother, and I've also spoken to Mallory, we believe it would be lovely to have a joining of Thorne and Haven families, and since we've agreed, I've set up a date with Creed and yourself."

What?

"No." The word is out of my mouth before I have time to think about it. They clearly don't know about Damien and me, and I'd like to keep it that way, but I'm most certainly not dating Creed Haven.

"I can't."

"Why?" Bradford's expression gives away more than he's letting on. *He knows.* "Because as far as I see it, you're our daughter, and if we'd like for you to join with the other powerful family in this town, to create a union worthy of royalty, I would think you'd jump at the chance."

He's toying with me. *Did he do this to Damien as well?* If he did, he'd have forced Damien to admit to something that I'd rather not think about—our relationship. If I can even call it that.

"What if Creed and I don't get along?" I ask, looking at my mother who's been silent all this time. "Is this something you agree with?" Even as I ask it, I recognize the flit of annoyance in her eyes at me.

"Damien is leaving tomorrow morning, you'll need to find your own way," Bradford tells me, in a tone that confirms he knows exactly what his son and I have been up to. If Damien didn't tell him, then he's obviously had eyes on us. And I have a feeling those eyes came in the form of Creed Haven.

"I'm capable of looking after myself," I bite out in frustration. "I've been doing it for most of my life." The moment the words are out of my mouth, I want to swallow them back and shrink into the darkness. I never meant to hurt my mother, but I know I have.

"You're just like your aunt," my mother finally speaks up. "Did she tell you about us? The family?"

"What?"

My mother pushes from the sofa and makes her way to a cabinet filled with bottles of alcohol. I watch her pour herself a shot of something, which she swallows back and refills her glass, before turning to regard me. I've watched her for so long that seeing her like this doesn't shock me. Not anymore.

"There are things you need to know about your father," my mother says, before swallowing the amber liquid like a shot and once more, she fills up the tumbler and waves it in the air. "I spent my life loving a man who treated me like shit." Her voice is filled with venom at her admission.

I know my parents didn't have the easiest marriage. I also know how painful it was for my mother when dad walked out, but I never knew why he left. And I didn't ever ask because the rage that fueled my mother, after he'd gone, scared me.

My stomach knots when she looks at me. Something's coming; I can feel it in my gut. I swallow back the tears that threaten to spill, and the moment she nears me, I know I'm going to break when my mother's secrets reveal themselves.

"Mallory, your favorite aunt," Mom spits the word as if it leaves a bad taste on her tongue, "Fucked your father. She then came to me in tears, begging forgiveness when she found out she was pregnant."

The sneer on my mother's face is clear. Her anger and hate for Mallory, her own sister, runs deep in her veins. I doubt they'll ever find common ground. My aunt had never mentioned she was pregnant, or even that she had a baby.

"What happened?"

My mother's gaze snaps to mine. "She had the baby. The child who she bore after her affair with my husband." Those familiar eyes glimmer with unrestrained rage. I've seen my mother in all sorts of moods, but this is new. There's something darker in her stare, and a cold shiver trickles down my spine, running from my neck all the way down to my tailbone. As if warning me that I don't want to hear what she has to say.

But I do.

As much as I wanted the truth, the answer, I'm not prepared for the words that tumble from her lips next. "She's the girl I raised as my own."

Her words sink in, permeating through me, but they don't make sense. Nothing about this makes sense. I watch my mother, who's smiling down at me with some sort of satisfaction. It's not affection, not motherly love, just coldness that I've become so accustomed to from her.

I spent my life wanting to hide in the shadows, in her shadow. And now that she's just muttered eight words that have my mind spinning out of control, I don't know why I'm even here.

"I don't understand." My voice is barely a whisper, drenched in pain and heartbreak. It feels as if the world is spinning too fast, and nothing makes sense.

"When she had the baby, you, she asked me to take care of you. Her fear of being shunned because she wasn't married had her begging for my help." Mother sips her drink, watching my reaction with glee. *How could someone be so malicious?* She's enjoying the pain etched on my face, reveling in just how much the agony I'm feeling is tearing at my chest.

The need to slice open my skin leaps into my mind. A craving to cut myself is at the forefront of my thoughts as it twists and turns, gnawing at me. I want so badly to release the pain in my chest, and I know I can do it with a single incision. My fingers tremble, and my breath is non-existent, as my lungs struggle to pull in air.

My emotions are once more collected inside my gut, where I can't find the words to voice them. Anxiety is back, clawing at me, reminding me of why that box in my bathroom is still there. It's as if it's calling to me.

The woman before me turns blurry, and I fight to keep my tears at bay, but I'm not strong. Not in this moment. When I blink, a single tear trickles down my cheek, but I don't swipe it away.

"I took you in, raised you with your father, before he decided to walk out." Her words are cool, as if she's detached herself from me, from my dad, and I understand she's been broken by him, but I'm innocent. I didn't *ask* for this.

This life I knew, that I believed in, is nothing more than a smokescreen.

"Why didn't you give me back to her?" I croak. My fingers dig into the armrests, as I watch her. "Why didn't Dad take me with him?"

"Things didn't work out like we wanted. Like he

wanted. Now that we're here, and Bradford has been so kind as to allow you to live here, even though you're not mine, I think we should be thankful."

"If that's how you see it, see me, I'll leave," I bite out, as anger surpasses the pain that's cloying at my lungs.

"Now, now," Bradford speaks up. "I think what your mother, uh, aunt is trying to say is that we want you here. Since you're a Thorne, because I would like to adopt you legally, I'd like to ask you to consider our proposal."

"What proposal?" I hate how childlike I sound. I hate that I'm feeling weakened by the news, but I can't stop myself.

"We'd like you and Creed to make a go of it. The year-end ball is coming up, and you can partner with him. In turn, I'll pay for your schooling, study anything you'd like, and when you turn twenty-one, you'll join with a Haven, we will have our first Thorne-Haven wedding."

He looks at me with a smile that confirms what I already knew when I first sat down, when he first told me about this. He knows about Damien and me. It's the only logical reason I can think of that would make him want to break us apart.

"What about Oxford?" I look at Marcia. She was the one who put the idea in my head, and now that it's taken root, I don't want to dismiss it.

"I've spoken to Bradford, and we feel it's best you stay

here," she informs me with a sneer.

"But why offer the option to me to—"

"I am your legal guardian. I can take, and I can give. What I say goes, and I'm informing you that you're to stay here, go to school here."

"I want to go to Oxford!" My voice bounces off the walls, as I push up from the chair. Tension thickens the air in the room, and I know I may have just fucked up everything. If they don't pay for my school, I can't afford it, and Damien is still under his father's thumb.

It feels as if everything is crumbling around me, and there's no way of me keeping it together now. I'm shaking. My body prickles with fear, and my heartbeat bangs loudly in my ears as blood rushes inside my veins. My fingers tremble, and my knees are wobbly. The thought of losing everything I've gained in the past few weeks makes it difficult to swallow.

"I can't do this now. Please." I turn to leave, racing for the door. I can't think straight. My mind is swirling with thoughts of my real mother, of my father.

"Twenty-four hours, Nesrin." Marcia's voice comes from behind me, cool and calm, but the threat in her words hangs heavily on me. I pull open the door and step out into the hallway, only to slam into a body that's hard as steel.

Finn.

"Whoa, little sis," he says with a chuckle, but the moment he really looks at me, noticing the tears making salty tracks down my cheeks, his arms pull me in. "What's going on?" Gently, he pulls me down the hall as we head into the gym where Cass is working out. Damien is nowhere to be found, and I don't know if he knows about my real mother or not but, right now, all I want is to be alone, to find my release from the pain that's collecting in my chest.

When emotions overwhelm me, it's the only thing that helps. But over the past few weeks, Damien has been there. He's been my solace in the dark, and now that he's hiding in his room, preparing to leave me, I don't know how else I'm going to cope.

"What's going on?" Cassian is at my side, and both of them seem to be holding me up, but I can't find the words. "I'll be back." Cassian's out the door, leaving me with Finn, who sits me down on the bench against the wall. He leaves to grab a bottle of water from the small cooler and hands it to me, once he's opened it.

Quietly, I offer a nod of thanks, before pressing it to my lips and taking a long drink. I don't know how to tell them what I've just learned because I can't come to terms with it just yet.

I saw Mallory today, and she said nothing. Even though we spoke for a couple of hours about why she's here, how she met Creed's dad, she never once gave me a reason to doubt this was all a coincidence. But as my mind plays out scenarios, I wonder if the woman who raised me as her own, Marcia, married Bradford for this reason, to one-up her sister, my mother.

"Nesrin?" Damien's voice cuts through the cloud of sadness that's taken hold of me. He's on his knees in front of me, his hands finding mine, holding them to his mouth. Blue eyes peek up at me, regarding me with pain, dancing like flames in the depths.

"I... I need to leave," I tell him, as I consider my options. I can't live here. And I certainly don't want to live in a house with Creed Haven. Even though he's done nothing to me personally, I know that if I have any chance at a life with Damien, I need to make a choice. I don't *have* to go to Oxford, there are other schools in London. I can apply for scholarships.

My grades were always perfect, and I know if I took a chance, I'd be able to get something. I am even willing to work part-time if I need to. Anything to be away from the lies that seep from the veins of the women I believed to be my mother, and my aunt.

"What happened?" Damien asks, and I realize he's been waiting for me to speak for a while. "I need you to talk to me."

I stare at the floor, focusing on the mat that covers the

area where Damien is kneeling. It's soft, smooth, and I try not to think about my world falling apart. But I need to tell him everything. He has a right to know.

"My mother, I mean... Marcia." My voice breaks, but I swallow past the lump in my throat and meet his intense gaze. "She's not my mother." The confusion in his expression is evident from the furrowing of his brows. "She took me in when I was born. My mother... My real mother is Mallory."

"What?" All three guys utter in unison, Cassian and Finn flank their brother, arms crossed, gazes locked on us. They've accepted me as one of their own, as their little sister, which made me feel like I'd found my place in the world.

"She just told me how Mallory had an affair with my father." I shake my head, still disbelieving the soap opera that my life feels like. "Mallory was worried because she wasn't married. My grandparents were strict. I knew that, even though they died when I was young, but even as a kid, they scared me."

"And Marcia took you in?"

I nod, feeling more tears spill from my lashes. "She agreed to raise me alongside my father, but even then, he didn't stay. He didn't want me. I feel alone. Broken."

"You're not alone," Damien assures me, his gaze locked on mine. He tugs me from the bench, pulling me into his lap, as we both fall back onto the soft mat, which I know they usually use for sparring. His arms wrap around me, warming me right down to my bones.

"You are never alone," Cassian tells me, as he takes a seat. "We're always here for you. You're with Damien now, he's chosen you, which means you're a Thorne."

"Your dad wants me with Creed. He wants a Thorne-Haven wedding."

Damien goes rigid beneath me. "No." The word is gritted out from the man holding me. "That's not happening. If he wants me to step down from running Thorne Corporation, I'll do it, but I'm not allowing you to be with Creed."

"Allowing me?" Even in the twisted events of this evening, I sass him. But the way his gaze bores into me, I know he's not joking right now. He doesn't have to worry about it, because I want him and only him.

"Creed can't have you." Finn agrees with his brother. "And he will understand you've already been claimed. The night of the masquerade ball, Damien made sure to show him that, he wouldn't come near you unless he wants a war."

"I just want to go, fly away and never come back," I tell them. Damien's arms tighten around me, holding me against his chest. I can feel his heart thudding against me, and the rhythm is calming.

His next words are a reassuring affirmation which makes every inch of my body release the anxiety that had earlier taken hold of me. "Then we'll go."

Damien

The Past

WHEN I OPEN MY EYES, I HEAR A NOISE DOWNSTAIRS, but confusion makes me peek over the covers. It's not morning yet, because the sun hasn't come up, but I can hear my mother speaking. Her voice carries up the stairs to my bedroom. The door is closed, and I can't hear what she's saying, but she sounds angry.

I don't like when Mom is angry. My stomach turns in knots, like when I'm meant to do my speech in the front of the class. I never liked people looking at me, and the kids at school aren't friendly.

Another shout comes from downstairs, and I push off

the bed, padding barefoot to the door, I slowly twist the handle and pull it open. Her voice is clearer now, and then I hear Daddy, too.

He says something, but his voice sounds like a growl. I'm scared when I move closer to the stairs to try to see what they're doing, but even from the landing, I can't.

My heart is beating so fast; it's making my ears beat like a drum of my favorite pop song. I know something is wrong because my mom is crying now.

"Please, Mark," she says to dad, but I don't hear him answer her. I tiptoe farther down the steps, and that's when I see them in the living room. Mom's face is wet, her makeup has made stripes down her cheeks as she looks at Dad.

He looks at her but doesn't hold her. Growing up, I always remember him holding her tightly when she was sad, but this time, it's different. In the next second, her hand comes up and smacks him across the cheek so hard, his head snaps to the side.

I stumble back, falling onto the carpet on the step.

"You're fucking crazy," he says to Mom, and I can hear he's angry. I've only heard him shout a few times, where I would hide under my bed out of fear, and this is just like those.

"You fucked this up!" Mom's scream is so loud, and I have to put my hands on my ears. "You're a fucking lying asshole!" I'm sure the windows will break each time mom shouts at him, but they don't.

Glass crashes onto the floor. Tears burn my eyes, and I stand quickly, racing into the bathroom and locking myself inside. My heart beats so loudly in my ears, I can't think about anything else. But nothing drowns out the sound of my parents' rage.

I'm scared.

My tears fall down my cheeks.

My chest aches from the anger I hear in their voices.

My stomach twists from the fight that seems so much worse than anything I've heard from them before.

Everything hurts because I wonder if it could've been something I did. Perhaps it's all my fault. Maybe they don't love each other because of me.

Another loud crash comes from downstairs, and I run to the toilet, just in time to puke up my dinner. My hands shake, as I hold onto the white bowl, the tightening becoming worse. When there's nothing more coming out of my mouth, I try to stand, and my legs wobble.

I open the tap. While rinsing my mouth, I see my dad's razor on the counter. I think about the first time I experienced calmness. When it happened; it was by mistake. An accident with a glass.

But now as I make the choice, I know it's more.

My fingers shake when I lift it, unlatching the silver

blade and holding it between my fingers. I turn, slide down onto my butt, and lift my shorts. I close my eyes after I press the silver metal to my skin and press it hard.

The pain makes me shiver, and more tears fall down my cheeks, but the moment I open my eyes and look at the blood, I can finally breathe again. It hurt, a lot, but I do it for a second time, two small lines on my tanned skin, the red staining my fingertips and the sharp object.

My chest doesn't feel tight anymore.

My stomach isn't in knots.

And I can finally feel my lungs inhale deeply.

As I close my eyes, all the fear and worry eases, the pain brings about serenity.

And I know this is the only way I'll ever find calm.

Nesrin

The Present

I PROMISED HER WE'D GO. MY FINGERS ARE LACED WITH hers, as we make our way up the stairs. She's quiet, contemplative, so I don't say anything, because I need her to make sure this is what she wants.

When we reach her bedroom door, I stop, waiting for her to say something, anything. I will walk away from Thorne Corporation if it means having her with me. I don't give a shit about the company if I don't have Nesrin.

"I want to run," she tells me, but she doesn't meet my stare. Her hand on the doorknob tightens because her knuckles turn white. She's tense, nervous. Her body trembles, as she stares at the door, instead of looking at me.

My brows furrow, not understanding her. "Run?"

"I want to go into the forest, I want to play hide and seek with you, but I want a burning rose. No more treating me like I'm fragile. The first time you took me on a run, it was merely a test. I want it all," she tells me, finally lifting her gaze to meet mine. My initial response is to say no, to refuse her immediately, but I have a feeling she *needs* this.

I can't stop my gaze from dropping to her legs, even though she's wearing clothes, I see beneath those.

"Fine. But you have to promise me something," I tell her, stepping in close, my palms landing on either side of her head, as I cage her in. "If you need to stop at any point, you tell me. You do not, and I mean do not, push past your limits."

She laughs. "Do I need a safe word?"

"Yeah." And I'm not even joking.

Nesrin ponders my response, her eyes sparking, as she nods. "Fine. It's Rose." I can't help but smile before pushing away from her and stepping back.

"Meet me in the greenhouse in ten minutes. Remember, don't wear anything that will get you hurt. Cover up," I tell her, before turning for my bedroom. "Oh and, Nesrin," I call to her before she steps over the threshold of her room, "don't wear panties. You won't be needing them."

I'm in the greenhouse, ready, waiting. The items I need are strapped to me—rope, knife, lighter. The rose I'm holding is deep red, the petals perfectly opened, splayed, just how I want Nesrin to be tonight.

With our folks at home, it's tricky to even consider fucking her anywhere in the house. Even though our bedrooms have doors, just the thought of them down the hall makes me anxious.

With a quick glance at the forest behind me, I allow the excitement to twist in my chest. My body is rigid with the need to run into the darkness and get lost amongst the trees. Just the thought of having her beside me has me on edge, in a good way.

"I'm ready for the real thing this time," she whispers when she steps into the glass house. She's dressed in tight black yoga pants, a tank top with her hoodie unzipped, and sneakers. She looks beautiful in the darkness, just like she did the first night we ran.

I hold the rose up, reaching for my lighter, I flick it to life. The flame dances over the petals, searing the perfection, turning the deep red to black. Nesrin's golden eyes are ablaze, just like the flower that's slowly turning to ash.

Once the bud is completely singed, I kill the flame and slip my lighter into my back pocket, before handing her the burnt rose. Her hand wraps around the stem, and I watch in awe as the crimson drips from the piercings of the thorns.

"You did that on purpose," I accuse her, and she can't refute me; she knows it's true. When Nesrin opens her hand, I grab her wrist, bringing her palm to my nose. Inhaling her scent has my mouth-watering, and I can't stop myself from leaning in to taste her. "Are you completely sure you want this?"

Her gaze flits to mine, her pupils dilate, and her lips part on a soft whisper of, *yes*.

"Then run," I order, low, barely audible, but when her feet move, I know she's heard me. I step out of the greenhouse, watching her path into the trees, and then I take off behind her. The moment I hit the tree line, I listen, slowing down just enough to pick up the footfalls on the ground.

When I hear the creak in a branch, I move to the left. My heart rate spiking with excitement, as I make my way through the shadows of the trees. Even though it's dark, I know my way through the maze before me. I wonder if she'll head toward the water, or if she'll run the other way.

A few meters later, I stop, listen, and close my eyes to focus on the sounds that skitter across the forest. A harsh breath echoes from my right-hand side, so I follow it. A smile playing on my lips, as I make way on the soft ground, and, seconds later, I see her in the sliver of light coming from the moon above us.

I grab at her, my fingers brushing along the material of her hoodie and a scream falls free from her, making me chuckle.

"I'm coming for you, wild rose," I warn her, as my cock thickens against my zipper. Fuck, I'm so ready for her right now. I want her heat wrapped around me like a vise.

She shoots forward, her breathing coming out in short, quick spurts that makes my desire for her burn through me like a blaze taking out everything in its way.

I'm about to grab at her again, when she twists to the left, making me race the wrong way because I couldn't slow down in time. Even through the trees, I can make her small form out, and the animal deep in my gut roars with happiness when another scream lurches from her as I make another grasp for her.

But my wild rose is quick, shocking me and she makes a break, racing from me on those slender, sexy legs. I fucking love this girl. The thought comes quickly, but I shake it away the next second, refocusing on the task at hand.

I can't think about that now.

Not yet.

Nesrin

MY LUNGS ARE BURNING, BUT I DON'T STOP. MY legs wobble with every step, but I focus on the adrenalin racing through me. Even though everything aches, I'm euphoric. The talk with my mother, the truth she revealed, no longer twists the anger in my gut. My chest is no longer tight with frustration at the lies.

I'm free.

The need to grab a blade, to open a wound in order to release my fears is no longer at the forefront of my mind. With every tentative step I take, hoping he finds me but also, praying he doesn't; I can't help but realize I can make it through whatever challenge comes my way.

It's a thin, sleek line between strength and weakness

for me. One small incident can tip me over the edge into the darkness, and I'll get lost inside myself.

The darkness engulfs me, holding me in its chilly embrace. I stop for a moment, completely lost. I took a turn somewhere along the way, thinking it would lead me to the lake, but it hasn't. I'm not sure where I am, but I do have my phone if I need it. I flicked off the GPS because I had a feeling Damien would be able to track me with it, but I could always turn it on when I've had enough.

But I'm not ready to go back.

I'm enjoying this far too much. A crunch from somewhere behind me has me freezing. The trees hide me, but something tells me Damien will find me, even if I was completely hidden.

I'll find you, even in the dark.

His words always linger on the edge of my fear. The promise is written on my heart, and I know no matter where I am, I'm safe because he's there. It eases the tension that tends to grip me. Another crack of a branch echoes through the forest, and my heartbeat kicks up a notch. It's louder, right in my ears, reminding me I'm alive.

I don't know what he has planned for when he catches me, and he will, but my stomach flutters with excitement. The next sound is even closer, and I push away from the tree, racing through the shadows, and that's when his movements become noticeable.

I'm taunting the hunter.

I'm teasing the beast.

Suddenly, he's on me. His body on top of mine, as we fall to the ground. The coolness against my cheek is only there for a second or two, before Damien pulls me to my feet, his grip on my wrists is solid. I find myself against one of the trees before he starts weaving a rope around my wrists.

"What are you doing?"

"You wanted to play," he responds, in a voice that sounds nothing like him. It causes my heart to stutter in my chest. The fear is intoxicating, but the excitement of what's to come is exhilarating.

Once I'm bound to the thick trunk, unable to get away from him again, he steps back and regards me. Even in the dark, his eyes seem luminous. Shards of silver light come from above us, the moon shining down, watching us, as we play our game.

Damien pulls a knife from his belt, the glint of metal shimmers, forcing a gasp to tumble from my lips.

"Open your mouth," he tells me. He takes a step toward me, stopping only once he's inches from me. When I open my mouth, he places the blade between my teeth and says, "bite down on this." I do, much to his satisfaction.

My eyes track him, as he drops down in front of me, his hands tugging at my yoga pants, pulling them down. He helps me out of them, and the cool night air tickles my exposed skin. A shiver races through me, causing my legs to shake, but Damien's hot mouth is on me, his tongue lapping at me, as his hands push my legs wider.

When I look down, the sight nearly undoes me. His blue eyes, now dark, are staring up at me, as he licks and laves at me as if I were his sustenance. Perhaps I am, but the moment two of his fingers dip inside me, my toes curl in my socks. My thighs shake, and the tightness in my lower stomach twists and teases, just like his mouth on my pussy.

He diminishes every fear, each anxious thought, and all my pain with a single touch. He doesn't relent the moment my orgasm hits, and a cry is ripped from my chest, muffled by the blade between my teeth, into the emptiness that surrounds us. He rises in one fluid motion. The hiss of his zipper is all I hear. I watch in awe, as he fists himself, the thickness that's about to fill me is hard and ready.

With his hands on my thighs, Damien lifts my legs, and I wrap them around his taut waist. He nudges my entrance, eyes glowing, smirk firmly in place, and sinks into me inch by torturously thick inch.

"Fuck," he hisses through clenched teeth. His forehead

touching mine, making our connection even closer. He doesn't move for a moment, allowing me to adjust before he pulls out slowly and thrusts back in. The gentle way he's fucking me causes tears to burn my eyes.

Emotion emanates from him like a cologne. It's not only about sex. It's also not just lust and need or desire, it's more. And he's showing me with his body. His mouth crashes to mine, stealing my moans and whimpers, as he moves inside me, filling me to the hilt, before teasing back out.

My hips undulate, my slick walls pulse around him, taking him in deep, needing him to fill a void I knew I always had. It haunted me for so long, but with him, it feels complete.

He drives in, hitting parts of me that are not just physical. He's nudging my heartache and fear, he's fucking my agony and anxiety, he's owning every part of me, and I allow it because I cannot refuse him anything.

Love doesn't find you when you want it or look for it. The feeling comes silently in the darkness and slices you open, burying itself in your veins, in your bones, right down to the marrow.

Love captures you when you least expect it, and it's a cut so deep, I'm afraid it will never heal if he were to walk away. But as he claims my mind, body, and soul, I am convinced that he can't leave me, just as much as I can't leave him.

I blink, and the heartbreak trickles down my cheeks in salty tracks. The kiss turns heated when Damien's tongue dances with mine. A soft, pain-filled connection that pours our emotions into each other. And as we fuck and kiss, and cry and moan, I realize I've fallen in love with him.

The same way he's telling me with his body how much he loves me.

Nesrin

THE SUN HASN'T RISEN WHEN I OPEN MY EYES. I KNOW today is the day I need to see my mom, Mallory. Last night, everything was too much to even consider going to her. If I had, I may have said things I shouldn't have said. It was safer to clear my head and think about what to tell her.

Now that I'm focused, I can go over and try to figure out how I'm going to deal with the truth. I also need to tell Marcia, who I now know is my aunt, that I want to leave with Damien. It's my life, my choice; I'm old enough to leave, she can't stop me.

After our run last night, Damien and I sat in his bedroom, looking over options for me to go to school in

London. Even though my dream would be Oxford, I've come to the conclusion that I would much rather be free of the lies in Thorne Haven, and the family I thought would love me, and find my own path.

If this had happened a few years ago, I'm not sure I could've been as strong as I am right now. Deep down, there is still a twinge of anxiety that twists in my gut, at the thought of what's going to happen today, but it's nothing compared to what I used to feel.

The run last night eased my need to cut. I told Damien I'd like to talk to a professional as well. And he promised the moment we got to London, he'd make an appointment with a couple of therapists who his dad is friends with, and I'll be able to meet with them, before settling on my choice. The thought of him supporting me definitely makes me feel special, and last night, something shifted between us. We may not have said the words, but they burned on the tip of my tongue.

If he hadn't been kissing me at the time, I may have muttered them out loud. But I'm not sure either of us is ready for that.

Pushing off the bed, I pad toward the bathroom to get ready for the day. If I don't do it now, I'll most probably hide out until Damien announces that we're leaving. He's delayed his flight till tonight, which gives me time to talk to Mallory and Marcia.

The moment I walk into the kitchen, Joy looks up with a smile on her face. She's always in a good mood, happy, affectionate, nothing like the woman I grew up with.

"How are you, dear?" Joy asks, offering me a mug of coffee, and a plate of toast dripping with honey. It's what I have every morning when I come down.

"I'm good. Tired, but okay. And you?"

"I'm always great. There's no reason to be sad, life may bring dark clouds, but the sun will always shine afterward." With a wink, she leaves me to eat in silence. I'm finishing up my toast when Marcia walks into the kitchen, her body language is rigid, and the air in the room cools considerably.

"Nesrin."

I open my mouth to greet her, but I have no idea what to call her, so all I say is, "Morning." I watch her move around the room, opening cabinets, trying to find the mugs. When she does, she fills it with coffee, before turning to me.

I'm nervous. It's strange. Now that I know the truth, it's almost as if we're no longer able to talk. But I know I need to.

"I'm going to London with Damien. Today, I'll be going

to see Mallory, mom, whatever she is to me." The words come out in a whoosh, and my throat tightens at the idea of what I'm about to do. "I want to be with Damien. And I don't care what barriers you and Bradford put in place. I'm done caring about people who lie to me."

I glance up to find shock painted on her features. But after a long while, she nods. "I should never have kept it a secret for so long, and I certainly shouldn't have told Mallory to lie to you either." Even though I don't want to fall into the trap of believing something that isn't true, I'm almost certain her voice is laced with guilt.

"No, you shouldn't have. Even when Dad left, that was the perfect moment to come clean, and you chose not to. I've struggled my whole life with depression, and you never cared. You never treated me like a caring mother should. But now, it makes sense, since you're *not* my mother."

At that moment, Damien saunters into the kitchen, and I'm fearful Marcia is going to kill him after my admission, but she lowers her head, shaking it slowly, as she looks at the floor.

"I've never been good with emotion. I had to be strong for so long, looking after my parents when they got sick, and I blamed Mallory for being the young, carefree person I wanted so badly to be." When she lifts her head, she looks directly at me. "I wanted to have my own life, but after you were old enough, I still couldn't bring myself to tell you the truth."

She sets the mug down, as Damien moves behind me, his hands on my shoulders, offering me his strength as the tears trickle down my cheeks. He doesn't kiss me or offer anything more than his hold on me, but it's enough.

"I'm sorry, Nesrin. I'm so sorry. And I know it's not something I can make up for with a meager apology, but for now, it's all I have."

I glance at Damien, and he pulls out my chair, allowing me to stand. I go to her, but I don't hug her, I don't even touch her. "I can't forgive you right now, it hurts far too much, but I can thank you for your apology. Perhaps one day, I'll be able to look at you without anger."

I turn around and head out of the kitchen, leaving her to mull over my words. Damien is beside me seconds later, his arm wrapping around my waist.

"Are you okay?"

I nod. "I am. Will you take me to see Mallory?"

"Of course." He's my rock. He's become my savior in ways I didn't realize I needed. And I love him for it. A smile curves my lips because, I know now, today will be the day I can finally admit it. I want to tell him how I feel.

Nesrin

THE FORTRESS IN FRONT OF US, AS WE MAKE OUR WAY up the drive, looms over the hill like a king sitting on his throne. My stomach somersaults at the thought of seeing her face to face, knowing the truth.

"Are you okay, wild rose?" Damien's voice captures my attention. I nod, but I don't know if it's the truth. His eyes are so blue today; they remind me of the ocean, shimmering with affection. With love.

"I will be. I just need her to tell me the truth. I know Marcia did, but she's my mother, Damien."

"I know. She should've been the one to come clean." His hand finds mine, his fingers tangling with my own. Just like before, he's the only thing keeping me afloat.

"You'll get through this. You're strong."

I glance at him. "I'm only strong because you're here. You're my strength." My voice is a husky whisper, filled with worry at my life taking a whole new path I never planned for.

"Listen to me," he says. "You've been strong all your life. I'm merely a life raft you hold onto every now and then. And I'll be by your side until you no longer want me."

"Why wouldn't I want you?"

"I mean if I tire you out with all the sex we'll be having, you may want to break up. But then again, why would you want to walk away from this face." He winks cockily, the smirk that I've come to love is firmly in place, and I can't help but giggle.

"Come on, Handsome," I say, pressing my lips to his. "Let's get this over with." I push open my door and meet Damien at the passenger side of the car, before walking up the path toward the entrance.

Creed steps out onto the gravel and offers us the once over, noticing our hands linked. A smirk curls his full lips. He's dressed in a black leather jacket, ripped jeans, and a dark band tee that looks like it's seen better days.

"The brand-new couple," he says when we reach him. "You two have certainly caused a stir."

Damien asks the question I have as well, "What do you mean?"

Creed meets the stare of his former best friend. "I just overheard Dad talking to Bradford. Apparently, your girl over here has decided jumping on your dick is better than mine. Just kidding." He chuckles, looking at us both, before saying, "Good luck. It's time you found someone worthy of you." His comment is directed at Damien, and I'm shocked when he holds out a hand. "I'm done playing war with my best friend." The tension between the two is strangled, but Damien grips his hand, and they shake on it. For a moment, I watch them connect. The friendship they had clearly meant something to them both. And when Creed walks off, I know Damien's happy they found common ground again.

We find Mallory in the kitchen, led there by the maid, who greeted us only a day ago. When we step into the spacious, modern room, my *mother* looks up, and her eyes widen in shock.

"I wasn't expecting you today," she says, her smile sickly sweet. *She doesn't know.* "Can I get you a coffee or something stronger?" Her gaze, that matches mine, flits between Damien and me.

"No. We... I wanted to talk to you." I'm shaking, my hands are trembling, even with Damien's fingers laced through mine. She doesn't miss a beat, noticing the physical connection.

"Oh." Her dark brows lift in surprise. "I heard you'd

spoken to your folks, well, your step—"

"You're my mother." The words whoosh out in one short breath, interrupting whatever she wanted to say. "Why didn't you tell me? I had to learn it from your sister." I'm so confused. My mind feels like it's been twisted in a thousand different directions and, right now, the only thing that makes sense is him—Damien.

Mallory's mouth opens, then shuts. The guilt that pains her expression is enough to tell me she certainly wasn't expecting this. *Neither was I, Mommy.*

"Can we sit? Talk?"

Her words send a burst of anger to my chest, warming me with emotions that I've always buried and allowed to flow free with the cuts on my thighs. I've never known how to express myself vocally but, right now, I find that the damn wall is about to crash wide open.

"I don't know why I'm even here. You pawned me off on your sister, so you could travel around the world and then marry a man we didn't know about. Not even bothering to tell us, your family. To have three new sons to look after, instead of caring about your daughter?" The anger that I'd been holding back floods through me, and it comes out as a tirade of words that I never knew I had been biting my tongue on. "I grew up idolizing you, looking up to you. I was depressed for most of my life because my dad walked out, and it was all because of you.”

“Nesrin, I didn’t mean—”

“No!” Releasing Damien’s hand, I take a step closer to her, nearing the woman who gave me life. “This time, you’re listening to me. I spent my life cutting myself because I didn’t know how to communicate. Your sister was cold, aloof, and she hated me from the moment I knew what that emotion meant.”

Behind me, I hear Damien’s feet shuffle on the ground. His boots confirming that he’s there, if I need him. He doesn’t make a sound to remind me of his presence. He doesn’t need to say a word. My silent anchor.

“I hurt myself time and again. I believed my father hated me, and I knew my mother did, too. Only, she wasn’t my mother. She was a woman who raised a little girl because her sister was too much of a fucking coward to step up and admit to her mistakes.”

“Please, Nesrin,” she pleads, but all I see is red.

“You know what, I spent my life *wanting* to be like you. But now I see that I’m, thankfully, nothing like you, and I never will be. Because you know what, *Mom*, I will always take responsibility for my misgivings. And when I do make a mistake, I’ll own up to it, no matter how painful it is.”

The words finally slow down, my throat burning, and my eyes filling with angry tears. I blink slowly, allowing them to trickle from me, to wash away the rage that's slowly burning through every vein in my body.

"I didn't mean for you to go through that. I believed she'd be there for you. Even though her love for her career took all her focus, I thought, I really thought, she'd love you."

No amount of apologies can make up for what I went through. I don't blame anyone for my choices. Even though I was a child and needed the stability and guidance of a parent, I was the one who picked up the blade. I knew what I was doing, even when I didn't realize it at the time.

"I'm disappointed that the woman I thought I knew is not the person I grew up with as my hero." My voice breaks, as the overload of emotions from the past couple of days takes its toll. "I'm leaving tonight. I won't be back for a long time. I don't know how to move past this pain," I tell her solemnly, gesturing between us. "But I know I'm strong. I'm so much stronger than either you or Mom, Marcia, gave me credit for. I've made mistakes, but I've admitted them, and I'm willing to work through them."

"Don't go. Stay, and we can get to know each other. There's a good school a town over. I'm sure Bradford will be happy for you to live there, or, if you'd like, you can stay here."

"No. I'm leaving. I need to get away from the lies, from

the darkness of you and your sister."

"Then promise me you'll write, text, call, something?" she pleads, grabbing my hands in hers and holding onto them. Those eyes that always sparkled with life, with happiness, are dull and filled with pain.

"I'll think about it."

"I just need you to know I loved you. When I found out I was pregnant, it was the happiest time of my life, but your father was in love with my sister, and… And I knew I would never be able to raise you on my own. All I wanted was for you to have a normal family."

"And all I ever wanted was a mother who loved me."

The tears flow freely now, hers and mine. The pain that hangs in the air between us is palpable. So thick, you could cut it with a knife.

"I should've stayed. I should've kept you with me, but when I lost your dad, when he chose her over me, it felt as if my world had been torn apart. And, knowing I had you should've been enough, but I was young and stupid." Her watery gaze locks on mine, and I see it, the guilt, the pain, the fear, everything. I can't imagine what it would be like to be in her shoes at that time. Perhaps I was overly harsh, maybe I'm too angry, and I should be more understanding.

I don't know.

This is new to me.

"I just... I need time," I tell her. "I need to be free for a while, and I'm going to London."

A small smile plays on her lips, and she glances at Damien. When I turn to look at him, I find him leaning against the door jamb, his arms folded across his chest, those sparkling orbs regarding me.

"Look after my girl," she tells him.

A parent should be there through your life to guide you when you're unsure, hold you when you're sad, and love you even when you're not whole. I never had that. But I'm strong, and I know I'll survive.

"She's a good girl," Damien tells her. "And I'll be by her side always. Even if she does push me away, I'm not giving up on her. I'm not her father," he speaks confidently, which makes my heart skip a beat.

I glance at Mallory again, taking in her expression, as she smiles at him and says, "Thank you." And I know I've found a good man.

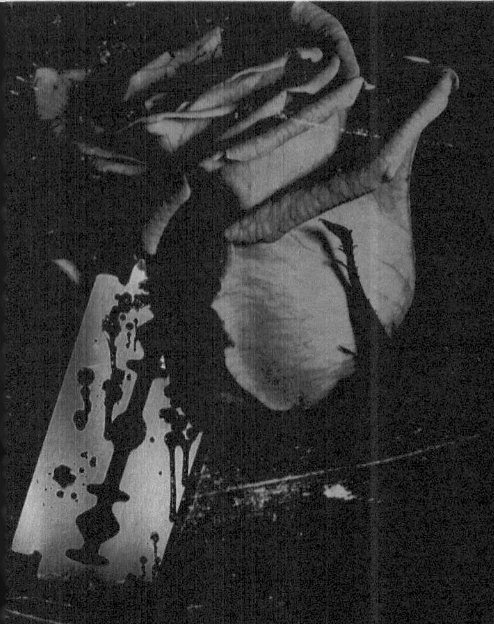

Damien

Even though Nesrin told Mallory she's coming to London with me, I don't know how Dad is going to take the news. The fact that he's holding my position in the company over my head is one thing, but he will threaten Nesrin's education, just to get what he wants.

Like I said, everything in life is a smokescreen. None of us are safe from a man who wields his power because of his fat bank account. He's hated me, and I him, since my mother left. I blamed him, and he blamed me, but now that he's replaced the first woman I loved, my mom, I know he wouldn't think twice to break Nesrin and me up.

"Are you deep in thought or just ignoring me?" Her

voice breaks through the dark clouds that hover over me like a foreboding threat.

"I can never ignore you," I tell her, honestly, casting a quick glance at her. Turning my attention back on the road, I take a left, instead of a right because it's time to tell her what I've decided. And she'll have to accept it. Because I'm not leaving her.

"Where are we going?"

"The lake." I don't look at her. I know her doubts are settling in now that she's heard how many people have lied to her, and I'm not going to be one of them. I put this off for so long, but it's time to come clean. To tell her how I feel.

When we reach the gravelly road, I pull to the side and kill the engine. She's nervous, I see her hands shake. Her tremble is visible even as she attempts to come across as confident and sure of herself.

"Come." I push open my door and exit the car, waiting for her at the front. When she reaches me, I offer her my hand and lace my fingers with hers.

We walk in silence the few meters to the large, silvery body of water. It's so still here, silence hangs heavily like a thick storm cloud. Stopping at the edge of the water, I turn to Nesrin.

My chest is tight with anxious energy, and my pulse is rioting wildly. I've never said this to anyone before. Not even Gen. And even when she craved these words from my lips, I could never offer them to her because I knew I wouldn't mean it, even if I said it.

"What's going on?" Her whispered question is more than I can take, and I breathe deeply, before looking into her eyes.

"I wanted to talk to you about something. When we get back to the house, I'm not sure what's going to happen. I don't know what my father is going to say when we tell him about us, about you going with me. He may want to strip my position at Thorne Corp."

"You can't do that, Damien. That's your legacy." Her insistence for me is sweet, but she doesn't get it, I'm not walking away from her because of this.

"I want you. I've wanted you since I saw you in the church that morning. Seeing you stand up for your mother, as she said her vows, you looked like a fucking angel, while I stood like a demon in the shadows."

Her eyes widen, the gold shimmering with emotion. I watch as the tears collect in her eyes. I hate seeing her sad, seeing her hurt, even when she does it to herself.

"When I told you I would be the one to break you, I meant it. I know I have that power, and I'm not saying that to be an overconfident asshole. But as much as I have the power to hurt you, you have that same hold over me."

"Damien—"

"Do you remember what you felt when I walked up behind you at the reception dinner and introduced myself?"

She nods, but she doesn't elaborate. We stare at each other for so long, the silence becomes an entity between us.

"Tell me, wild rose."

"Anger, jealousy, and attraction." I can't help but smile at her answer.

"Anger?"

"Yes, because you were an asshole." Her lips pout, playfully, and there's a whisper of a smile on her pretty face.

"That I know." I chuckle. "And why jealousy?"

She drops her gaze to the ground, her focus shifts away from me for a moment, before those golden orbs lock on my blue ones.

"Because I wanted to be the girl giving you pleasure."

That's the answer I wanted. "And I wanted it too. I craved it so much, it drove me crazy. And, at first, I fought it, that need to have you. But when we got home, I gave in to my hunger and here we are."

"Here we are."

"I love you," I exhale in a whoosh of nervous breath. "I love you, Nesrin. I don't know how, or why, but you're everything to me. And a job, a fucking legacy, it means nothing if you're not by my side."

"Damien—"

I interrupt her once more. "If you don't feel—"

"I love you, too." This time, it's her who whispers it to me, and, for a moment, I think I didn't hear her right. "I love you, too." Her voice, more forceful, and I pull her into my arms, my mouth trailing soft kisses from her forehead to her mouth, capturing her lips and tasting her, as if it's the first fucking time.

Her flavor intoxicates me, making my body tense with the need to be inside her. Her tongue swipes along mine, hot and warm. The duel has my cock hardening, wanting her, craving her, just like I've wanted since the moment I laid eyes on her.

The delicate touch of her hands sears me when she runs them over my shoulders, locking around my neck, and I pull her up against me by the cheeks of her pert little ass. Her legs wrap around my waist, her heat at my crotch, tempting me to take this further.

"I… I…" her whimpers tumble from her kiss-swollen lips. Reluctantly, I pull away from her, breaking the kiss to meet her gaze. "I can't believe I love you," she whispers.

A smile graces my expression. I love her like this—innocent and shy—but I also love her fire. "I love you, so fucking much. You've consumed my every thought, and I can't live without you. But I don't want you to rush into something that you may regret later on."

I know she's only eighteen. I can't ask her to promise her life to me. But what scares me is that if I did ask her, I know she'd say yes.

"We can take it slow," she tells me, her shyness dissipating, and her confidence burning through. "Each day will be different, but every day, I'll be with you. That's all I want."

"And you're sure you want to fly across the world with me?" I ask, knowing it's a big change. Her life is here, well, most of her life.

"I do. I've decided on my major, and I know I want to pursue my career in psychology." I'm still holding onto her, as she tells me this. Her eyes shimmer with excitement at her admission. She's going to do amazing things. I know she is. Pride swells in my chest, and I nod.

"Then that's what you'll do." I know if she puts her mind to something, she'll accomplish it. "Are you ready to tell them?"

Her pulse riots at the spot just under her ear. I want to lick it, taste her rhythm, but I wait for her response first.

"Let's do it."

The smile that graces her expression warms me from the depths of my soul -- the same one that I always believed was dark and broken. Somehow, this girl with golden eyes, has walked into my life and healed what I never thought would be mended.

Nesrin

THE HOUSE IS QUIET, BUT DAMIEN LEADS ME THROUGH to the office, where I heard the truth about who my mother was. The room is lit by the sun streaming through the window. His father is sitting behind his desk, and when those familiar blue eyes dart up, he notices our connection, our interlocked hands, before he even takes note of our expressions.

"What can I do for the two of you?" he asks, as he leans back in the large, leather office chair that makes him look like a king rather than a man.

"We need to talk," Damien informs him, pulling me along behind him. We reach the two chairs that face the large, dark mahogany desk, and Damien turns to me, gesturing for me to sit. I do. My legs are weak as my heart pitter-patters in my chest, and my stomach is in knots. The anxiety that I've quelled easily, while beside Damien, is twisting painfully in my gut.

"Then talk," Bradford says, before laying his hands across his stomach. He's not fat, but he has a paunch that's evidence of his lavish lifestyle.

Damien is silent for a short while before he sits down, his gaze on his father. "Nesrin and I will be flying out tonight. She wants to study in London, and I want to take over the England office." His voice is confident, not even a hint at how nervous he must be.

"Are you telling me that you want to live as a couple?" Bradford's eyes widen considerably, and his dark brows lift to his hairline. Shock is clear on his face.

"Yes, she's not my sister, she's not my blood." My heart sinks when Bradford shakes his head. My stomach topples to my feet when he pushes to his feet, and I'm almost certain he's about to lash out. But he doesn't. Nerves have a hold of me, and as if Damien can feel my worry, he reaches for my hand and gives it a squeeze.

"I don't like it," Bradford says. "This is wrong. It's not.... normal," he speaks with authority.

"What's not normal, Dad? The fact that I found someone who makes me feel like I can finally be happy?" The strain in Damien's voice makes my chest tighten. He wants me, as much as I do him. And he loves me. He told me so. I watch him fight for us, as he rises in one fluid motion and places his palms on the smooth top of his father's desk.

"Damien, I expected better than this," Bradford tells him. "You were here to look after her, not get between her legs." I can't help but wince at the words. "If you leave, you will not be on the board of Thorne Corp. I cannot explain to them that my son is gallivanting with an eighteen-year-old *child*."

"I am not a child," I bite out, pushing to my feet. I can't allow Damien to fight for me on his own. And I need Bradford to see that I'm willing to stand up for the relationship that's formed between us. "You may not think this is real and, who knows what will happen in five or ten years, but I want to be with Damien. I love him. And if that's not something you can accept, then so be it."

He opens his mouth, then closes it, and I wonder, briefly, if he's shocked that I just said what I did. Fire blazes in my veins, determination sinking into the marrow of my bones.

"Love is love. It doesn't matter who it's with." Those are my final words before he turns away. He looks out of the window, surveying the garden below, as he seems to ponder my retort.

"I have a challenge for you both." He glances at us. "If you leave, Damien, then you're on your own. You'll live together, and if you can survive a year alone, without the job at Thorne Corp, and still feel this way, I will allow it. And you will take over for me."

"That's easy enough," Damien tells his father with the confidence of a soldier racing into battle. "And when I prove you wrong on every count, I want an apology."

Bradford grins as if his son had just told him a joke. I've seen this man smile, but this isn't an expression of happiness; it's one of malicious satisfaction. He doesn't believe we can do it.

"And you," Bradford says, meeting my gaze. "I'll pay for you to attend Oxford. Even though you're truly a Haven now, because of who your mother is, I will not have a woman who's standing beside my son go to some underrated school."

"I can't—"

"It's not an option." He waves me off. "If you can't accept it, then you can walk out of here without my blessing."

I want to argue and tell him that his *blessing* is nothing but his control over our lives. Even though his son is nearly thirty, he still treats him like a child. But I don't. I accept it for what it is.

"Thank you."

He dismisses us then, waving toward the door. Damien

takes my hand. We make our way to the patio where we find Finn and Cass talking. They glance up, smiles on their faces. Finn stands, making his way toward me.

"Little sis," he says, pulling me into a hug. "You're official now."

"What?"

"You and D," Finn tells me as if I should've known that he knew.

"I'm happy for you both," Cassian tells us, with a grin on his handsome face. His gaze lingering on Damien, and the happiness in his eyes sparkle playfully. Cass has always been the more reserved brother, whereas Finn was playful and almost immature.

But I wouldn't have them any other way.

"I love you both," I tell them.

"See, D-man," Finn says, "She loves us more than you." We laugh, as we settle into easy conversation about moving to London and our future together. And I know everything is going to be okay.

Damien

The private plane is quiet. The solace is welcome. Nesrin's staring out of the window, and I have a feeling she's about to start a conversation that's been lingering in her mind for a while.

Since the night of the party, I know Creed set this in motion, and it's time I finished it. But I don't know how to bring it up without her prompting it. I rise, heading to the bar to grab a bourbon. With my back to her, I can feel her eyes burning into me.

"Can I ask you a question?"

"Sure," I respond, not looking at her. This is it. The moment of truth.

"What happened between you and Creed?" My chest

tightens when I remember that night. When I recall watching my best friend take it a step too far, and the accident that caused us all to walk away.

"One night, when I had just turned twenty-one, Creed and I wanted to challenge each other in the forest. It was a duel of sorts." I speak, looking through the small window—which is black—forcing me to see my reflection. "We took Gen and her sister to the woods, gave them a rose each and told them to run. Creed wanted her sister, and I had Gen."

I finally turn to see her nose crinkle at my words. This isn't going to be easy to hear, but I need her to know.

"I ran, it was exhilarating, and I lost myself to the euphoria of freedom." Golden eyes watch me intently. "Somewhere in the darkness, I heard a scream. It was piercing. I made my way toward it, following the sounds that came from deep in the forest."

Nesrin's on the edge of her seat, her lips slightly parted, her chest rising and falling, and her hands twisting in her lap.

"Creed was there, standing back when I reached a clearing. I didn't see it at first, but when Gen came up behind me, she screamed so loud, the sound pierced the woods, and I realized what was lying on the ground."

Ice races through my veins. The memory still haunts me. I blamed Creed all these years. I walked away from that fucking life, but Nesrin took me right back. The only difference is, I kept her safe.

"Damien?" My girl is on her feet, making her way toward me. I swallow my drink before I look at her again.

"Gen's sister was killed that night. It could've been an accident, but I was still plagued by guilt," I admit, as a gasp of shock falls from Nesrin's lips. "And we watched it happen." The words are out of my mouth before I have time to think. "Thorne Haven has far too many secrets, not even the people who live there like to talk about it."

"What happened, though?"

"Do you remember when I told you the forest is dangerous?" She nods, and I know she's recalling the threat I threw at her that night. "There are certain parts of the forest that have been set up by hunters to make sure we don't get any wild animals, or anything like that out here. We know where they are, but someone not used to the forest can get themselves hurt, badly."

Nesrin visibly shudders. I don't need to tell her what happened. "But you blamed Creed for it?" Confusion creases her brows, causing them to furrow.

"The man who killed Gen's sister is Creed Haven." My admission has her mouth returning to a shocked O, and her eyes spark with surprise. "We had a fight that night. Creed told me it was an accident, that she took a wrong turn and he tried to warn her, but..." My words taper off into nothing, into the darkness. The memory of that night haunts me, every fucking day. "Creed told the police he had found her like that. They didn't know about our game, and he kept it that way, telling them we were out for a walk and she got angry and ran off."

"What about you and Gen?"

"We told them that we didn't see what had happened, which is the truth. In the end they ruled it as an accident, since it was a trap set out by hunters. I blamed Creed for being a murderer. He hated me because I thought the worst of him. But there was nothing else that made sense. I didn't see him do it, but deep down, I wonder if he ever *did* try to stop her."

"So, you still don't know what happened for sure? Like if Creed did it on purpose," Nesrin whispers, shock still ringing in her voice.

Shaking my head, I can't help but sigh. "I don't know if Creed led her down that path on purpose, no, or if she just veered off our normal route through the forest, but before the scream, I didn't hear him shout to her. Voices carry in those woods, and I have a feeling he just let her go."

"I don't even know what to say."

"You don't have to say anything at all. It's over, we're here, and I want you to focus on us. On your studies and on your new life." I pull her into my arms, and thank god, she's here because I could never be without her.

Even though we have had our challenges, I'm thankful she chose me. Each time I wake up, looking at her, I know I've done something right in my life.

"I love you so much, Damien," Nesrin whispers into my shirt, and I can't help the smile that graces my lips.

"I love you too, wild rose," I admit the truth. I tried to fight it, tried to steer clear of her, but each time I saw her, I was drawn in. I had no choice in the matter. She was always going to be mine.

Six Months Later

SUMMER IN LONDON IS NOT ALWAYS CONSISTENT, BUT today is a beautiful sunny day. My dress swishes around my thighs, as I make my way through the throng of tourists that fill the sidewalk.

When I chose Damien over everything else, leaving it all behind, I knew I had to make a life that I wanted, instead of what my mother had dictated to me.

We shocked everyone in Thorne Haven when we walked out of the manor and didn't turn around. My therapist tells me I'll be okay if I focus on talking about my feelings, rather than bottling them up. I've been seeing her twice a week, and each time I come out of her office, I do feel stronger.

I haven't reached for a blade in so long, and I'm proud of myself. Damien's smile when we talk about my emotions, about my fears and dreams, makes it easier to focus on the good times and work through the bad.

It's not easy, but it's worth it. Hurting myself was not the way to deal with my heartache. I know that now. And I finally feel like *me*.

After the first month of us being here, Bradford Thorne flew out to London to see his son. That's when the offer came. When he finally relented and admitted the truth.

Marcia, who I grew up knowing as my mother, but was actually my aunt, knew about her sister marrying a Haven. She learned about the wealth Mallory had found herself living with, and she wanted it all to herself.

I recall the conversation with such clarity, it's as if it happened just yesterday.

"She was always jealous of her sister," Bradford tells Damien and me, as we sit in our living room in our North London apartment. His hands tremble as he holds onto the tumbler. He came to us because he's sick, and he wanted his eldest son to step up to the head of the table. Damien will run Thorne Corporation alongside Cassian and Finn. All three brothers will be in charge of their own departments. Damien as CEO, Cassian as COO,

and Finn as the CFO.

"But I don't understand why she would marry you and want me to be with Creed," I tell him. It's one of the things that never made sense, but after her last conversation with me, I realized I never wanted to be near her again.

"My wife is a complicated woman. Even though she was jealous, deep down, she wanted the best for you." He regards me with an earnest stare. "She just didn't know how else to keep you in town, and…" His words falter for a moment, as he regards his son. "We didn't expect you'd fall in love with Damien."

I nod slowly, my gaze sweeping across the room to the man I love. His blue eyes hold me hostage, and the affection I find there leaves me breathless.

The cocky smirk that I've come to crave appears, and I know he's not focused on the conversation right now. Shaking my head, I turn back to Bradford.

"I just don't want to hide from her when I visit. I'm a grown woman, and she needs to accept me as I am. She raised me, gave me a home when I didn't even know I needed one, but the hate between my mother and Marcia needs to come to an end. The past is in the past."

Bradford nods. "I agree. And that's why we would like you to come home for Christmas. Stay at the manor, so we can be a family." He looks so pained when he says this. And I realize it must be difficult for him to put up with Marcia. She's definitely hard work.

"We'll come," Damien answers his father, before reaching for my hand and lacing his fingers through mine.

"Good. Now let's get some dinner, I'm starving."

That was how we finally found our way back to the family we thought we had lost forever. That night, Bradford gave Damien the contract, which they signed at the dinner table.

When the office door opens, I glance up to see Damien saunter through. He's taken off his tie, his light blue shirt has been tugged from his slacks, and the top three buttons are undone. He looks tired, but his smile is ever-present.

"I was thinking we should go out for dinner tonight," he tells me, as he closes the distance between us. His lips capture mine for a sweet, chaste kiss before he straightens.

"Sure, where did you have in mind?"

"It's a surprise, just get dressed, something... fancy, and I'll shower and get ready." With a wink, he turns and leaves me to finish up an email to my mother, Mallory.

epilogue
Damien

Six Months Later

I'M NERVOUS. I'M FUCKING SHAKING THE MOMENT I walk into the warmth of our apartment. It's almost Christmas, and even though we were meant to fly out tonight, it's Nesrin's birthday, and I wanted to celebrate with a gift that I'm scared she won't accept.

When I shut the door behind me, I take in the view from our living room, which looks out over the university where my girl is studying. The yellow, glittering lights shimmer in the distance from the student residences. Since we moved to England a year ago, things have changed considerably.

Nesrin is at school, studying for her psychology degree, while I travel to London to attend meetings twice a week. Other than that, I work from home, ensuring I can spend time with her. Even though I know she's not walking away from me, there's always a lingering fear that I'll lose her. I don't know why.

She's beautiful, intelligent, and, at times, I wonder what the hell she sees in me. Besides my good looks, of course.

"You're home," she says, padding barefoot toward me. She's wearing a pair of fluffy PJs, with roses all over them. The blue and pink buds look soft to the touch.

"I've missed you." I grip her hips, pulling her toward me. She's my anchor to happiness, and I am never letting her go. Pressing my lips to hers, I savor her flavor which, at the moment, is chocolate and coffee. "Did you finish all that candy I got you?"

Her guilty smile tells me she did. "Perhaps. But you've been gone for two days." Her pout is cute. She's right, though. With the company expanding into Europe, I've been away, but all I've thought about is being here with her.

"I have something for you." I lace my fingers with hers. "Come, let's sit." We make our way to the living room, where the roaring fire dances behind the black grate.

I allow her to sit on the sofa, before I shrug off my coat,

throwing it on the armchair, and then I reach into my pocket, my fingers wrap around the box, and my heart skips a million beats at the thought of finally doing this.

"What is it?" she asks, practically bouncing with excitement, as I stand so still, fear gripping me.

Inhaling a deep breath, I settle in beside her. Those golden eyes are locked on my hand, but she can't see the small box yet.

"Look at me." The order comes out firmly, and she lifts her gaze to mine. "I've thought about this for so long. The year with you has been nothing short of perfect. Being beside you, watching you flourish, seeing you blossom into a woman has been magical. I'm not one for soppy shit," I tell her, causing a giggle to fall free from her lips. "But I need to tell you how you've changed my life."

"I love you, Damien. You know that."

"I do. And yet, at times, I feel as if you're going to disappear. I know you won't. I believe it, but sometimes, my mind plays tricks on me."

"Don't let it. I'm always going to be yours. Even though your father didn't believe it himself, you've seen the change in him. He knows, he can see what we mean to each other."

"And that's why I asked him to send me something."

"What?" There's a small crease between her brows as confusion paints her pretty face. "When I called Dad and asked him for this, I knew he'd help. A friend of his had made my mother's ring and my grandmother's ring. And now, he's made the one I'm going to give you, Nesrin."

I finally pull my hand away from my pocket. Flicking the box lid open, I hold it out to her. "Nesrin Anne Ellington," I say, using the name she chose to use. "I love you. I'll always love you. And I want you to spend each day making me the man I've always wanted to be. I want you to be Nesrin Anne Thorne, if that's what you want. I'd like to show you just how much you mean to me, with every waking moment and each night in your dreams."

Her eyes widen in shock. The ring is gold, just like her eyes, but the stone is set in a small rosebud, which sits atop the golden band. The center of the bud is a deep blue gemstone, a Lapis Lazuli.

"This is..." Tears fill her eyes, and I hold the breath that I pull into my lungs, as I wait for her answer. "This is beautiful," she whispers, picking up the ring, twisting it around, looking at every inch of it, before lifting her teary gaze to mine.

"I can't live without you. Marry me, please?" I've never begged, never pleaded with a woman. I've never wanted to. Until her.

"Yes. Yes. I want to love you forever." I slip the ring on the finger of her left hand before she leaps into my lap and wraps her arms around my neck. Her body flush with mine has a groan rumbling in my chest.

"I'm going to fuck you now."

Nesrin rolls her eyes. "My fiancé, ever the romantic." And, I know that no day will pass that she doesn't challenge me. Doesn't make me a better man. And I wouldn't have it any other way.

THE END

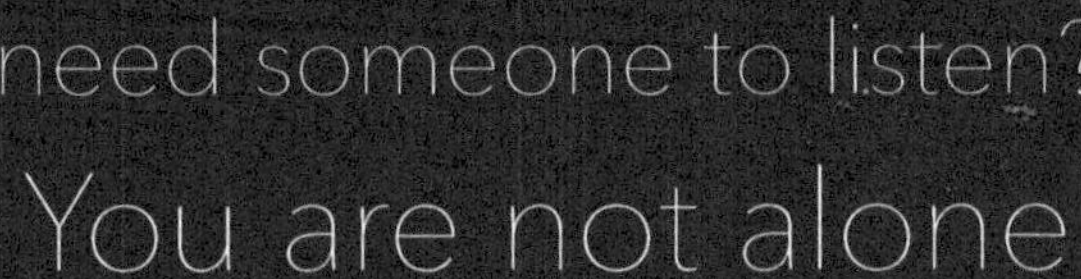

If you're struggling, feeling depressed, or thinking of harming yourself, please seek help. Below are a few places you can reach out to.

United States
https://twloha.com

United Kingdom
www.supportline.org.uk

Australia
https://www.lifeline.org.au

Canada
https://ontario.cmha.ca

South Africa
www.sadag.org

Are you ready?

Book Two in the Thornes & Roses Series.

Add Cassian's story, the next book in the series is now live!

A High so Sweet
https://danirene.com/book/a-high-so-sweet/

acknowledgements
Thank you

Thank you for reading Nesrin and Damien's story. This was one of the most difficult books for me, because Nesrin's journey isn't easy. Delving into her mind was tough because her anxiety made mine spike. But if you've reached this part of the book, you've hopefully fallen in love with these characters as much as I have. And hopefully, you're excited for Cassian's book!

I want to thank my BETA reader, Michelle Myers (Digital Dirty Girl Book Blog) for falling in love with Damien and Nesrin the same way I did. Thank you for all your insight.

To my editor, Rebecca Barney (Rebecca's Fairest Reviews), thank you for polishing these two characters and their journey to perfectly. Your advice and comments always ensure my book is shiny and ready for readers.

To my proofer, Brian (Illuminate Author Services), as always, a huge thank you for all your hard work on catching those final changes.

To my readers, the amazing ladies in my reader group, The Deviants, thank you for always being so incredible, and to my Captive Angels for pimping my ass out, you ladies ROCK!

To the author colleagues who read A Cut so Deep, and helped share and promote it, thank you so freaking much! I love you ladies!

And to the bloggers and bookstagrammers who were so excited to meet these characters. I truly hope the book lived up to your expectations. Thank you for always taking time out of your busy lives to help support and promote me. Your love is humbling.

Mad love,

Dani xo

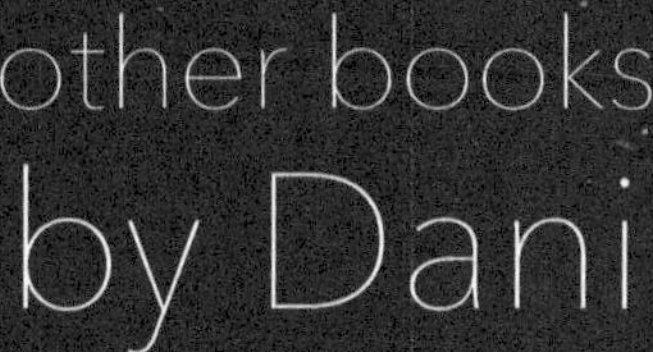

other books
by Dani

Head over to my website to find all my titles!

https://danirene.com/books/

You can also find me on Kiss, Radish, WattPad

about
the author

Dani is a USA Today Bestselling Author of dark and deviant romance with a seductive edge.

Originally from Cape Town, South Africa, she now lives in the UK with her better half who does all the cooking while she writes all the words. When she's not writing, she can be found binge-watching the latest TV series, or working on graphic design either for herself, or other indie authors.

She enjoys reading books about handsome villains and feisty heroines, mostly dark, always seductive, and sometimes depraved. She has a healthy addiction to tattoos, coffee, and ice cream.

www.danirene.com | info@danirene.com